for George Scithers,
despite his innate wickness

OTHER BOOKS BY DARRELL SCHWEITZER

fiction

WE ARE ALL LEGENDS
THE SHATTERED GODDESS
CONAN THE DELIVERER

nonfiction

THE DREAM QUEST OF H. P. LOVECRAFT
CONAN'S WORLD AND ROBERT E. HOWARD
PATHWAYS TO ELFLAND: THE WRITINGS OF LORD DUNSANY
ON WRITING SCIENCE FICTION: THE EDITORS STRIKE BACK
[with George H. Scithers and John M. Ford]
WRITING FANTASY [with Joel Rosenberg]
SCIENCE FICTION VOICES #1 (interviews)
SCIENCE FICTION VOICES #5 (interviews)

as editor:

DISCOVERING MODERN HORROR FICTION
DISCOVERING STEPHEN KING
DISCOVERING H. P. LOVECRAFT
EXPLORING FANTASY WORLDS
TALES FROM THE SPACEPORT BAR
[with George Scithers]

Tom O'Bedlam is a **madman**! Who else could succor the King of Elves, or save the earth from becoming a sphere of ice, or rescue the captives of the Autumn King. Who else but a madman would even believe these threats were real?

In these pages you will find a plethora of other wonders and horrors: the restless ghost of Emperor Nero — a versatile lady named Lilith Circe McSiren — a boy whose belief in the reality of comics makes them all too real — Thalanod, magical city deep in a desert oasis, where no man ages or grows ill — a Titan disguised as an island — a variety of gods, demons, telepathic crocodiles, and other fascinating and fabulous creatures — a bountiful feast for the fan of horror and fantasy.

Here to delight you is Darrell Schweitzer's first collection, loaded with the irresistible fantasy artwork of Stephen E. Fabian!

Tom O'Bedlam's Night Out
and Other Strange Excursions

by Darrell Schweitzer

illustrated by STEPHEN E. FABIAN

W. PAUL GANLEY: PUBLISHER
BUFFALO, NEW YORK
1985

Artwork in this book: Copyright © 1985 by Stephen E. Fabian
Remainder of this book: Copyright © 1985 by Darrell Schweitzer
No part of this book may be reprinted without the permission of:
W. PAUL GANLEY: PUBLISHER, P. O. Box 149, Amherst Branch,
Buffalo, New York 14226-0149.

Tom O'Bedlam's Night Out, from FANTASTIC, Sept., 1977.
© 1977 by Ultimate Publishing Co., Inc.
Raving Lunacy, from AMAZING, July, 1981. © 1981 by Ultimate Publishing Co., Inc.
Continued Lunacy, From AMAZING, March, 1983. © 1983 by TSR, Inc.
The Story of a Dādar, from AMAZING, June, 1982. © 1982 by Ultimate Publishing Co., Inc.
A Lantern Maker of Ai Hanlo, From AMAZING, July, 1984. © 1984 by TSR, Inc.
The Story of Obbok, from WHISPERS #2, Dec., 1973. © 1973 by Stuart David Schiff
The Pretenses of Hinyar, from AMRA 69. © 1981 by the Terminus, Owlswick, & Ft. Mudge Electrick Street Railway Gazette
The Story of the Brown Man, from FANTASY CROSSWINDS #1, Jan., 1977. © 1977 by Jonathan Bacon
The Last of the Shadow Titans, from AMAZING, July, 1985. © 1985 by TSR, Inc.
The Stranger from Baal-ad-Theon, Copyright © 1985 by Darrell Schweitzer
The Bermuda Triangle Explained, Copyright © 1985 by Darrell Schweitzer
The Adventure in the House of Phaon, Copyright © 1985 by Darrell Schweitzer
The Last Child of Masferigon, Copyright © 1985 by Darrell Schweitzer and John Gregory Betancourt
A Vision of Rembathene, from FANTASY CROSSROADS 10/11, March, 1977. © 1977 by Jonathan Bacon
Jungle Eyes, from TWILIGHT ZONE, June, 1985. © 1985 by TZ Publications
Sunrise, from PULPSMITH, Winter, 1983. © 1983 by The Generalist Association, Inc.
The Game of Sand and Fire, from THE DRAGON #51, as "A Part of the Game." © 1981 by TRS Hobbies, Inc. Revised version Copyright © 1985 by Darrell Schweitzer
The Wings of the White Bird, from MYRDDIN 4. © 1978 by Lawson W. Hill. Revised version Copyright © 1985 by Darrell Schweitzer

Library of Congress catalogue card number 85-80505
Paper cover edition: ISBN 0-932445-14-4
Hard cover edition: ISBN 0-932445-15-2
Deluxe edition: ISBN 0-932445-16-0

FIRST EDITION

CONTENTS

- 9 TOM O'BEDLAM'S NIGHT OUT
- 18 RAVING LUNACY
- 32 CONTINUED LUNACY
- 47 THE STORY OF A DĀDAR
- 67 A LANTERN MAKER OF AI HANLO
- 77 THE STORY OF OBBOK
- 83 THE OUTCAST (poem)
- 85 THE PRETENSES OF HINYAR
- 93 THE STORY OF THE BROWN MAN
- 101 THE LAST OF THE SHADOW TITANS
- 119 THE STRANGER FROM BAAL-AD-THEON
- 129 THE BERMUDA TRIANGLE EXPLAINED
- 139 THE ADVENTURE IN THE HOUSE OF PHAON
- 153 THE LAST CHILD OF MASFERIGON
- 159 A VISION OF REMBATHENE
- 167 JUNGLE EYES
- 173 SUNRISE
- 179 THE GAME OF SAND AND FIRE
- 186 THE WINGS OF THE WHITE BIRD

TOM O'BEDLAM'S NIGHT OUT

"Swill! Filth! Horse piss!" yelled the ragged man as he threw his bowl onto the stone floor.

"Ah, Tom," said the gaoler. "Be grateful for what ye got."

"Put something in this slop! Meat! A man needs meat to be strong!"

"But meat's expensive, Tom. If ye had two pennies I'd give ye meat, but ye don't, so be quiet or else I'll call the doctor to purge your ill humours."

"I'll get two copper pennies then. I will!"

"Ha! A thief ye will be too? For that they'll hang ye, Tom. Stay a loon and be safe."

And laughing, the gaoler left.

Sad Tom, mad Tom, tattered Tom, removed a bar from his window on this night of All Hallows, in the year of Our Lord 1537. He tied his blanket into a rope and climbed down to the muddy street below. He wandered through shadows and empty lanes beneath a round full moon, and the first person he met was met a half mile away, near the edge of King Harry's good town of London, and this person was a little boy.

"Are you the bogey-man?" he was asked, and if ever an answer was likely that was it.

But Tom made a face and waved his arms and stuck out his tongue and sputtered, "No! I'm the Devil! Gobblegobblegobble!" and the child ran away in terror, screaming that he had seen the Devil.

Tom laughed. He went a little further and met a maid with a bucket in hand.

"Going a'milking?" said Tom. "Not a good night for that. The Devil's loose I hear."

"I'm not milking, sir," replied she, drawing back.

"Then you should! You should!" He pinched her with both hands in two places where she would not be touched. The maid let out a shriek, Tom a yelp of delight, and the two of them were quickly parted. Tom continued on until the houses thinned out and the stink of the city was behind him. He came to a field, in the middle of which a rock moved.

It was a boulder larger than a man and much heavier too, and yet it moved up and down as if an unseen giant were hefting it.

Then suddenly it flew up, up, up, and a star winked as it passed by.

"Won't be back till tomorrow," said a little piping voice. Tom looked down and saw a little man standing where the stone had been, a fellow not more than five inches tall and clad in an oak leaf.

"You are very strong," said Tom. "You must eat fine meat to get that way."

"Indeed," said the man. "The thighs of men roasted, the breasts of maids toasted, little babies whole and raw, your mother's rump, I eat them all——"

"I think I must be getting back. I can't be out this late." Tom began to run, but the little man's voice followed him.

"Wait! You I shall not eat, for the King of Elves holds court tonight and he has summoned you. There's a great reward waiting for you."

Tom stopped, turned around, and came back.

"A reward?"

"Yes. Follow me."

He followed, over fields and fences and walls, through hedges and trees, along roads and over them, into a swamp and out again, all the while falling behind as the other ignored the obstacles that so tormented Tom.

"Slow down," he called out at last, "or I'll lose you."

"You're not lost. You're found. You're here."

And Tom emerged from a final thicket of thorns onto a wide plain where there was a great bonfire tended by witches, and before long he came to the old log which was the throne of the King of Elves. He saw that the King was not tiny, but tall as a mortal man, with a robe of soft green and a flowing red beard. The Queen of Elves sat beside the King, also dressed in green, and there were strings of acorns in her hair. The King spoke.

"Thomas, you have been called here by me to be my champion. You must joust for me as one must every year for my honour with the enemy. If you are victorious a wish will be granted to you from the fullest resources of my magic."

"And if I lose?"

"Why then," laughed the King, "my tithe to Hell will be paid until next year."

Tom knew he was in dire peril then, but he knew also that there was no escape through the throngs around him, so he made the best of it and joined the feast that was being held for the occasion. He joked with the gnomes and dwarves, took fairies by the dozens into his lap, and he ate well of meats no one has tasted in a thousand years. He drank deep of the molten liquor they brewed, and would have forgotten his predicament entirely had not a bent old man with a white beard trailing along the ground, with lantern and thorn branch in hand and a mangy dog trailing behind, come into the midst of them wailing, "Hellgate is open. The time has come. The foe has arrived. The time has come."

"Who is that?" whispered Tom to one beside him.

"The Man In The Moon, although presently not in the Moon," was the reply.

"And the foe?"

"Look."

The crowd drew away from the fire as it flamed brighter than ever, and out of the middle of it came one who was unmistakably Satan himself, and after him a knight on a black horse wearing black armor, with the face of a skull revealed beneath his upraised visor. His lance was aflame and his eyes seemed to be. Smoke snorted from the nostrils of his mount.

Greetings were exchanged between the Devil and the King, and the Lord of Elves called on Tom.

"Rise and come forward, champion, and fight in my name."

"But——I have no horse——"

"Then take one, made of air." The King waved his hand and the dust beneath Tom's feet began to stir. He was caught in a whirlwind and raised up. He felt the muscles of a horse rippling beneath him. He felt a saddle, and his feet found stirrups, but to his eye there was nothing except a dim shape, like a cloud. His steed whinnied and stamped.

"I have no lance," said Tom.

"Then take one." A burning twig was brought from the edge of the fire.

"**This** is a lance?"

"Take it," commanded the King and Tom took it by the end that wasn't afire. As soon as he touched it it lengthened and grew and became a fine, flaming lance indeed.

"Now the battle shall begin," said the King.

"But I lack a helmet," said Tom, desperate for excuses.

"Take one then." The same witch who had handed him the twig now offered a leaf, and he put it on his head where it became a silver helmet with two slits to see through. She gave him also a plate which expanded into a shield, and she said a word and his rags were armor. Now without any more ways to delay the inevitable, Tom gulped hard and muttered a prayer to the Saviour. As he did the whole company hissed like a thousand snakes, and the King said angrily, "**Speak not such words!**"

In silence Tom was led away from the fire on his horse of wind and dust, and the black knight followed to a place where there was plenty of room for combat. Only the King and the Devil stood near.

"Now fight," said the King, and Tom was terrified.

"But wait. I'm not ready. I don't know——"

"What don't you know?"

"Who am I fighting?"

"The same one who comes every year for this."

"You mean——nobody has ever beat him?"

"Tom, I have great hopes for you."

"Well, who is he?"

"The Knight of Ghosts and Shadows. His name is Kamathakalamailetheknafor."

"**What**?"

"Such is his name. It is said that no mortal can repeat it, and thus none can gain power over him."

"Then how shall I——?"

"Good luck, my champion."

A trumpet sounded. The Knight of Ghosts and Shadows lowered his visor, and his lance. With no further warning he spurred his horse and charged. Tom in his confusion fumbled for the invisible rein of his barely visible steed. At the same time he kicked it in the ribs and the creature bolted forward. His lance was up, then down, then swaying side to side. When the two met Tom's point missed his opponent entirely, while the other's crashed into his shield and broke it like the old plate it was. The force of the blow sent Tom tumbling to the ground.

He landed with a clang of metal and lay stunned. When next he was aware the Knight stood over him with a red hot sword upraised, and helpless Tom, who had raved wilder things before, cried out, "Oh spare me, Kamathakalamailetheknafor, please!"

And the Knight of Ghosts and Shadows paused and began to sway, and then he fell over backwards. At the same time Tom's armor became his rags again, and with the weight off him he was able to sit up. He saw his smoldering spear on the ground a good way off, and at his feet was a skeleton in a rusty suit, which crumbled as he watched, became only a heap of bones, then dust, then nothing at all.

The King of Elves lifted him to his feet, and all shouted his praises except Satan, who scowled and stalked back into the fire, took the flames with him and shut the door to Hell. By the light of the stars and the moon another feast was held, and this time Tom was treated like a God.

"Now Champion," said the King after a while. "What reward will you take?"

"I——I——uh——hadn't thought——I don't know."

"Would you like to be King of India?"

"I don't know."

"Well then know." And the Elfking took a wand and touched Tom on the head with it. All the folk around him vanished, and the field did also. For a minute Tom was King of India, sitting on his throne while eunuchs fanned him with huge feathers, and a hundred African maidens danced before him."

"It's awfully hot there," he said when he came back, "and I don't know how to rule anyway."

"Then do you desire riches?"

"Riches?"

"All the gold in the mountains of the Moon. Look up."

Tom looked up at the full moon which still had no man in it, and he felt himself floating. As if he were made of smoke he

rose above the earth. Below him the field grew small and vanished, and he saw all of England, then all the sea, then all the world. The round face of the moon grew larger, until it filled the whole sky. Then he was falling down, not up, into the valleys and mountains of the moon. He came to a stop in the middle of a barren plain and saw huge ingots the size of elephants strewn about, and mountains of pure gold in the distance, and even a volcano which spewed forth a golden stream. Then he was back on earth again and he said, "I could never carry that."

"Will you make up your mind, soon?" The King was growing impatient. "Dawn will be coming soon and you must choose before then."

And Tom, afraid of losing all the riches and power and privilege in the world, could say nothing at all.

"Well, think," said the King. "What did you most recently wish for? What did you want this morning?"

"Two copper pennies," blurted Tom, before he knew he'd said it.

"Done! Two copper pennies you shall have."

"Wait, I——"

"Two copper pennies." The King clapped his hands and did a little dance, and his shape began to change. He shifted into something not at all human, and he shrank and darkened, and sprouted feathers. His neck grew disproportionately long; his lips grew out from his face and became a bill; his arms flattened into wings. The King had turned himself into a black swan. Tom looked on in amazement, and he began to feel sick. He seemed to be falling. His limbs would not obey him, and he looked up to see how the Man Not In The Moon, the witches, and even the dwarves towered over him. In the place of his hands he discovered black feathers, and knew then that he had become a swan too.

"Follow," said the King in a voice that sounded odd coming from the bill of a swan.

The two of them took to the air. It was natural for Tom, like running or jumping. It seemed that he had always known how to fly. He soared with the King away from the field, away from the Isle of Britain entirely, over the channel, across France, and above another sea. The moon was a lantern to light their way, and when clouds closed beneath them there was yet another ocean, this one all of glowing mist. They overtook night owls in their flight, and bats, and even a witch on her broom. All were left behind as Tom followed the King until land was beneath them again. They dropped lower, passed two artificial mountains, and followed a river. They came at last to a hidden place, to the catacombs of Nephren-Ka in the forgotten valley of Hadoth by the banks of the Nile, to the tomb of a Pharaoh the histories never mention. At the door of the tomb they became men very briefly, then serpents, and on their bellies they wriggled between the stones, down into the deepest vault where the coffin of the Black Pharaoh lay. The snake who was the Elfking caused there to be a faint light, and Tom could see the grim, shrivelled face of the Pharaoh, and the two copper coins laid on his eyes.

"There are your pennies, Tom," said the King. "Take them in your mouth and come away. There isn't much time."

And so Tom wriggled over the corpse of the one who had rested there so many centuries and scooped up the two pennies off the eyes to reveal a hateful glare undiminished by time. He screamed at the sight and nearly swallowed the coins. The light went out, and in complete darkness the Elfking spoke.

"Come! Hurry!"

The two of them crawled back between the stones, and up out of the tomb. Tom followed the other only by the rustling of the King's dry body, and by smell, which was much more acute than it had been when he had a human nose. At last dim light appeared overhead, and they emerged onto the desert sand. To the east the sky was beginning to brighten.

"Be quick," said the King. "If daylight catches us we can never resume our true forms." He changed them both into swans once more, and off they flew, racing the dawn all the way back to England.

This time the clouds beneath them were not a sea but a land, a wondrous country brought alive by the sun, and hidden to those who dwell only on the ground. Tom thought he saw hills and valleys, bright castles with tall white towers overlooking glowing fields. Where the clouds broke there were vast cateracts dropping to the unimaginable world below.

They flew on until London was beneath them, and the swan that was the Elfking said to Tom, "Go now where you will, and touch ground only when you have arrived, for when you do you'll be a man again." Then he folded his wings and dropped away into the retreating darkness, and was seen no more.

Tom winged on, over the palace, over the bridge and the Thames, until he came to Bishopgate. He swooped very low and a night watchman saw him, and wondered what was the meaning of this strange thing, this swan with coins in its bill. The watchman came for a closer look as Tom dropped behind a fence. He found him there, looking dazed, but there was no swan. Tom had changed, spit out the coins, and pocketted them the instant before the guard arrived. He was recognized.

"You! What are you doing loose? You know where you belong."

"I know, and I've nowhere else to go."

"Then I'll take you back." The watchman took Tom by the scruff of the neck and dragged him through the still empty and dark streets as morning began to break over the city. He came to a familiar old building with a wooden sign swinging over the door which read:

BETHLEHEM HOSPITAL
FOR THE DEMENTED
God Help all ye
who enter here.

"Is this one of yours?" demanded the guard of the gaoler.

"It is."

"Then see that he doesn't get out again."

When the watchman was gone, Tom said, "I've got the two pennies, like I said I would."

"Did ye now? Indeed."

"In fact and also in deed."

"Quick! Show me them before anyone else wakes up."

Tom gave him the two coins, and the gaoler puzzled over the unfamiliar designs on them.

"Will you put meat in my soup now?"

The gaoler dropped one penny in his pocket, and held up the other. "The first is to make up for the trouble ye caused by running away, but the second will buy ye something for your dinner, as long as ye tell me where ye got them."

Tom told him the whole story, leaving out no details, and distorting it very little. When he was done he was not believed, as he had feared. The gaoler looked at him silently for a moment with a mixture of disgust and pity, then sighed, "Ah Tom, you're mad as ever and nothing will change that."

He put Tom back in his cell, and dropped the second coin in with the first, but the two did not rest there. The end was not yet, not quite anyway.

The gaoler sent a boy down into the cellar to kill a rat for the soup, then forgot about Tom altogether. He paced back and forth desperately, waiting for the long hours to pass until the shops would open, the coins like red-hot coals in his pocket, so eager was he to spend them. The gaoler was not a thrifty man.

At last a steeple clock struck nine, and the time was come. He ran out into the street, past windows filled with tempting things, and made his first stop an inn. Inside, he ordered a drink, had one of his new pennies changed, and it was only a moment before the innkeeper was turning the coin over and over in his hand and muttering, "This money isn't English. And it isn't French, or Spanish."

Just then the innkeeper's wife came by. She took one look and pronounced, "It's not money at all. It's fake!"

"Fake! Fraud! Counterfeit!" The cry was raised by all there, by all who stood in the street outside, and a mob formed. They chased the gaoler back the way he had come, yelling, and a sheriff joined them, and several guardsmen with pikes.

When they got to the hospital the crowd huddled outside while the sheriff and the guards went in one minute and came out the next with the offender in custody.

"'Tis death to counterfeit," the sheriff intoned righteously.

"**What**?" came a voice. "Would you put to death a poor lunatic that doesn't know right from wrong?"

Everyone turned, and there was Tom standing in the street. He'd climbed out of the window again and come down to see what all the excitement was about. His eyes met the gaoler's and no

words were spoken, but a message was passed:
Help me Tom. They'll kill me if ye don't. I'll do anything. Please.

"Who are you?" demanded the sheriff.

"I'm the keeper."

"What? He's the keeper!"

"Oh no, he's a lunatic. We let him play his game of being the keeper to keep him good. Otherwise he's violent. His wit's diseased."

And at that moment the gaoler was so astonished that he looked the part.

"You mean," said the sheriff, "that he's——**mad**?"

"Quite"

"Then he belongs in a cell, not out here loose!"

"He does."

The sheriff ordered the guards, "You there! Take him inside and lock him in a cell."

They did, and from their looks when they came out you'd think they had been handling a leper.

"Thank you," said Tom. "You've all been very helpful."

"See that he doesn't get out again," said the sheriff. "If he does, lunatic or not, I'll have his head."

"I'll keep him safe. Don't worry."

Some hours later Tom found the rat meat the boy had left, and he put it in the gaoler's soup.

"Here's meat for you," said Tom, "and I won't charge you for it. Not anything. Not a penny."

"Ah Tom," the other sighed, "Ye're the soul of kindness."

RAVING LUNACY

"I am mad north by north-west, and in any other direction things are not much better."
———The Collected Works of Anonymous

There were lunatics aplenty on the roads in those days; it was a splendid time to be mad. All too many filled the halls of Bethlehem Mercy Hospital, better known as Bedlam ("God help all ye who enter here!"), and so it was that some of those whose condition was unquestionable, who could not be taken for mere rogues or frauds, were sent out into the world to beg. It was cheaper. It looked good in the account books. It provided endless amusement to passersby.

Thus, a curious person named Tom——between eight and eighty, taller than a cricket and shorter than an oak——who had never been even suspected of sanity, and an equally certain Nicholas, formerly a gaoler of the place but now fallen on difficult times, set forth to win their bacon. They wandered among the other distracted, fantastical fellows blowing horns, ringing little bells, making strange faces at people, and singing stranger songs.

One day they met an old man dressed all in black.

"A coin, sirrah? A trivial, tiny, tsk-tsk penny of a coin?"

"Oh no," said he, trembling as he leaned on his cane. "I can give you nothing, for I am suffering from the ague, and must pay all I have to a doctor of physick to get rid of my ills."

"But we can drive them away with a few verses," said Tom, and he nudged his companion. The two of them leaned on their crooked staves, swayed from side to side in time, and sang:

"From the hag and the hungry goblin
That into rags would rend ye,
All spirits stand
By the naked man
In the Book of Moons defend ye!"

And the old man laughed, gave each of them a small coin, and went on his way. It is not recorded if he was cured or not.

And they came upon a miser, counting up his money. He was in the back of a wagon doing it, hugging his bags of gold, surrounded by ruffians to guard him.

"A coin? A coin for two poor souls bereft of wit and will?"

"Go to, go to," said the ruffians, "and go away, before we knock your teeth down yer throat an' out yer arse."

And the two madmen sang:
> "Grim king of ghosts make haste,
>   And bring hither all your train;
>   See how the pale moon does waste,
>   And just now is in the wane.
>   Come you night-hags, with all your charms,
>   And revelling witches away,
>   Hug me close in your arms;
>   To you my respects I'll pay."

Hearing this, the miser was run through with dread, for he knew that the waning moon of the song was his own fortune and perhaps his life, and the night-hags, well — overall those words could bring down upon one anything from whirlwinds to breaking wind, to boils, to elf-shot, to sour milk, to a kick in the butt and a visit from (not so, in this respect, in fact a greedy old bugger) Good King Harry's tax collectors. He barked a command, and the wagon was off in a clatter.

On that same day, a few hours later, Tom and his friend sat by the roadside, lazily dangling bells from their fingers, when they had a third encounter.

There came the tread of many feet, the jangling of metal on metal.

The two sprang up, mumbling lines from idiotic old songs, but before they could launch fully into their routine, they found themselves face-to-face with a sheriff and half a dozen men at arms with pikes and steel helmets. The sheriff looked o'er his left shoulder, and a grim look looked he, and then he turned around because it was more comfortable and glared. The men-at-arms were scarcely more cheerful. Only one had to repress a snicker.

And the sheriff handed a paper to Nick, who twitched his head sideways and said, "Alas, a poor demented soul like me can't read."

So the sheriff snatched it back, let out a **harumph**, cleared his throat, and read (in pompous black letter, if it is possible to vocalise a typeface):

"Be it known that **Nicholas Block,** formerly keeper of the Bethlehem Hospital For The Moonstruck, Hag-Ridden, Melt-a'-Brained, And Generally Addled, shall be charged with the foul offense of **counterfeiting,** for which he may be hanged, on account of the affair of two unlikely pennies, as has been previously related in a doubtful history yclept, to-wit, and without further ado, "Tom O'Bedlam's Night Out," and unless that same **Nicholas Block** can, within thirty days of this notice, prove himself to be truly beyond his wit's end, that is to say mad and not just pretending, all rights shall be forfeited, all contracts void, licences revoked, & off with his head, if the hangman doesn't get there first. Signed, Lord High Judge To His Majesty's Court, Honorius Muckamuck, Etcetera, Etcetera, Gesundheit, Amen. Anno MDXXXVIII. **God Save The King!**"

"From what may we save him, pray tell?" asked Nicholas Block,

as if he hadn't understood any of the foregoing.
"You surely know," said the sheriff, "that it's wicked to pretend. Why, all the **false** madmen in this country ought to be locked up, and will be, at the very least!"
"For the public good," said Tom, solemnly.
"For that very reason. So, Nicholas Block, show yourself out of your head within the month, or else."
"You could go **mad** with the effort," said the man-at-arms who had had to repress the snicker. He could no longer, and threw a coin to Tom, who caught it, put it between his teeth, bit off a piece, and swallowed.
"Hmm, good," he said, and swallowed the rest.
Now there was a whole chorus of snickers, and the sheriff was too busy snarling at his men to notice until too late that Nick had snatched the pronouncement out of his hand, torn it into strips, thrown his head back, and was in the process of swallowing them one by one.
Everyone was laughing except the sheriff, whose face was as fierce as a heathen idol. Some people have no sense of humor.

* * *

As dusk came upon them that same day, Tom and Nick came upon a carriage stopped in the middle of the road. Three men were grunting and straining as they strove to replace a broken wheel. A distance away from them two ladies stood, fluttering fans in front of their faces even though the air was getting cool. They both started as the two ragged figures approached.
Tom blew a blast on his horn, evicting a mouse which had been dwelling in it, and sang:
"The spirits white as lightning,
Would on me travels guile me.
The moon would shake
And the stars would quake,
Whenever they espied me."
"How terrible! Brave fellow!" the ladies laughed.
Not to be outdone, Nick broke in:
"I slept not till the Conquest;
Till then I never waked;
Till the roguish boy
Of love where I lay
Found me and stript me naked."
At this one lady rolled her eyes to heaven in feigned dismay and said, "Well that's certainly **odd**!"
But the other applauded. "Poor, poor wretch," said she, and, seeing that Nick was barefoot, she took a pair of bell-tipped slippers out of her luggage and gave them to him.
"I thank ye, ma'am, from the bottom of my empty skull, which is bottomless, 'tis said."
He put the slippers on his hands, stood on them, and ran along the highway, over a hill and out of sight, his toes waving in the

air.

"I think you've **got it**," said Tom when he caught up with him, and they both lay in the grass, gasping for breath. "That was the craziest thing I've ever seen."

"Then **why** doesn't the judge believe me? Aren't I as mad as can be?"

"His Honor doesn't think so."

"But I've raved. I've ranted."

"So have lawyers."

"I've seen rare and terrible visions."

"John the Apostle saw so many he filled a book with them and called it **Revelations.** Now would ye be so blasphemous a knave as to call him mad?"

"Well... no —— but I'm no bloody saint neither! Tom, you've helped me before, even when I didn't deserve it. What am I to do?"

"**Do** is just it. Don't think, **do**. We lunatics follow our fancies. It's a way of looking at the world, madness is, and the world looking back at you, and running shrieking from what it sees. An unphiloslopical —— er, untrilotropical —— an unphilo**sophical** philosophy. And if you can't mouth gibberish like this, you haven't a chance..."

The two of them sat still as the evening darkened, and the shadows flowed like the tide from behind the houses and out of the forests and covered the land. The sky was a deep blue, the sun an orange trace in the west. The first stars appeared. Night hawks flew. Cowbells rang far away as the herds were driven home.

At last Tom rose and said, "Stay here a while. I won't be gone long."

"Where are you going?"

"To find the answer, of course. Everything is written in the Book of Moons. You just have to know how to read it."

He walked alone across the darkened fields until he came to an old pagan place, ringed with upturned stones. He climbed atop a horizontal piece, which lay across two vertical ones, and looked to the east.

At first the moon was only a glimmer between the trees on a distant hill, then a brightness like a signal fire, and then it was slowly gliding into the sky, full in all its glory and roundness, and the Man In The Moon, his thorn branch, staff, and dog hidden in the brilliant glare of his lantern, looked down on the world.

He winked.

In response, Tom howled. He called out to the moon itself, not the man, in a language which has no words and is lost to ordinary folk. He addressed it as mother, lover, and goddess of the night, and he asked of it a favor, that a way might be found out of his friend's difficulties. The answer came as the spirit of the moon filled him and it seemed that all the world was filled with soft light and he was floating on it like water. He was quiet. The

world was quiet. There were none of the usual night sounds. He leaned back, as if asleep in the peace of the moon.
And fell off the stone.
The darkness was a riot of chirps and rustlings.
The Man In The Moon winked again.

*   *   *

When he returned to where he had left him, Tom found Nick on all fours, staring intently at a clump of reeds.
"Tom! Hush! Be careful! I've had a vision and you might step on it!"
"Don't be afraid. I won't squash it."
"You don't understand. It was a little man, a hand high — look!"
"There's a lot of that going around."
But even as he spoke, Tom looked, and he saw something moving out of the reeds.
It was a box, revealed by the moonlight to be intricately carven. At first it seemed to be moving of its own accord, but then he saw that it was carried by a little man only half as large as it was. The fellow was plainly exhausted. At any moment he might drop dead, crushed by his burden.
"Please sirs," came a diminutive voice. "**Can I put it down**?"
Nick looked to his friend quizzically.
"First tell us," said Tom, "why you have to ask permission."
"It's part of the curse. Five thousand years ago the wizard said I couldn't put it down without being told to, but if someone else were to take the box, **he** could do whatever he liked——"
But Nick broke in, "For mercy's sake, let him rest." And to the elf: "Yes, put it down. Then explain."
The man seemed to evaporate, and the box fell to the ground. He was not to be seen. The companions leaned forward, wondering if he'd been mashed, and jumped back again as a black snake whipped out from under and pressed the latch with its snout.
The lid flipped open, and a thing emerged to confound the eye. A puff of smoke hovered over the spot. In a flicker there followed an explosion of something off-white, like dirty milk, followed by a shapeless mass of flesh wriggling free, a glob far larger than the box. Finally an old woman stood there, leaning on a cane. She was archetypically hideous with a long, warty nose that almost touched her chin, a trace of whiskers around her mouth, a wide assortment of blemishes and boils on her face and bags under the eyes, and an evil grin which exposed green, irregularly spaced teeth. For the barest instant she could hardly stand astride the box, but then she grew like a skin being inflated until her glittering eyes were on the same level as those of Tom and Nick, who were crouched down on their haunches. That would make her about three feet tall.
The serpent coiled up one leg. She took it in hand and held it to her breast, where it vanished into her clothing.

Tittering, she hobbled over the open plain, still leaning on her stick, yet going at such a pace she could have outraced a stallion.

"Oh God," said Nick, "**what** have we let loose?"

"I think we'll find out," said Tom.

* * *

Dejected, afraid, they wandered in search of a place to spend the night. Nick took the empty box with him in hope that someone could tell them something about it.

At length they came to a hollow log large enough to accommodate the both of them, and they crawled inside, falling at once into a troubled sleep.

In the middle of the night Tom sat up suddenly and looked outside. What he saw made his heart skip a beat with terror. Nick was out there, chained and bound, surrounded by the sheriff and his men. Their helmets and blades gleamed in the moonlight.

They had forced Nick to kneel down, and one of them held him by the hair and pulled his head forward until it was all he could do to maintain his balance.

A gigantic executioner, bare-chested and hooded in black, hefted an enormous axe over the exposed neck.

Tom noticed that all of them took special care not to turn their backs to Nick. The reason for this was obvious: all of them were hollow behind. They had only three sides to their bodies and were open on the fourth. They stood and moved like sails filled with wind.

The axe rose and was about to fall.

"Stop!" He scrambled out of the log and charged. One hand passed into the executioner's open back and out through his front, which felt like a mass of dusty spiderwebs. There was a pop, and all the apparitions vanished save for the executioner who, now two-dimensional like a sheet of paper caught in the wind, whirled and tumbled over the fields. Scarcely comprehending the impulse, Tom chased after him.

"Wait! Come back here! Explain all this!"

But the executioner blew on, until at last he caught around something standing upright and flapped, like a flag tangled around its pole.

Tom crashed into whatever it was and found it as unyielding as stone.

The 'flag' wrapped itself over his face. He felt and smelled the heat and sweat of the executioner's body for a minute or two, but then hands other than his own were tearing the thing away.

He found himself in the arms of the green-toothed crone. She tittered again, then spoke very clearly the words "Grandmother Grey," and let go of him. She hobbled jerkily away as she had before, impossibly fast.

As he was watching her vanish in the distance, something struck Tom on the head. The world blinked out and back into existence, and he found himself inside the log. He had hit his head sitting up, and before that he had been dreaming.

At the same moment Nick was coming in the other end of the log.

"Tom," said he, "I know I'm mad, of course, but still it was the strangest thing. I dreamed that I was standing at a crossroads, where a highwayman was hanging from a gibbet. He was slowly turning in the cold wind, muttering to himself. Then I woke up because it was so cold, and I was really there, barefoot in the snow beneath a body rotating in the wind."

"**Snow**?"

There was no need to answer. Outside, even though it was the middle of July, snow drifted down out of a steely sky.

"It's Grandmother Grey," said Tom, his breath coming in white puffs. "She did all this."

"That's what the hanged man said."

* * *

The day did not really dawn. The sky faded somewhat into a murky twilight. Height and distance were lost in the swirling flakes. Already the landscape was covered with a rolling white blanket, the rough surface of twigs, leaves, grass, and stones smoothed over and buried.

The two companions huddled in their log, tearing strips from their doublets (as neither had a cloak) to tie around their feet. The slippers the lady had given Nick the previous evening proved useful after all.

The world was otherwise empty. There were no travellers on the road. Doubtless everyone had either found shelter or perished in the night.

"I think..." Nick said, his words interrupted with grunts as he struggled with a knot which would not stay knotted, "that we... will have to put an end to what we've begun..."

"Beard the beast in its lair," said Tom.

"Does Grandmother Grey have a beard?"

"If you look closely, yes she does."

"Who is she, anyway?"

"No sane mind could believe it, but she is the mother of Darkness nevertheless. She hates all things warm and alive. She hates color, and bleaches it out of everything she touches. She can only stand pure white——snow——and the grey of twilight, the black of the inside of a tomb. And I think she will tolerate blue, if it's a corpse. You know:

"From Grandmother Grey till the break of day,
I'll flee until I'm frozen.
Till the sky turns black
And me bones all crack,
And I'm in the grave she's chosen."

"But where did she come from?"

"Where?" quoth Tom. "The story goes that an old god wanted to create the human race, so he drank a potion, planning to spit us all out, but he belched, and there she was. One look at her and he gave up, which is why you and I are sons of Adam and Eve, not someone else."

The two of them rose, wrapped their rags as tightly around themselves as they could, took staves in hand, and set out, faces into the wind. Tom shivered and looked down on a dead crow, and several still blooming flowers bending with the wind. He wished he could have the executioner of his dream with him now, flapping as a cloak. Anything. It was so cold.

The bells on Nick's slippers tinkled mournfully.

* * *

A mountain rose in the middle of the plain, at the very spot where the box had been opened. When the snow was no more than a sprinkle, and even before that, when farmers merely shrugged at the unseasonable chill and hoped it would be warm again by morning, the thing was there. It condensed out of the air faster than the snow could fall, but the flakes added to it, as if a hundred fell there for each one somewhere else. The heap on the ground grew into a drift, then into a cold mound, like something a heathen king of winter would be buried under, and it continued to rise until cliffs of pale ice towered over the countryside. Fields and forests were swallowed up by the expanding base. People fled from it in long lines along the roads, sunk in up to their knees, leading their cattle and carrying what goods could be borne away.

There was a preacher who stood in a tree exhorting the people to fall down then and there and repent, for surely God's judgment was on the land for their wickedness. He was ignored. The wind drove the refugees on, until the holy man was alone.

He was astonished to see Tom and Nick coming from the direction in which the others had gone.

"Stop! You can't go toward the mountain! You must be out of your minds!"

"Yea verily, verily, I say unto you verily verily you're right the first time," said Tom.

"Verily," said Nick between chattering teeth.

"The Devil!" said the holy man.

"No, it's too cold for him. Grandmother Grey."

* * *

The mountain rose black against the sky out of which the snow whirled. The wind blew and blew. The peaks creaked and rumbled as they drove higher into the murk. It was the hour before noon.

As Tom and Nick began to climb, they felt they were on a treadmill, because the distance would increase for every step they took. But then they got ahead of it, and were carried aloft on the still growing mountain.

The snow was so thick around them they were blinded in a white void. At times they could see a few drifts and blocks of ice, at other times nothing. There was no sense of altitude, as they could neither see top nor bottom. Instead, they drifted in a directionless universe by themselves as the snow whirled around them. The only colors were white and grey and the only sensation was cold.

When they got to the top they saw to their astonishment that the snow wasn't falling out of heaven the way it does in a natural winter. It rose in a column out of a huge stone chimney the same way ashes are expelled from a volcano. Then the wind caught the flakes and spread them over the world.

"Hello!" cried Nick, leaning over the opening, face into the blast.

"Hush! We're uninvited. It's best we come unannounced."

There was a precarious stairway cut around the inside of the crater, spiralling down into the heart of the mountain. Doubtless someone's grandmother used it for comings and goings, and perhaps it was also trod upon by monsters and snow elves, slithered over by ice snakes, and Tom could well imagine frost dragons following it as they drifted up from the bottom on their silvery wings.

But now it was empty. From below, if they listened carefully over the shrieking wind, the two companions could hear the sound of hammering, like a smith at a forge.

Which is exactly what it was.

When they had at last completed their descent, both of them ghastly pale from the cold and beyond all shivering, having braved the incredible fury of the upward current, they found themselves standing on a polished floor of ice as smooth and slippery as a mirror. Carefully sliding along the wall, they came to a doorway and entered a foundry, where a naked blue giant, twice as tall as mortal man and four times as massive, labored over a forge.

No heat came from his fire. The flickering blue flames were as frigid as the rest of the place. The giant would stoke them for a while, then go to his bellows, and they would burst up. Out of them he would draw with a pair of tongs what seemed to be a ball of pure Cold, an abstract thing made concrete: it was glassy with a trace of silver. An azure light flickered at its core. This ball he would place on his anvil and pound with a hammer until it shattered into millions of snowflakes, which the wind would suck out of the room and up the chimney.

He worked for several minutes, his back to the two humans, but then Nick scratched behind a numb ear and an icicle fell to the floor, shattering.

"Whozzat?" The giant whirled about, revealing a chest covered with white hairs and a face which sported an oversized blue nose. All his body was blue, of course, but it was a dirty-white blue, like a corpse abandoned in a wintry field. His nose, however, was a brilliant, almost glowing sapphire. Even under such circumstances, and as fierce and unnatural as he looked, the nose was impressive.

"Whorryyyou?"

"Who are **you**?" asked Tom. "We asked first."

"Nnnooo." The giant wheezed, and his breath was as piercing as any blizzard.

"In that case you'll have to excuse us, since we are both lunatics and have trouble keeping track of such things. Your pardon, grave, noble, heroic, hardworking sir."

"**Huhh**?" The giant looked around, as if seeking advice. Then he scratched his shaggy head — dandruff fell like snowflakes or snowflakes like dandruff, one or the other — and at last comprehended the flattery. He stood up straight, chest out, shoulders back, gut sucked in, smiled, and said carefully, with great pride, "I am The Great Snog. I am far greater than The Lesser Snog, who isn't here."

"Where is he?" Nick interrupted. Tom scowled at him, but The Great Snog was non-plussed.

"Out running errands for his ggrrandmother. I wish he werrre hhhhere. I neeed someone to wwwworkk the bbbellowss. Ittt slows mmme downnn."

"We're just the ones," said Tom. "Being mad, we desire what sane men dread, so we'd like nothing more than the whole world covered with ice and snow."

"Yesssss... ssso nice... quiet and cold and dark. Grandmother will like you... At least you're not hhhere to ssteal my nose. There was a hhhero hhhere once, but Grandmother warned me. Hhis name wasss Sigulf... or Siglop... something like that."

"He stole your nose?"

"Nnnooo. We gggot him. Grandmother sssays if sssomebody stole my nose, my power to make cccold would be loss**tt**. But we gott**t** him. **There**."

The two of them looked where a massive finger pointed, and beheld the hero in all his Teutonic glory, clad in horned helmet and elf-wrought byrnie, with magic sword in hand—and frozen in a block of ice and hung on the wall of the cave as a trophy.

"We'll have to meet your grandmother sometime," said Tom. "But now to work."

Nick looked at him askance, wondering just what the plan was.

The two of them labored at the bellows and the production of pure cold doubled, then tripled, then quintupled as The Great Snog hammered away in a frenzy of enthusiasm, happy to have such willing assistants. The Lesser Snog was always so quarrelsome. He never appreciated good work. So The Great Snog was happy. Audiences were scarce in his trade. He wanted to show them what he could do.

As he worked, he sang a frigid tune. So cold it had gotten in the room by that point that his breath froze, dropping from his lips to the floor in a tinkle. As each piece shattered, a word was released, and the song drifted upward: "It's... snowing... it's blowing... the... world... in... darkness**s**... gggrowinggg...."

The tune was rather like **It's raining/it's pouring/the old man is**

snoring/ etc., although the giant was badly off key.
  After a while his efforts got the better of him, and he was heaving with exhaustion.
  "Musssttt snnooozzze..."
  "Yes," said Tom. "Take a nap. Don't worry. We'll take over for you."
  The giant lay down, while Tom beat out the pure cold, and Nick operated the bellows. After a while The Great Snog was fast asleep.
  The two of them stopped. The air cleared as only a slight residue of snowflakes went up the chimney.
  "Now what?" Nick asked.
  "Steal his nose, of course."
  The Great Snog snored. There was a sucking sound as he inhaled, and then he spat out little globs of ice, which cracked as they hit the ground and released the other half of the snore.
  "We'd best hurry," said Nick. "How do we get it off."
  "Pull, I suppose."
  "No, Tom, I think I have a better idea. Let's melt him."
  "What? In all this cold? If you weren't mad, I'd say that was the silliest thing I'd ever heard."
  "No, watch."
  And as Tom watched he tore off a piece of his underclothing, which was still dry, and set it afire with flint and steel from his pocket. Tom tore off a piece of his garments and touched it to the flame. Both of them sneaked gingerly over to the sleeping Snog.
  "Tom, when I hold him down, you grab the nose."
  Both of them stood stealthily above their victim, then simultaneously dropped the burning cloths onto the giant's face. There was a burst of steam, and The Great Snog awoke with a roar. Both of them leapt onto him, Nick struggling to hold the cloths on him. The three of them rolled and tumbled. The cavern shook with their shouts.
  The nose came off in Tom's hand, and the giant stopped moving. He leaned like an awkward statue in a half crouching, half kneeling position, clutching at his face, crushing Tom and Nick under either arm. Relieved, they wriggled free.
  Tom held up the nose for Nick to see.
  "Let's find Grandmother Grey," he said.
  From the back of the foundry there was another set of stairs going down, down, down, into limitless darkness.
  At the bottom of that was a door marked PRIVATE in glowing letters.
  "This must be her chamber," said Tom. He blew on the doorknob and his warm, human breath must have melted any locks. The door swung inward silently.
  It was indeed her chamber. There was a bed of downy snow, with icicles for posts and a headboard decorated with crystalline curlicues. An ice cat, looking like the masterwork of some genius

glassblower, sat curled on the pillow. When Nick stroked it, the animal purred, and little clouds of snowflakes drifted out of its nostrils.

On the nightstand were two mirrors, one of ice, to reflect, and the other of darkness, through which one could look out over the world and see how the devastation was coming along.

In open jars were Grandmother Grey's cosmetics: blue-black lipstick, ashen grey face powder, and eyeshadow made from the blood of frozen corpses.

This room led to another door marked: POSITIVELY NO ONE ALLOWED, AND THAT MEANS YOU, SNOGS #1 AND #2.

"Even more private," said Tom.

"Fortunately, neither of us is a Snog, greater or lesser."

They opened it. A shriek came from within.

"Who **dares** disturb me in my bath?"

This room contained a frozen pool as wide as a small lake, in the middle of which lay Grandmother Grey, held by the ice so that only her hands and face were above its surface. Her hair spread out in all directions a few inches down, held rigid by the ice, like the petals of a withered flower. A dim blue light emanated from the bottom of the pool and reflected off the domed ceiling, filling the room. She was wearing sunglasses.

The two walked out to her.

"Have you still got the box," Tom whispered.

"Yes, here it is." Nick gave it to him. He opened it, slipped the nose inside, then closed it again.

"A curse on you both!" screamed Grandmother Grey. "You will be the very last to freeze and you'll feel the cold the longest."

"Ah, Grandmother, you recognise us. We've met your grandson, the one with the spectacular nose."

Tom opened the box and tilted it, so she could see what was inside.

"No! You can't!" Faster than the eye could see, she reached out with her left hand, and her face and her right hand disappeared, and her whole body flowed like smoke out the hole in the ice where her left wrist had been. Like a gaseous serpent she writhed and wriggled around Tom and the box. He trembled but didn't drop it.

Her hand was the only definitely shaped part of her left. This crawled spider-like into the box and the rest followed, settling over the nose until the mist was entirely within, and defined by the four square sides.

"Now!" yelled Nick.

"Yes, now," said Tom, snapping the lid closed.

And the winter witch let out a long, woeful "Eeeeek!" but before she could move it was too late. Tom fingered the latch into place.

At that very moment the air temperature began to rise. The surface of the bath turned into ankle-deep slush. Tom and Nick left the place as quickly as they could. On the way out, Tom noticed that the ice mirror was dripping and the cat had drowned in the bedsheets. The Great Snog remained where he had stiffened, but the Nordic hero, whoever he was, was beginning to thaw out. It was a treacherous and slippery way up the stairs out of the mountain, but the way down the outside was easier because the mountain was shrinking even as they descended, and there was less far to go. Still Tom held onto the box tightly, lest he accidentally drop it, the lid spring open on contact with the earth, and this all start again.

"You realise," he said to Nick as he gave him the box, when the two of them stood in a muddy field as the sun set in a clear sky, "that you'll have to carry this box for the rest of your life, never once putting it down."

"But... but..." Nick sputtered. "I'd have to be **mad** to do that!"

"And, when you're dying, you'll have to find someone else to carry it."

* * *

But, to return to the more immediate:

The rest of that summer was not like any other. Leaves had fallen from the trees, crops were ruined, and many of the birds had died. But others returned, and some flowers bloomed. It was hard for a while after that, but people were thankful enough that the world was saved. Sober historians, of course, have left no record of the blizzard of the summer of 1538. It was too preposterous. Theologians said little about it either, finding no precedent in Scripture.

Tom and Nick sat by the side of the same road a month later, singing the same songs and dangling the same bells, when again they heard the tramp of iron-shod feet and the clank of arms.

"You there, Nicholas Block," barked the sheriff. "You have not proven yourself mad, so come with us."

"No, no, sir, by all that's holy, I dare not, for if I do, you'll take this box away and set it down, and the witch of winter will escape with her grandson's nose, and the snow will start again." He trembled and held onto the box desperately. And he told the entire story of his adventure, as it happened.

"Why," exclaimed the sheriff, "that's the most **absurd** thing I have ever heard! 'Sblood, fool, **ye're out of yer bloody head!**"

CONTINUED LUNACY

The city of London creaked and groaned in the cold wind. Shutters rattled like the dentures of shivering old men. Sometimes you could hear children shouting, carriages rumbling over cobblestones, pedlars hawking their wares, or even the cries of seagulls circling over the Thames, but for the most part the wind was lord of the city that day.

It was a clear, crisp day in September or October (one of those months) in the year something-or-other, when Harry Tudor was still on the throne and had just gotten rid of another wife (everyone had stopped counting; it was dangerous), and on this day Tom of Bedlam and his friend Nick, who had been Nick the Gaoler and was now Nick the Lunatic, sat in a muddy alleyway bemoaning their lot. And shivering.

Now sitting and bemoaning (and shivering) are not good things for madmen to do, because it makes them less amusing, and when they present no spectacle, passers-by are less likely to drop coins in their cups. It is a matter of sheer economics. But the air was so fresh that day that all the stink and foggy humors of the city seemed to have dissipated, and it was enough to make even a madman clearheaded.

Tom fingered the intricately carven wooden box he always carried. In it Grandmother Grey was imprisoned, the Winter Witch, and if ever it touched the ground the lid would fly off and out she would come, quick to build herself a house of ice and then a mountain, from which snow would belch and bellow out of a cold forge in the mountain's heart and cover everything. Nick and Tom both knew. They'd seen it happen. But, while the two of them could pass the box back and forth, they could never get rid of it. This put a strain on them, since they could never sleep at the same time, and when begging and making general fools of themselves they worked best as a team, which meant one was always tired. That might make one of them drop the box, which could well bring the end of the world this time.

The problem was convincing people. You had to be out of your mind to believe a story like that.

"Ah, there is a shortage of true lunatics," said Tom.

"Aye, there is at that," said Nick, "but 'tis strange. Did ye not say but a little while ago that there were lunatics aplenty, that it was a splendid time to be mad?"

"Ah, there is a shortage of true lunatics. There are the

pretenders, the common tramps and beggars, those who howl because their heads are filled with devils, those whose wits are not scrambled, but merely absent. It's the ones with the true vision, the ones that see the world cockeyed and upside down and inside out — these, these are getting scarce. None of the others are our kind of people."

"Aye, they are not. I wonder where they have gone."

"Who speaks with the flying night hags anymore? Who grimly grapples with the great king of ghosts and ghouls and all his gruesome crew? Who talks in riddles that don't mean anything, but do? Who reads from the Book of Moons, which has no page nor print nor cover?"

"Aye! There is a shortage of folk such as that!"

"What are we going to do about it?"

"No idea."

"The old ways are passing, I fear. But at least I've been remembered in song. Have you heard?"

Not waiting for an answer Tom sang, coarsely, off key, with the instrumental accompaniment of a fart:

"For to see mad Tom of Bedlam,
Ten thousand miles I'd travel.
Mad Maudlin goes on dirty toes,
for to save her shoes from gravel."

At that Nick laughed and hooted, stood up on his hands and ran around in a little circle, splashing mud. The bells on his cap jingled the tune. Someone opened a window and tossed out a coin. He flipped rightside up just in time to catch it in his teeth, but bit down too late and swallowed the penny, then hiccoughed, and had it in his hand.

"A fine song! Fine! But who is Mad Maudlin?"

"Oh, and alas," said Tom, rolling his eyes to heaven, "a maudlin tale it is."

Nick was up on his hands again, his toes wriggling in the air, firmly at attention.

"She was an old lady with a hole in her head," said Tom. "You have not heard? On cold winter nights the wind would blow over the hole like your breath over the mouth of a bottle, and it would make a mournful sound. In the spring, wrens nested in there. In summer she used it to store dried fruit. She had been a fruit seller once, you see. But one summer the days were too hot and too long, and she stayed out for too many hours, and her brain dried up. It shrivelled. The next morning she mistook it for a prune and had it for breakfast. After that all her fancy was gone. She was one of those witless souls I spoke of. Eventually she fell into the Thames and was eaten by a crocodile."

"A crocodile? **Here**?"

"A crocodile! **Here**!" shouted several bystanders and overhangers. Windows and doors slammed shut. Bolts and bars dropped. There had been rumors of crocodiles in the gutters and puddles of the city for almost a year now, ever since an African ambassador's crocodile-hide purse had been cut, and later thrown into a sewer. Spontaneous generation, a learned doctor called it. Others claimed a Papist plot.

"No," said Tom, looking this way and that along the now deserted alley. "This crocodile was filled with a vision even when he was in the egg, a sense of grand destiny. So all his days he swam from his home along the Nile, charting his course by the stars, feeding on seagulls that took him for a log and tried to rest on his nose. It was the will of forces far, far beyond his humble crocodilian self, the very purpose of his existence, that he should devour this lady. And she, being hollow-headed, floated down the river and out to sea. They met halfway, somewhere near Spain, and his quest was ended."

"Oh." Nick sat down again. "Then it was she who took all the charm of lunacy away with her, and that's why life's no good anymore."

"But you still live it."

They sat absolutely still for a minute, as a patrol of the watch came by, armed with pikes, looking for crocodiles and Papists.

"Alas," said Nick when they were gone, looking at his toes which were as dirty as they could ever be, "if the old lady saved her shoes from gravel, I save the gravel from my shoes, not having any."

"And why have you no shoes, Nicholas?" intoned Tom. This was rehearsed, part of their repertoire.

"Because I ate them. I do it every spring on May Day, to make the summer come in."

"Yes, it is one of your best tricks."

"Aye, it is." Nick wrapped his arms around his body and shivered. "So I can't give it up. But times be hard and purses lean, and the air too cold too soon. If I haven't saved enough to buy new shoes by winter, my feet will freeze and snap off."

"I think I have the best solution. I don't wear out any soles, but still I am shod."

Tom's shoes didn't wear out any soles because they were bottomless. They were tied around his ankles. Sometimes they twirled completely around and his feet stuck out.

"But ye don't have to eat them every year to make the summer come in. If only winter wouldn't come so soon. If only autumn would hold off——"

"**You could ask this of the one in charge**," a voice suddenly whispered inside Tom's head. Startled as he was, he found himself repeating those very words.

"The one **in charge**?" Nick exclaimed. "Oh no! Not me! I'm still healthy. I'm not ready to meet **him**! 'Sblood, Tom, how can ye say such things?"

"Well we are both stark, staring mad, don't you forget, and besides ——" And once more the voice whispered. There was something dry and crinkly in its tone. Blank-faced, Tom repeated, "**Seek the court of the Autumn King. Vast is his realm and** beautiful, both far away and near... The matter is between you and him. Take a day. Take a week. I shall wait here like a true friend."

"Well... all right. Ye'd better hold on to the box till I get back." Nick backed away slowly, mystified. Tom didn't seem to be aware of him. Then he laughed, "Why I'd have to be out of my head to do such a thing!" And Tom laughed too, and Nick went off singing, jangling his bells. He made one penny, two, but not enough, not enough.

Tom stared after him, still in a daze. The whole episode was... disquieting. What voice had spoken? He stirred and heard the dry crinkling by his right ear, reached up, and found a dead, dried leaf caught in his hair. It was yellow, with patches of brown, the first fallen of the new season.

* * *

Tom slept in a huddle against a wall for a night, for seven, curled up with the box between his knees. By day he wandered among the clutter, looking up at the leaning, rickety houses which sometimes touched overhead to shut out the sun. Tier upon tier they rose, more like ragged, dark cliffs than real houses. The cold mud of London oozed between his toes, caked his feet and became the soles of his shoes for winter. But each noon and each sunset he would return to that same alley, to see if Nick had returned. He had not. The sky was clear. The air was cool. More autumn leaves drifted on the wind.

Near to midnight on the seventh night it came to be somehow, in dream or delirium as he slept, that Tom's mind and that of the crocodile met and merged and held converse. He felt claws dragging through the cold water, and the sting of salt in leathery nostrils, and he knew a longing for the warm, muddy, still place where the creature had been born. Deep down and far away, the monster's heart beat like the muted thunder of a drum.

"After all that trouble, did she taste good at least?"

"Southward, southward, and east I swim, through the surging seas. The Pillars of Hercules are behind me now, and soon the waters will grow warm. I can faintly taste my lovely Nile mud. Ah, to be home, to bask in the sun, to devour antelopes and Arab children... No, no, no, little man, no, crazy man, she was tough and stringy and sour. She had not bathed in seventy-three years, and was too ripe for the palate. I can understand now why her own kind did not eat her. But it was my fate, and the gods ordained it, and it was written, and it was (so an errant Norseman explained to my great-great-great-grand egg-layer ere I was even a hatchling) my doom, my inexorable destiny to perform this thing, so I did, and now I only hope that fate and all the rest will leave me alone. I shall tell the tale to the Holy Ancestral Crocodile when I die, and drift against the current, up the river to its secret source in the hidden valley of Hadoth, where Nephren-Ka, the crocodile that walked like a man——"

"I know. I've been there."

"The Holy Ancestral Crocodile is huger than any other. He is ten leagues in length with his tail uncurled. He rests in the sacred mud, waiting for all scaly folk in the end, and if they have interesting stories to tell, he does not eat them, at least not right away."

"Is eating all you think about? I'm glad I'm not a crocodile."

"In a way, you are, my little one, my morsel. Ah! Why couldn't I have eaten you instead? You even sound delicious. But it is Fate and the gods, and none can deny them. You cannot escape Fate either, little man. You too drift along the river, away from what you want and where you will, mayhap knowing a little of whither you are bound, borne on the current of years like a chip of wood, like a leaf, like a maiden's tattered skirt after I've had my supper... Listen, little one. You shall drift where your friend has, since it is your task to save him from his deadly peril, which is perilous, I assure you, and deadly, and a waste of perfectly good meat."

"**What peril?**"

"Southward, southward, and east I swim, through the surging seas. I taste the silt of my beloved Nile..."

"Would you excuse me? It's dawn here and I have to wake up."

Tom found himself on the street, with the box in his lap. The dawn dawned. The morning morned. Nick didn't come back. The day was far colder than any that had preceded it, as if they were the advance guard and this one was the real thing. Even sane people remarked on it. Those with extra sense and extra money wore extra hose, heavy hats, and thick capes. The rest shivered. The wind blew and blew. The city groaned and creaked. Countless shutters clacked. Tom was getting worried. It was his fate, he knew now, to find out what this was all about.

* * *

He sang as he stalked through the streets, not because he was happy, but out of habit, because it was expected of him, and when he did so no one bothered him on his way. His agitation came out in the song:

"The palsie plague these pounces,
　　When I prig your pigs or pullen;
St. Peter's pie will plop in your eye,
　　Perhaps, perchance, per——
And he ended up sputtering "P's."

Where the city ended and the country widened into fields, he came to a graveyard at the end of a lane. Beyond its walls men and women labored at the harvest. Within, a tall, tall person with horns on his head, a long face, and a pointed cap made of brittle leaves sat swaying back and forth on a tombstone, wailing mournfully as the wind passed through him. He was that thin, his clothes like rags wrapped around a few sticks, and, yes, the wind really did blow through him.

"What are you blubbering about?"

"I, sir," said the other, "am a mooncalf, and I am weeping because my mother, the moon, left me behind last night. She came to touch all the world with her light, and I to dance in it, but she sank too quickly in the sky. I ran and ran, but she was below the horizon before I got there. It is lonely here on Earth. So far you alone have noticed me. Are all the others blind?"

"Something like that. But I cannot tarry. My friend went to see the King of Autumn on a certain matter, and now I fear he is in terrible danger. A crocodile told me, you see——"

"Yes, I see. We superlunary creatures see many things. But can you not see that your woes are not nearly as great as mine, being forgotten by the Moon?" The tall fellow started weeping again.

"Stop that! Stop that, you puss-brained whoreson oaf! I don't care about the Moon. I care about this king. I have to find him."

"That's simple. I know that..."

"Then **tell** me, or by God's wounds I'll——"

"You'll find him in Autumn. Go until you find a leaf that has changed color. Let that be your roadmark. Follow it to another, and another, until you come to a place where all are colored and brittle, and that is the place you seek."

Tom bowed low and backed away, eager to get going.

"But wait! Now that I have told you this, you must do a favor for me!"

"Later, later. I shall gladly do it later. Now I must save my friend." Tom started to run, but in the blink of an eye the creature was off the gravestone and standing in front of him. He had to crane his neck way back to see its face, so tall did the thing stand. The body swayed in the wind, like a wobbly tower.

Then the tower seemed to crumble. The mooncalf leaned down, and down, telescoping on itself, and handed Tom its head, which still spoke, even when removed from its shoulders.

"You really must accept my head as a present. I don't need it. Really. I'm too tall already. It keeps getting knocked off when I go through doorways."

"No——no——I'd have to be **mad** to accept such a thing!"

"But you **are** mad! Don't use that excuse. We superlunary creatures see a lot——"

The head was tossed. It bounced off Tom's chest, hit the ground, bounced again, and the teeth clamped onto his leg, just below the knee. He danced and hopped to shake it off, but it would not budge.

The headless body collapsed into a pile of leaves and twigs.

"What do you want?" cried Tom. "What do you want?"

"The Autumn King sent me," the head mumbled through a mouthful of leg. "Promised he'd send me back to the Moon if I helped. Told me to delay you, until he was ready. I won't let you go until you tell me all about your times, your travels, travails, troubles——"

But here the thing underestimated Tom. He began to tell his tales, sing his songs, and he did so with the special intensity of the mind-boggled, the cracked, the melt-a-brained, and before long the listener was all those things, and babbling, retelling any ten of Tom's stories at once, backwards as often as not, and between babbles it lost its grip on Tom's leg. When it hit the ground, the flesh crumbled away like dust, and all that remained was a skull which indeed did look more like a calf's than a man's.

Farther down the road Tom met a man of God, and his fancy moved him to warn, "Be warned, parson, be warned. Beware of crocodiles. Beware and be warned."

"But there are no crocodiles in England," said the parson. "You poor wretch, you must be half-crocked at least. I shall pray for you, that your wits be made whole again." Pray he did, but he didn't give Tom a penny, nor did he heed the warning. (Then again, if everyone did, these dire dooms would never come to pass, and prophets could never say, "Behold, verily, I told you so," and no one would pay them. It's sheer economics.) Sure enough, years later he was called to missionary work in a remote land, where he was eaten by a savage disguised as a crocodile. But that does not concern us here.

["What a waste," said the crocodile in Tom's mind. "It sounds more interesting. Southward and southward I swim..."]

* * *

Tom saw no one for a long time. He wandered along roads and beaten paths until there were no more, and then he crossed fields and climbed hillsides thick with goldenrod and the humming of bees. In the quiet, beneath the clear sky, his jumble of thoughts seemed to untangle and run smoothly, like a stream which has passed the rapids. He began to forget himself, to drift over the land like a milkweed seed on a puff of delicate silk.

He startled a herd of deer in a meadow and they scampered away, white tails flashing.

Several days passed. He spied them faintly against the sunset, huge shapes like figures carved of golden smoke, and the spirit of one day nudged another and said in a voice like the stirring of dust, "He can see us. He isn't like the others."

And Tom was vaguely reminded of who he was and what he had set out to do. He shook the box he carried.

"Grandmother Grey, did you think I'd forget and drop you? Oh, no."

There was no response from within.

He came to a forest without a name, which touches every land like the tides of the sea. It has its inlets and bays, some so small they are scarcely noticed, others huge, but all of them leading just as surely to vast expanses. When there are only green distances in all directions, when the sounds of the world are shut out and strange flowers bloom in the green darkness without fear of the sun, when one can sense something different in the air, something magical, then one has entered that forest of which all others are shadows and reflections. It is no mere wood. It does not open on the other side into the fields of men, but, ultimately, into Faery.

When Tom had come to that place, he knew it. One night he slept and dreamt of the crocodile swimming south. It was aware of him, but did not speak. The next night he dreamt only of endless, windy distances, and he seemed to be clinging to a pendulum, swinging back and forth beyond the edge of the world. On the third night he heard Nick's voice, far away and far below. He couldn't see anything. He felt rustling, dry leaves all around him. He reached out. The ground gave way. It was as if he lay on the lip of a well and Nick were at the bottom, whimpering, "Tom, Tom, it's cold, cold, and so dark." Then his friend was weeping.

He awoke with a start, sat up, and saw that the leaves on the trees all around him had changed from green to gold, to red and orange, even to a dirty brown which crumbled to the touch.

Birds sang in the branches, but they were not summer birds.

A monarch butterfly drifted by on its way south.

"Hurry," said Tom. "Don't be lazy. Don't be late."

"Fie, fie," it replied. "I am the signal. I am the sign. The Autumn King does not come until I have gone."

And it went.

Tom walked the way it had come, following the golden leaves. Wherever the colors were densest, there he went. Where even a single living leaf remained, he turned away. At last he came to the center of the forest, where the underbrush gave way completely to the hollowness between the trees, but leaves were piled in such huge heaps that armies of men could have been buried in them. Branches leaned low, heavily laden. The mounds clogged the way almost entirely, rising far over his head in some places. The forest was hushed, expectant. The wind had stopped. With each step, the crunching of leaves became a diffuse rumble, like an avalanche of tiny pebbles, echoing into the distance.

He was entering a mountain range of fallen leaves, often sunk to his belt buckle, even when he stayed in the shallowest parts. His legs heaved up great masses as he went. He held onto the box tightly, lest he trip and Grandmother Grey get loose.

If all the leaves that had ever fallen were gathered in one place, never to sink down into the mud, it seemed to Tom, the accumulation might be like this.

Gradually he perceived that some of the leaf mounds were deliberately shaped. Some resembled walls, with definite, if irregular battlements. Others formed towers, climbing the thickest trunks to hide their tops in the leafy canopy above.

There was a fluttering by his ear. He thought it was another butterfly, but when he turned his head, he saw that it was a single leaf, hovering in mid-air. Another rose beside it, with no wind to hold it up, and another, and another, swirling into a mass, assuming an outline, an oblong shape which refined itself and acquired a head, arms, and legs, and even a face, with fine features made of leaf fragments, all of them in motion, like a million ants racing through a transparent mold.

The thing's rustling slowly formed words.

"Who...are...you...?"

Tom bowed with exaggerated courtesy.

"I am come to see your king, good sir. Can you take me to him?"

"Yes..."

As Tom watched, astonished, the creature's face became familiar. It's features were those of a butcher he had known, who had tired of his trade one day and wandered into the countryside, still wearing his bloody apron, never to return. Then the face shifted, subtly at first, and became Whistling Jack the Gypsy, who had also not been seen in a long time. Then there was Nick, frightened and lonely.

"No!" cried Tom. "You shan't have him!" He grabbed a stick and struck at the creature, but the stick passed right through, and it collapsed into a pile of leaves.

Windows and doors opened all around him. The leaf castle was alive with light, glaring in the twilight of the deep forest. A gate swung slowly inward, releasing a blast of damp air, which smelled of earth and rotten logs.

Tom hesitated, and all the leaves around him stirred furiously. Then, seeing no other recourse, he went in.

The gate closed behind him far quicker than it had opened. For a while he stood in complete darkness. The damp earth smell was stronger, the ground underfoot muddy and bare, save for a few scattered twigs.

Then the leaves began to glow, red, gold, yellow, all the colors of Fall, and he could see. Before him sat a hunched-over giant clad in a gown of leaves of every hue, crowned with a golden crown, attended by a dozen leaf men. But the most remarkable thing about him was his beard. It was brown, streaked with gold and red, filled with leaves, and so massive and long that it had to be divided in the middle and draped over either of the king's shoulders, until it rose up in long, heavy loops like hammocks stuffed with leaves, and merged with the ceiling. Tom looked up, and could not tell where the leaves of the beard ended and the leaves of the castle wall began, and then he realised that **they didn't**. The entire place, and those enormous mounds outside, were all part of it. He was standing **inside** the Autumn King's beard.

"You have found my house," thundered the king.

Tom bowed very low, but careful not to touch his box to the ground.

"And I have found your magnificent beard, and it please your majesty. Or it found me."

"Of old, many men came to this place to offer sacrifice, that their harvests might be plentiful, that the autumn would be long and soften the winter, that their fields would remain fertile through the long sleep. And I would touch those fields and spread my beard over them, making them my own, protecting them from the coming snows."

"Ma-majesty... **What** did they offer in sacrifice?"

"Oh, anything. Fruits and nuts. Animals, or sometimes each other. Or just prayers. I didn't really care. I just liked the attention."

"Ah..."

"And that box you have there, is it a sacrifice for me?"

Tom hadn't thought of it like that. He wondered what would happen if he gave the box to the king. But he didn't dare find out.

"No, alas, it isn't. You wouldn't like what's inside."

At this the box stirred as if indignant, and almost slipped from Tom's hands. He held onto it so firmly his knuckles went white.

"That's how it is," said the king. "You little folk, you mortals have no respect for your gods anymore."

"Majesty, Oh great one, no offense is meant, but these days we worship but one God, for to do more would be... pagan."

Suddenly leaves dropped from the ceiling into heaps, surrounding Tom. They rose into fierce-looking guards armed with pointed stakes and clubs.

"Little Man," said the Autumn King grimly, "whether your kind admit it or not, there are still spirits of the seasons, of the forest, of the waters. Long and long ago the eyes of all mortals were open, and they saw these spirits, but of late they have become clouded. Now very few see me, or hear when I call. Only the different ones such as yourself. But being different will not save you. You **will** give me a gift in sacrifice, or else you'll join my kingdom. Do you think I caused you to be brought here for no reason? Look!"

A wall parted, and out came a procession of people, strangers to Tom. Each stared ahead, vacantly. Each bore a paint brush in one hand and a little pot in the other. They shuffled past, smelling of Earth, as if they'd lain in it for a long time before being summoned. Some of them, Tom noticed, were skeletal enough that he could see through them.

Twenty or thirty went by, and then came one he recognized. It was Nick. Tom called his name, but he did not answer. For an instant their eyes met, and the look in Nick's was one of hopeless despair. All of his merriment, the very life of him had been stolen away. He was an empty vessel, shuffling with the rest. A soundless message passed between them, as if to say, **Help me Tom. I can't go on like this for ever and ever. I'd rather be in Hell.**

"What...?" gasped Tom. "Why...?" This was impossible. It was ugly and **insane**, which was a species of lunacy he wasn't at all comfortable with.

"Let me answer all your questions," said the king. "Here." He drew a glass bottle out of some fold in his robe. It was clear, and stoppered with a cork. Inside hundreds of motes of light drifted, like lethargic fireflies. "These are the souls of my subjects. As long as they are here, and not in their bodies, I control both body and soul. Their bodies do not age or die, and their souls do not progress toward eternity. They are mine, all mine. Some have been here for thousands of years. Now, since few men see me or hear me anymore, it is harder for me to add to their number. It is a wonderful gift you have, to be able to see things others don't, but it does have its dangers. Why do I do it? You'll notice that each year, when I come into my power, all the leaves change color. That takes work. Nothing is free in this world. My task it is, my duty and burden, to supply each of my subjects with paintbrush and paint pot, and send them to color all the leaves they can, before winter comes along and ruins everything. They do good work, but I need all the help I can get."

"I can see that..."

"Now then, you have come here because you can perceive my kingdom. Either you shall join it, or do something special for me. It's as simple as that."

"Will you release my friend Nick if I do?"

"For two, it has to be twice as special."

"Then I shall be doubly amusing, Majesty." Again Tom bowed low. This, he knew, was serious business. He wasn't working for pennies or new shoes now.

He sat down on the floor and twiddled his thumbs, staring blankly into space.

"Well, get on with it!" cried the king. "We are not amused!"

"I am mad, sir, lord, great king, and I can't do anything too sensible, lest I lose hold of myself. Alas, if you insist!" He got up on his hands, the way Nick always did, and ran around the room, crashing into several of the leaf guards, reducing them to heaps. He held the carven box in his teeth. Then he flipped over, and sat again, twiddling his thumbs. Slowly the leaf men reformed themselves. A minute passed, two. The king began to fidget. He was about to signal his guards when Tom began to sing. He sang all of his famous songs, about himself, about Mad Maudlin, the Knight of Ghosts and Shadows, the visit to Satan's kitchen and what he ate there (and how well it was done, and what sort of seasoning was used) and even the story of the crocodile. He wished he knew some of the stories told to the Holy Ancestral Crocodile over the eons, but he didn't, and had to make them up:

How Lledddenyyachllyll Vnarghullew created the world in six days, one ahead of Jehovah, and would have gotten the upper hand if only his children could have called out his name before Adam and Eve called out the other one. Unfortunately there were no Welshmen present, and nobody could pronounce it.

How the world was wrought in four days by an obese fellow

with an extra eyeball in his navel, who then placed it on the back of a turtle. But the turtle heard so much about the marvels above him that he came out to have a look, then concluded that so massive a thing could never be supported by an empty turtle shell. He was right.

(There were forty-six creation stories, all of them different. "Collect the whole series," said Tom.)

How Delicious Donald the farmer opened a pea pod and found a beautiful maiden inside. By magic she shrunk him down, and they moved in, and lived happily until his shrewish wife made soup out of the pod. He was awarded his name posthumously.

[**The best so far,** said the crocodile, who was listening in.]

How Tedius of Thebes was sent by his king to slay the Stymphalian Bore, how the two met, and got along splendidly. (It was a long story, involving lots of ants and a granary. Tom abridged it.)

How the wizard Etelven Thios was murdered, and came back again, and was murdered, and came back, again and again, each time in diminished condition, until he grew on his last victim as a hangnail. And still won out.

How the Russo-Saxon warrior Hrothgarovitch Hngrotwitheowfnogfnogski met the Welshman who would have made a creation's worth of difference if he'd just opened his mouth at the right moment, and battled him to the death polysyllabically.

Of folk marvelously disfigured, that do have their heads beneath their shoulders, and what their table manners are like. (Awful.)

Of the old woman who opened her ragged cloak at sunset to release a black bird from within, and another, and another, until the sky was made dark and she had diminished into a pile of old clothes.

(There were a hundred and fourteen stories of the world's odd folk, only half of them Tom's autobiography.)

And so on. He told mermaid stories and monster stories, tales of shipwrecks and ghosts and cyclopses and crocodiles [**At last, I get some recognition!** hissed the crocodile], and heroic thrilling sagas and heart-throbbing tragedy (but the Autumn King's heart, being made of leaves, did not throb), and warm domestic comedy (the warmest involving houses burning down), the old yarn about the back street knee-deep in blood (an alley gory), and the one about the Ghost Goat Man of Alexandria, who herded his phantom charges through the great library, where they devoured only bad books, becoming the world's first literary critics and relegating the tale of their own existence to oral tradition.

And so on

And more.

Many in rhyme.

"You know," said the Autumn King when Tom was done and panting for breath, "if you hadn't become a lunatic, you would have had quite a career as a storyteller. But for me there's just one problem."

"What's... that?" (gasp, pant, wheeze)

"We spirits often lack the finer points of humanity. It probably comes from not having souls."

"And?"

"I have no imagination. I don't like stories. Sorry."

"Then what **does** amuse you?" asked Tom, nearly in despair.

"I don't know really. When I'm alone I dream strange dreams, filled with darkness and dead leaves and the smell of earth, and I don't understand them myself. But no one has ever succeeded in amusing me, try as they may. I'm **sure** I don't like riddles. They always try riddles. The same old routine. You know: what is your name? What is your favorite color? Then some nonsense about African swallows. Nuada! It bores me to tears!"

Tom was almost ready to give up, but there was one last hope. He hoped that the king had an ego. He too would like to be celebrated in song, surely. Tom knew how it felt, so he sang, hoarsely:

"Oh the Autumn King, his crown
   is of gold, is of gold;
Red and yellow are his robes
   with each fold;
And with his breath so cold
   the summer does grow old,
And the leaves go tumbling down
   to the ground, to the ground.
The leaves go tumbling down
   to the ground."

There was silence in the whole forest, and the palace was hushed. The Autumn King smiled broadly, and seemed content.

"Will you release Nick now?" Tom blurted at last.

"No. Now that I have your song, I don't need you to sing it, so I'll keep you both to paint leaves. There is always work to be done."

"You tricked me!"

The king smiled again. "That, I admit, does amuse me. But just a little."

Then he laughed, and his beard shook. The castle trembled. Leaves rained down from the ceiling. Tom felt dry, scratchy hands seize him by the ankles as the leaf level rose like water in the hold of a sinking ship. Then the leaves rose higher and they had him by the knees, then the waist, and he was caught. He could not budge. Still the king rocked with laughter. Tom recalled the look he'd seen on Nick's face at the last, and never did he know more pitiless terror than at that moment.

It was as the leaves rose to his chin, and he held the carven box he still carried on high, that he realised that, frozen world or no, **nothing** could be worse than what was happening to him just now.

He flung the box in a long arch across the throne room, over the rustling leaves. It landed in the king's lap, but he was too convulsed with laughter to notice, and it fell onto the ground at the foot of the throne. The leaves closed over Tom's eyes at that instant, but he heard a familiar, screeching voice, and there was a flash of blue light. Through the leaves came a blast of frigid wind. Then there were no leaves around him anymore, only snow, an intense whirlwind of a blizzard confined in the tiny space of the room.

"You! You! You!" shrieked Grandmother Grey in the middle of it. "You dare to make my lovely winters mild! You dare to put color into my pretty dead leaves, when it is my task to freeze away all colors except white and grey and corpse-blue! **How dare you**?"

"Just when I have everything painted and right, **you wreck it**, and I have to start all over again!"

Tom caught a glimpse of the two of them wrestling as he fled the hall. The air was filled with flashes of blue and orange light. Snow and leaves and mud pelted him in the face. The walls were collapsing. He ran to the door, pushed, and saw the forest outside, the trees writhing before the sudden wind, leaves ripped from the branches and filling the sky like a cloud of locusts.

Then there was only darkness for a long time. And cold. The Autumn King and the Winter Witch agreed on that much.

* * *

The rest is mud. When next Tom was aware, he found himself clawing upward through half-frozen, leafy mud. Other shapes rose around him. He was afraid for a moment that these were things akin to the leaf creatures, but then one of them wiped the slime off its face, blinked, and said, "Hello, Tom."

It was Nick good as new, although much muddier.

[Ah, mud, mud, beautiful mud, said the crocodile. **Home at last, in my warm, soft Nile mud. I rest, digesting an antelope and a child. This is the life. Mud is a good place to end a story.**]

All those people now returned to mortal life eventually told of their adventures. Some had to learn new languages, since theirs were ancient. Two or three were arrested for paganism while dancing around Stonehenge, but the rest remained, astonished by the changes the world had gone through since whenever.

To tell such a story, much less to have experienced it and to believe it, requires that one be mad, truly so, in the visionary sense.

Ah, and to hear it. That is almost as good. Then to tell it to others...

Once again there were lunatics aplenty. There hasn't been a shortage since.

THE STORY OF A DĀDAR

It was in the time of the death of the Goddess that the thing happened, when the Earth rolled wildly in the dark spaces without any hand to guide it, or so the poets tell us, when Dark Powers and Bright drifted across the land, and all things were in disorder.

It was also in the open grasslands that it happened, beyond the end of the forests, where you can walk for three days due south and come to the frontier of Randelcaine. All was strange to me. I had never been there before, where not a tree was to be seen, anymore than I had been to a place where there are no stars. All that afternoon, my wife Tamda and I drove our wagon through the familiar woods. Slowly the trees began to seem farther apart, and there was more underbrush. I remember how the heat of the day faded quite quickly, and the long, red rays of the setting sun filtered between the trunks, almost parallel to the ground, giving the undersides of the leaves a final burst of color before twilight came on. The trees ahead of us stood in silhouette like black pillars, those behind us, in glory. Above, little birds and winged lizards fluttered in the branches. I reflected that these things had always been thus, even in the earliest times, when the great cities of the Earth's mightier days stood new and shining, and other gods and goddesses, the predecessors of the one which had just died, ruled the sky. Those ancients could just as well have been seeing this sunset and this forest through my eyes.

Then a wagon wheel sank axle-deep in mud, and I didn't have time to reflect on anything. The two of us struggled and gasped in pained breaths that we weren't young anymore. If only our son were still with us... But he had gone away to serve the Religion. What is religion when your wheel is stuck?

When at last the wagon rolled free, stars peered down between the branches. The night air seemed very cold. We sat still, panting, until Tamda had the good sense to get our cloaks, lest the chill get into us.

So it was that we emerged from the forest in darkness. At first I was hardly aware that there were no more trees. It seemed merely that there were more stars, but then the moon came up and revealed the vast dark carpet of the plain rising and falling before us. Imagine a fish, which had always inhabited the dark and narrow crags among the rocks at the bottom of the sea, suddenly rising up, into the open wonder of the sea itself. So it was. Overhead the Autumn Hunter was high in the sky. The

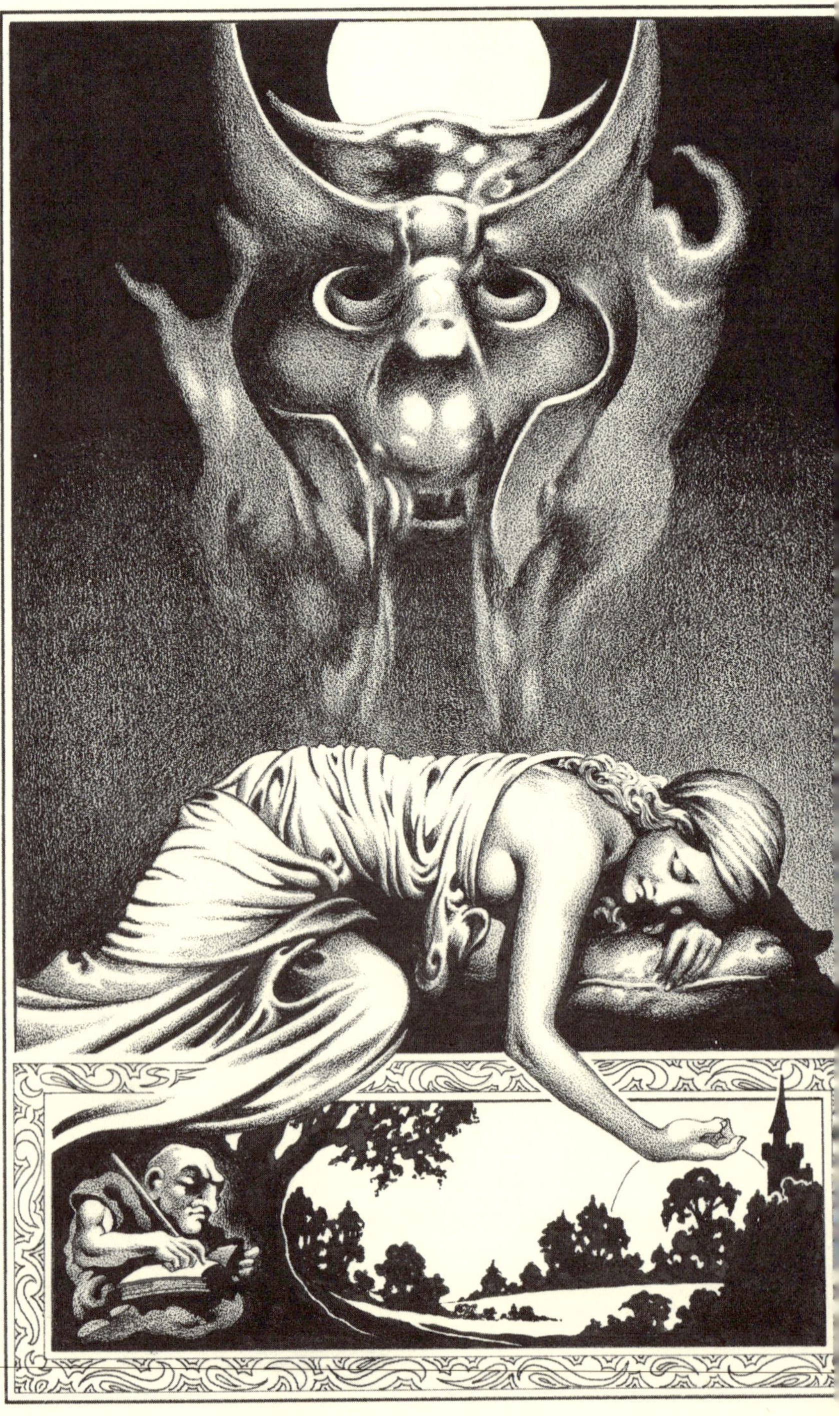

Polar Dragon turned behind us, and the Harpist was rising. By these signs we knew our way. Neither of us wanted to stop for the night. I suppose plainsmen feel the same way, their first night in the forest. So we pushed on, and shortly before dawn reached our destination.

The village glowed on the plain like a beast with a thousand eyes, reclining there, alive with torches. We would never have found it otherwise. The houses were all curving humps of sod, hollowed out and walled with logs. Had they not been lit, we would have passed them in the night, thinking them little hills.

We were expected. Everyone was awake and waiting. A man in a plumed helmet took our horse by the bridle and led us to a building larger than all the others.

"Are you Pandiphar Nen?" asked the chieftain who stood at the door.

"Yes. You sent for me," I said. "You understand, then, that I do not heal broken bones, or cure any sickness which can be cured with a herb or a little spell?"

"Yes, I do, or I would not have sent for you."

"The price is high."

"Please, bargain later. It is my daughter, sore afflicted. She has... left us. Her mind is in darkness, far underground."

Tamda and I climbed down from the wagon seat. I got my bag out of the back. We were shown inside. The house had but one room, and a fire burned in the middle floor. The smoke hole wasn't large enough, and the air was thick. On a pile of hides to one side a maiden lay, her eyes open, but her gaze distracted. She did not seem aware of us. She rolled her head and muttered to herself. I listened for a moment, catching a few words, but most of it was strange to me.

"Put the fire out," I said to those who had come in with us. "And leave us alone." This was done. I waited for the smoke to clear.

Then I made a mixture of the ground root of the death tree, the water of life, common flour to hold it all together, plus other ingredients, including something called Agda's Toe. Agda was my master, to whom I had been apprenticed when I was fifteen, some thirty years before. Then I had believed he had an infinite supply of toes, which could be regrown whenever he cut them off and sold them to pharmacies all over the world, but of late I had had my doubts. He never took off his shoes in public.

I ate a spoonful of the mixture and washed it down with wine. I sang the song of the false death, with Tamda at my side to make sure that I did not truly die. She would hold my wrist and take my pulse, counting one heartbeat a minute, and listen for a shallow breath about as often. If I got into trouble she would shout my name and call me back. She alone had this power.

I departed. At once my awareness was out of my body, sharing that of the girl. I saw through her eyes. Tamda and I stood absolutely still, distorted out of shape, like tall sculptures of glowing jade. The room was full of a white mist, and in it swam things like the luminous skeletons of fishes, and some, like impossible herons made of coral sticks, walked on a surface below the floor, wading in the earth. They sang to me, trying to lull me into sleep within a sleep, but I paid them no heed. They were common spirits of the air. I had seen them many times before.

I turned inward. Indeed, the girl's soul was far beneath the earth. I had a sensation of sinking a long way in thick, muddy darkness before I had an impression of a hunched shape, like something carven out of rough, dirty stone, embedded in her.

I began to draw the spirit out. Literally. I drew it. By a trick known only to healers, I was both deep inside the girl's soul and in my own body. I was aware as my hands took up drawing paper and charcoal and began to sketch the image of the spirit. When I was a child I had always had an urge to draw things in the dirt, on walls, hides, scraps of paper, anything, and my father always boxed my ears and told me not to waste my time. But when I began to draw things he had seen in his dreams, and things others saw in theirs, he understood my talent. Everything after that, even my apprenticeship to Agda, was a refinement of technique and nothing more.

I knew what to do from much experience. As my hand moved over the paper, I wrestled with the thing inside the girl. Soon I saw it more clearly, a frog-like king clad in robes of living marble. He had long, webbed claws like a beast, but his face bespoke vast intelligence and age. I understood him to be a creature from some earlier age of the Earth, trying to return now that the Goddess was dead. His eyes seemed to speak to me, saying, "Why should I not have this girl, and walk beneath the sky again?"

"You shall not have her," I said in the language of the dream, and as I spoke, my hand completed the drawing. Then my body got to its feet, stood over the girl, and with a pair of tongs reached into her mouth, pulling out first my spirit, then the other. It was like flying up out of a mountain through a little hole in the top, into my own hand.

"Pandiphar Nen," said my wife, and with the sound I came into myself. I was whole and fully awake. The white mist and the things in it were gone. The task should have been over, the second spirit I'd extracted should have melted into the air now that I had captured its image.

But the stone king was standing before us. Tamda screamed. It turned to stare into my eyes, and its gaze caught me as surely as any prey is ever charmed by a snake. I was helpless.

"**Dadar**," it said. "Know that I was placed here to bring this message to you from worlds beyond the world. I am sent by your creator. Know that you are a dadar, a wizard's shadow and not a man, a hollow thing like a serpent's skin filled with wind, pretending to be a serpent, deluding itself. The master shall make himself known shortly, and then you shall be sent on the task for which he made you, his dadar."

Then, howling, the creature went through the closed door of the house like a battering ram, scattering wood and screaming at the villagers outside.

I was in a daze, only half aware of anything.

"Let us get away from here," Tamda was saying. "They'll think we're witches. Hurry, before they regain their courage. Forget about the payment."

"I don't understand," was all I could say. "It wasn't supposed to happen like that."

She gathered our things and bundled me into the back of the wagon. No one interfered as she drove away from the village.

The wagon rattled around me. Sunlight burned through the canvas cover. I lay in the stuffy heat, thinking.

The problem, and the reason I felt so much dread, was that I **did** understand what had happened. My spotty education was more than enough to include everything I needed to know. Some wizard had directed me, his dadar, into that village for his own ends. I knew full well what a dadar was. The world has never been thick with them, but they have been around since the very beginning. They are projections, like a shadow cast by a man standing before a campfire at night, but somehow the shadow is given flesh and breath and a semblance of consciousness. Hamdo, the First Man, made one. He had shaped with his hands the egg from which all mankind was to be born, but while he slept by the River of Life, a toad came along and swallowed it. Then a serpent swallowed the toad and a fox swallowed the serpent, and was in turn devoured by a lion, which fell prey to a bull, which was eaten by a dragon, which in turn was swallowed by an Earth Thing for which there is no name, which before long found itself residing in the belly of a Sky Thing which remained similarly nameless. Therefore Hamdo climbed the mountain on which the sky turns, charmed the Sky Thing to sleep with his singing ── for he was the greatest of all singers ── and then, on the mountaintop, he made a dadar of himself, and put a feather in one of its hands and a burning torch in the other. He went it inside the Sky Thing to make it regurgitate the Earth Thing, the dragon, the bull, the lion, and so forth. From inside the toad it cut itself free, rescuing the egg. Things were different in those days, I suspect. Animals don't eat like that now. But the dadar was still a dadar, a reflection in the mirror of Hamdo.

More recently, the philosopher Telechronos spent so much time brooding among the ruins of the Old Places that he nearly went mad. He made a dadar for company. It became his leading disciple.

And a king of the Heshites was found to be a dadar. The priests gathered to break the link between the dadar and its master, lest some unseen, malevolent wizard lead the country to doom. The link was broken and the king crumbled into dust. A dadar is an unstable, insubstantial thing, like a collection of dust motes blown into shape by the wind.

Thus I feared every sound, every movement, every change in the direction of the wind, lest these be enough to unmake me. All the confidence I had gained in the years of my life ran away like water. I was nothing. An illusion, even to **myself.** A speck of dust drifting between the years.

I wept like a child abandoned in the cold and the dark.

And I argued: can an illusion weep? Can its tears make a blanket wet? But then, how could I, with the senses of a dadar, know the blanket to be real, or the wagon, or the tears?

I looked up front and saw only the horse nodding as it walked, and Tamda huddled at the reins. I did not speak to her, nor did she turn to speak to me. I think she was nearly as afraid as was I.

And I argued: But I have sired two sons. Two? One died when the cold of winter settled into him and spring did not drive it forth, but even in death he was real. He did not vanish like a burst bubble. And the other——he lives yet. Just this year he was called by a voice within him to journey south to the holy city of Ai Hanlo. I walked with him a long way, then wept when he passed from sight around a bend in the forest path. Does this not make me a man?

I was back to weeping. All roads of thought seemed to lead there.

I looked up again and saw that the sky was beginning to darken.

"Stop," I said to Tamda, and she reined the horse. She was trembling as we made camp. We went through the motions of settling down to supper, but suddenly she was in my arms and sobbing.

"Please... don't go away. Don't leave me. I'm too old to learn to be without you."

I was sobbing too. "I love you. Does that not make me a man? How can I prove it? Can a shadow feel such a thing?"

"I don't know. What is going on? Are we both mad?"

"No, it isn't that. I'm sure."

"I wish it were. To be mad is to be filled with passion, and at least that's real."

Although both of us were tired and hungry, we made love there on the ground as the stars came out. But even as I did I was haunted by the thought that a shadow may make a shadow's love and know nothing better.

Later, it was Tamda who put into words what I was groping for. She gave me a plan for action.

"You must find this wizard whose dadar you are," she said, "and kill him. Then you'll be free. You won't fade away. I'm sure of it. We must go to him when he summons you." She took a sheathed knife and put it inside my shirt. "When the time comes, surprise him."

Then I got up and fetched my folio of drawing paper. I sat down beside her and paged through the book. I stopped to stare at the image of the frog king. I couldn't help but admire the artistry. It was good work. When I wasn't practicing my more esoteric skill, I simply drew. Sometimes I sold the pictures in towns we passed through. Sometimes I even sold the ones I'd made while healing, after the spirits were dispersed and we didn't need them anymore.

I began to draw. I closed my eyes and let my hand drift. It didn't seem to want to make any marks. I felt my hand slide along the page, the charcoal only touching paper seven — eight? — nine times?

Then I opened my eyes and saw that I'd made a fair outline of the Autumn Hunter, which vanishes from the southern sky as the year ends.

"We travel south," I said.

When first I looked over the plain by day, I thought of the fish from the deep ocean crags — now bursting out of the water altogether, into the air. As far as I could see, green and brown grasses rippled beneath the sun. Here and there stood a scrubby tree. A herd of antelopes grazed far away. Once we passed quite near to a green-scaled thing walking upright on thin legs, fluttering useless wings in annoyance at our presence. It stood twice as tall as a man, but looked harmless, even comical. I had heard of such creatures, half-shaped, still forming. They are said to emerge whenever one age ends and another begins. I had heard they were commoner in the south, as if the strangeness radiated from the holy city of Ai Hanlo, where the actual bones of the Goddess lay.

The journey was comforting. I relished every new experience more than I had any since I was a boy. But then the melancholy thought arose that it was only because I was about to lose these things, all sensations, all perception, even my very self, that they seemed more rare and exquisite.

Tamda slept in the back of the wagon while I drove. Horses are supposed to be able to detect supernatural creatures pretending to be men, but ours behaved normally for me.

The plain was divided by a winding silver line, which I knew to be the Endless River. It was said to engirdle the world. My son said he would follow it on the way to the holy city. I stopped by the bank to water the horse and to bathe. Tamda awoke and prepared a soup with river water. Later, I took up pen and paper and began to draw.

She watched me intently.

"Is it a message from our enemy?"

It wasn't. A bird bobbing on a reed had caught my fancy, and I made a picture of it. It was a charming little sketch, the sort some rich lady would pay well for.

Later, in a town called Toradesh, by a bend in the river, a man came to us, begging that we rid his father of the spirit which possessed him. There were many people around, and I could not refuse. Tamda and I were shown into a basement room, where an old man was kept tied to a bed. His eyes were wide with his madness. He did not blink. There was foam at the corners of his mouth. He stank of filth.

The picture I drew was of a long flight of stairs, winding down into the darkness. Once I had departed from my body, I was on those sodden, wooden stairs, descending into a region of dampness and decay. At the bottom I waded knee-deep in mud until I came to a slime-covered door. I pulled on an iron ring to open it, but the wood was so soft that the metal came away in my hand. I kicked the hole thus begun until it was big enough for me to wriggle through.

On the other side something massive and hunched over, dark with glowing eyes, sat nearly buried in the muck.

"Begone!" I said. "I command you, leave this place. Be vomitted up and leave this man."

The thing turned to me and laughed. Its voice was that of a child, but hideous, as if the child had never grown up, but lost all innocence and wallowed in cruelty for a thousand years.

"Gladly would I leave, **dadar,** for the soul of this man is rotten and there is not much left of it. But you have no soul, so where would I go?"

"If I have no soul, what is this standing before you?"

"It is the dadar of a dadar, the image of an image, the rippling of water made by another wave. **Dadar,** Etash Wesa made you, and sends you as a present to his brother, Emdo Wesa. There is enmity between them, which you shall consummate. More than that you need not know. Your actions are his, your thoughts his. From now on, he shall guide you."

In the blinking of an eye I was back in the basement room, and the old man was mad as ever. Tamda let out a startled cry. She had not called me. The townspeople scowled and muttered something about "theatrical fake." Tamda tried to calm them. We had failed, she told them, and thus would demand no payment. We left the town at once. It may have only been the subtle and remote workings of Etash Wesa, directing my fate, which prevented us from being smeared with dung and driven out with rods. Someone mentioned that as the traditional punishment for frauds.

I was drifting. Sometimes in a dream I would see a hill or a bend in the road or men poling a raft along the river. Sometimes I would draw pictures of these things, or awaken to find that I had drawn them. Especially in these cases, when the image was firmly in my mind, I could be sure that sooner or later I would behold those things while waking. I drove the wagon when I could, letting instinct which I knew to be the instructions of my maker be my guide.

I didn't have any doubt now that I truly was a dadar, a thing like dust carried in the wind. I was going to confront Emdo Wesa.

Then what? Would some other secret of my nature be revealed?

Once I fancied that in the presence of Emdo Wesa I would explode into flame, consuming both of us. For this purpose alone I had been created. The rest was random happenstance.

Tamda said little as the miles went by. She knew she was losing me. Sometimes when she did speak she mentioned things I could not recall at all, as if I were slipping away from myself, becoming two, real and unreal, a reflection again reflected.

I awoke in the middle of the day, the reins at my feet. The horse had wandered to the side of the road to graze, pulling the wagon askew. How had I gotten there? I didn't remember any morning. Last I remembered, we were travelling nearly into the sunset. Tamda was asleep in the back.

I had a vision of a man in an iridescent robe, bent over a steaming pot. I could not see his face. His back was toward me. He was missing the last three fingers of his right hand. With thumb and forefinger only he reached into the pot, immersing his arm all the way to the shoulder——and yet the pot wasn't a third that deep——and as he did there was a scratching inside my chest, as if a huge spider within me began to stir. I gagged. It was coming up my throat, into my mouth.

Then it retreated back inside me and there was a sudden, intense pain. It had wrapped its legs around my heart, and was squeezing, until blood rushed to my temples and my head and chest were about to——

I awoke with a scream. A flock of startled birds rose all around me, wheeling in the twilight of early dawn.

I was sitting by a campfire in the middle of the grassland. There was no sign of Tamda or the wagon.

Flames crackled. There was no other sound except that of the birds. I let out a grunt of surprise.

"What's the matter? Don't you know where you are?"

I looked up, regarding the speaker, saying nothing. He stood opposite me, a spear with a rabbit impaled on it in his gloved hands. He had a long beard, brown hair streaked with grey, and he wore a long robe alternately striped blue and red. For an instant I feared he was the man from my vision, but by the way his hands worked, spitting the rabbit over the fire, I was sure he had all his fingers. I guessed him to be slightly younger than myself, and by his speech, a foreigner. He seemed to take my presence for granted, as if we had met before this instant. Carefully, trying not to reveal the gaps in my memory, I got him to tell me what I wanted to know.

"You may have heard of my country," he said. "Here in the north the people say the air is so thick in Zabortash that men carry it around in buckets, into which they dunk their heads when they want to breathe. They blame our foul dispositions on this. But these things are slanderous lies. Am I not a man, like any other?" He smiled when he spoke, and I felt sure he was deliberately mocking me. This was a new terror, but I forced myself to remain calm. I allowed that he seemed a man, like any other.

"Now you, on the other hand," he went on, "seem strange. Last night when you came upon my humble camp, you were like one walking in his sleep. 'Who are you?' you asked, and I said 'I am Kabor Asha,' but a few minutes later you asked again, and again I answered, and it seemed that your mind wandered even farther than your body did. Most strange."

He offered me some of the rabbit. When we were done eating, he noticed that I was watching him as he wiped his gloves clean, without removing them.

"You are wondering why I don't take them off and wash them, of course. I can't, you see, because I am not alone. In my country no magician bares his hands in public. It's obscene."

"You are... a magician?"

"That's another rumor they have here in the north, that everyone in Zabortash is a magician. It's not true, but there are so many that there is no work for many. That is why I wander, you see, to practice my art."

And again I wondered if he were mocking me, but I made no sign. An idea came to me. Another magician could help me against my enemy. At the very least, it would complicate Etash Wesa's plans. So words poured out of me in a torrent. I was well into my story before I realized what I was doing. Then there was nothing to do but finish. I told him all.

"I know of Emdo Wesa," he said when I had finished. "I can take you to him. Then the whole unpleasant business will be over and you'll be free."

"Wait! What business? What am I supposed to do? Who are you? How do you know——?"

Before I could do anything he stood over me. He had opened his robe. Beneath he wore some sort of armor. The scales glittered blue and black, close against his skin. I had a sudden fear that it wasn't armor at all, that he was some kind of reptile

———

The cloak closed over me, covering my head as he knelt to embrace me, hugging me to his chest.

His flesh was cold and hard as iron. I couldn't feel any heart beating.

"Help! Wait! Where is my wife? What have you done——"

"You didn't tell me you had a wife," he said as he pushed me over backwards and tumbled onto me.

The ground did not catch us. We were falling off a precipice, tumbling over and over in the air, the wind roaring by us, for a long time. I screamed and struggled, and then all the strength went out of me and I hung limp. He straightened out from our hunched position and stopped somersaulting. I could see nothing but darkness beneath his cloak, but somehow I had the impression that he bore me in his arms like a bird of prey carrying off a fish.

The fish, from out of the crag, wandering into the wide ocean, bursting into the air, snatched away by a sea hawk——
—— falling among faint lights, false images behind my eyelids, but then stars, as pure and clear as any seen by night over the open plain, as if Kabor Asha had all the universe inside him.

We stopped falling without any impact or even a cessation of motion. My vertigo simply faded slowly away, and after a time I felt solid ground beneath my feet.

He took his robe off me, and I saw that we stood on a little hill before a vast city which rose up tier upon tier, like something carven out of a mountain. Every stone, every wall, every rooftop of it was of dull black stone, and it stood silent and empty against a steel grey sky. As far as I could see the ground was bare and dusty grey. Every color, every trace of life seemed drained out of this place.

"Behold the holy city of Ai Hanlo," said my guide and captor, "where lie the bones of the Goddess. But this is not the Ai Hanlo to which pilgrims flock, where the Guardian rules over half a million citizens. No, this is one of the shadows of the city, in a world of shadows. Where the bones of the Goddess lie all magic intersects, all powers are centered. All shadows come together here, branching out into separate worlds. Thus, in a sense, all practitioners of deepest magic, not that petty and shallow stuff you yourself use, the sort you can see on any streetcorner in Zabortash, but the deepest, most secret magic, which partakes of the inner nature of things; all who know this and immerse themselves into it — all these dwell in Ai Hanlo, alone, in some shadow or other, where ordinary men cannot follow. In this particular shadow Emdo Wesa dwells. You must go to him."

I looked up at the city in dread. It was no city, but some monster, waiting to devour me in the labyrinths of its mouth, to dissolve me utterly.

Dadar though I was, if I had any will, I would resist.

I ran down the hill, away from the city, away from the one who called himself Kabor Asha.

"Stop! Fool!"

The spider in my chest scurried to my heart and squeezed and sank its fangs deep. I screamed once, but the sound broke into gurgling, and the pain filled me.

The next thing I knew the Zaborman was helping me to my feet. I was numb and weak. I could not fight him.

"Don't try to run away," he said. "Listen to me. I can still help you. I can be your friend."

"Who are you really? You didn't find me just by chance."

"No, I did not. Let me merely say that I am one who wants to see you complete your mission and go free. I want to help you do what Etash Wesa has sent you to do, and get it over with."

"You seem to know what I must do."

"Yes, I do. It is quite simple. You will find Emdo sleeping. Reach beneath his pillow and take out the jewelled dagger you find there. With it, cut his throat from ear to ear."

"Why should I murder a man I do not know, with whom I have no quarrel?"

"Because you were created for that very reason. Be comforted. You have no more guilt in this than does the dagger."

"That's very comforting," I said bitterly. "What happens to me afterwards?"

"In all honesty, I do not know. You could go on for a while, the way ripples do in a pool, even after the stone that made them comes to rest on the bottom. If so, take that as reward for services rendered."

So, filled with helpless dread, like a victim led to slaughter, even though I was supposed to do the slaughtering, I let him guide me through the dark gate of this shadow Ai Hanlo, through the wide squares, up streets so steep that steps were cut in them, below gaping empty windows, to that gate beyond which, in the real city, no common man was allowed to go. But no guards stopped us, and we entered the inner city, the vast complex containing the palace of the Guardian and — in all the shadows too? — the bones of the Goddess resting in holy splendor. All the while the air was still and dry, not warm, not cold, giving no sensation at all. There was an overwhelming odor of must, like that of a tomb which had not been opened for a dozen centuries. We came to the topmost part of the palace, the very summit of the mountain, to a great chamber beneath a black dome. In the true city the dome was golden, and was said to glow with the sunset hours after the rest of the world was dark.

In that vast, empty room, by the faint light of the grey sky coming in through a skylight, I could make out two vast mosaics on the floor, one of a lady dressed in black, with stars in her hair, and another, of the lady's twin, in flowing white, with a tree in one hand and the blazing sun in the other. The Goddess, in her bright and dark aspects, as she was before she fell from the heavens and shattered into a million pieces, which we know as the Powers.

Where the feet of the two images came together, there was a dais, and on it a throne. A man sat there asleep, his head on an armrest. I had expected him in a bed, the pillow beneath his head. But, no, he was sitting on it.

We crept closer, climbing the few steps until we stood by the throne. We stood over the sleeping man. He was very thin. I could not make out his features.

"Take the dagger, and do what you must," said Kabor Asha, and as he spoke he stepped down from the dais. "Do it!" he whispered to me. "Hurry! Fear not; it is a magic weapon, the only one which can pierce him. Now carefully draw it out."

The hilt was sticking out from beneath the pillow. Delicately, I took hold of it and inched it away. The task was easier than I had expected. The thing slid out of a scabbard, which remained beneath the pillow. Once I froze in abject terror as my victim's

eyelids fluttered, but he did not wake.
"Do what you must!"
I felt as if I were about to slay myself, as if the first prick of the blade would burst me like a bubble. But then I told myself, well, I had been created for this. What years I had lived, I had lived. What man can avoid his appointed doom? My life is done, I thought. There are more painful ways to die than merely winking out of existence.

I took the sleeping man firmly by the hair, and quickly, savagely, before he could react, I slashed his throat so deeply that I felt the blade touch his neck bone.

I winced, and braced myself for oblivion, but nothing happened.
Nothing.
There was no blood from the open throat. Only a little dust dribbled from the wound, and the body deflated, like a punctured waterbag, until it was no more than a crumpled mass.

The one who had brought me here ascended the dais again.
"What does this mean?" I asked. "Why doesn't he die like a man?"
"I can explain. Give me the knife."
Without thinking, I gave it to him.
He slammed it hilt-deep into my heart.
There was——
——I——
——the beginning of pain; a scream, my knees like running sand

——stood still. He held me up, impaled on the blade, frozen forever in an impossible dance of death.
"Dadar," he said. "I can explain. He does not die like a man because he is not a man. He is a thing like a dadar, like you. A reflection of a reflection. You have killed one of your own number. Dadar, it is all clear to you when you know that I am Emdo Wesa, the one my brother sent you to murder."

Hearing came first. Footsteps. The sound of a small metal instrument being dropped into a glass jar. Breathing. Slowly, images coalesced out of the air. Bright areas became torches set in a wall. A drifting smear became a more unified shape, and wore the face of Emdo Wesa, whom I had known as Kabor Asha the Zaborman.

Was he with me, even beyond death?
I shook my head to clear it, and was aware of my body. I was spread-eagled to a table, and was stripped to the waist. Emdo Wesa, holding a sharp knife, bent over me. Impossibly because I felt no pain, there was an immense gaping hole in my chest. I felt sure he could have ducked his head into it. And yet, I was numb, and blood did not spurt out. I watched almost with disinterest, as if all were part of a remote pageant performed by spirits in some other plane of existence. In the shadows.

"You know," laughed the wizard, seeing that I was awake, "you could say it was obvious from the beginning that my brother had a hand in this."

He put down the knife and reached into the cavity. His gloves were off and I could see that he indeed lacked three fingers. In their place light flickered.

He drew out a severed hand, totally covered with blood. From out of my chest. He took a ring off one of the fingers, then threw the hand away like so much garbage.

"Yes," he said, examining the ring. "It is my brother's hand. His last one. He used the other to make another dadar. How long ago was that? I don't remember. Oh, I should tell you something. To make a dadar, the wizard must cut off a piece of his living flesh. You have to amputate something. Dadars are not made frivolously. So far I have had but three enemies I could not otherwise deal with, and each cost me a finger to make a dadar. But my brother, I believe, is more quarrelsome. He has lots of enemies. He has changed himself hideously. I won't tell you the cause of our feud, because it would go on an on, and I don't care to spend that much time doing so, but I will say this. The world, all the worlds, would be better off without him. He is a monster."

"M——monster..."

Emdo Wesa smiled and said softly. "Don't strain yourself, my friend. Don't try to speak."

"Who...? Friend...?"

"Now you have a good mind, for a dadar. I must compliment my brother on his workmanship. Or you shall, when you see him. You are so full of questions. Let me set your mind at rest and answer a few. First, know that sorcery changes the sorcerer. Every act makes him a little less a part of the human world. It has to be done with moderation. Otherwise, like my brother, one will drift like an anchorless ship, far, far into strangeness. He has. I don't think his mind works at all like a human one anymore. But he is still clever. Why did he create you, and let you live unsuspecting for forty-five years before using you? It is because I have long journeyed outside of time, and forty-five years in this world has no duration outside. When I looked back into time, to see how things were going, at a point years ahead of where I departed, I saw you killing me in my sleep. It was no illusion, but a true thing. So I had to arrange for another to die in my place. **That** was what I had seen. Then I was able to come back some days before the event, encounter you, and make sure things occurred as planned. Thus my brother was thwarted."

Fear, nausea, and delirium washed over me. I felt like I would vomit out my insides, but nothing came. I screamed my wife's name.

"Tamda is not with you anymore," said Emdo Wesa. "It is useless to call her."

He reached somewhere beyond the range of vision and came back with a still beating heart in his hands.

"No... Tamda! You——monster!"

"Calm yourself. Calm yourself. I didn't say where I got this. It is for you, that you might live." He placed it in my chest. "You don't think I... no, how could you? I am not some inhuman fiend like my brother. I am a man, like anyone else. I am human. I have feeling. I can perceive beauty, know sorrow and joy. I haven't lost that. **I am moved by compassion.** I know what love is, even the love of a dadar."

His breath came out like smoke. By the light of the torches I could see that what I had taken to be tight-fitting scale armor was really his flesh. His three ghostly fingers flickered as he sewed up the wound.

I screamed again.

He walked along the table, toward my face, the knife in hand once more.

I thought that my being on the hill outside the shadow city, with Emdo Wesa beside me, was all a dream, something conjured by my desperate mind in my last moments of life. But the scene had duration, and I felt hard ground beneath me, and I touched my body and found that it was real. I groped under my shirt and encountered a tender spot, where the wound had been closed and still had a thread holding it. Much to my surprise I also encountered the dagger my wife had given me. Obviously my new master had nothing to fear from ordinary blades.

One side of my face tingled. There was something subtly wrong with my vision, as if one eye perceived things more intensely than did the other.

I looked at Emdo Wesa. He had a bandage over one side of his face, covering an eye.

Again I was a dadar.

"I am returning you to my brother," he said. "I shall see everything you see and do. When the time comes, I shall direct you. When your task is completed, I promise you, I shall release you."

"How can I ever believe that?"

"Why, you have my word, as a human being."

There is another gap in my memory here. I made to answer, but when I looked up I saw a clear, blue sky. Surf crashed nearby, and the air was filled with spray. I was no longer in the shadowland, but on a beach somewhere in the real world, on a bright, chilly day, and the wizard was no longer with me.

I had come to the ocean. I had looked upon lakes before, and rivers, but never the ocean. I had only heard of it, from those who had travelled far. Water stretched to the horizon, a vast array of whitecapped waves marching toward me like the ranks of some endless army, only to break into foam at my feet. The wonder of it almost overcame the terror of what had gone before. For this, it was almost worth what I had endured. Perhaps, I thought, I had gone mad, and had imagined all that had gone before in my madness, and in my distracted state wandered over the world until at last I came to the shore of the sea. That was how I had come here.

But then I saw that there were no footsteps in the sand. I walked up a step, and then there was a single set. I was not wet, so I had not come out of the waves, to have my tracks washed away behind me. No, I had been deposited here, out of the air.

When I pulled up my shirt, I saw the closed wound on my chest, red and swollen, the end of the black thread sticking out of it. It hurt when I breathed deeply.

Everything was true. I could not weep. All the salt water in creation was before me, so what would my tears amount to? Besides, I had expended them all before.

Anyway, a dadar is not a man, and his tears are all illusions.

I prayed to the bones of the Goddess, wherever they might be, and I called on the Bright Powers, repeating the names of them that I knew. But what are the prayers of a dadar?

Then I knelt down and began to draw in the wet sand. My hand moved by itself. Only when I realized what I was doing did I take out my dagger and use it as a stylus.

I made a crude outline. It was only a suggestion of a shape, and there were no colors to it, of course, but somehow this act set my senses spreading like smoke over the land and sea. I felt every wave in its rising, every grain of sand pressing against the rest, here concealing a shell, there a stone. I felt the chill of the great depths and the crushing currents beyond the reach of the sun. I heard the long and ancient song of the whales, a fragment of that single, endless poem which the leviathans have called out to one another since the beginning of the world. I seemed to pass out of my body for a while. There was no sensation. Then came a vague sense of direction, as if I were being led by invisible hands to the edge of an abyss.

I became aware of the drawing again. It had grown far more elaborate. My gaze drifted from it to the sky, and I saw that the sky was no longer blue, but a vivid, burning red, and I looked out over the ocean, which was now an ocean of blood, new and thick and spurting from some torn artery as huge as creation.

An object broke the surface near the horizon. It was little more than a speck, but it grew larger as it neared me, moving like a ship even though it had no sail or oarsmen to propel it. It was a rectangular box, rising and falling in the waves of blood, drawing ever nearer the shore, until I could discern quite clearly that it was a coffin of intricate and antique workmanship, embossed in gold and covered with strange hieroglyphs.

My will was not my own. Of its own volition my body rose and waded into the sea, till blood rose above my waist. My mind wanted to flee, but remained there, helpless, until the coffin was within arm's reach. Then it ceased to rise and fall, but remained perfectly still, oblivious to the movement of the waves around it.

I watched with the terror of inevitability, like some prey cornered by the hunter when there is no further place to run, as the lid silently rose. Within was darkness, not merely an absence of light, but a living, substantial thing.

And slowly this darkness faded, and my new eye penetrated it. I saw Etash Wesa, the enemy against whom I had been sent, the one who had remained on earth for so long, never venturing out of time, the one who had fought so many feuds with so many enemies.

Indeed, by the look of him, Etash Wesa had made many, many dadars. His almost shapeless pink bulk floated inside the coffin, awash in blood, slowly turning over. In the gouged-out bulk which had been a head, there was an opening — I couldn't call it a mouth — which mewed and babbled and spat blood when it rose above the surface. One stubby remnant of an arm twitched like a useless flipper. And yet, this was no helpless thing. Sometimes I knew it was almost infinitely aware and powerful, and that it had grown far, far away from the humanity that spawned it, until it no longer saw or felt as men did. I think it touched my mind then, and its presence was an intense, exquisite torture beyond the ability of words to describe or the mind to conceive. No one thought can encompass the mind of Etash Wesa.

In its twisted way, with something other than a voice, it seemed to be saying, "My dadar? Where is my dadar? I have been separated from it, and yet I shall find it."

The greatest terror of all those I had known was that Etash Wesa would indeed find me. I could look on him no more. Somehow I could move again. Screaming, I stumbled onto the beach. I obliterated the drawing. I covered my eyes with my hands. I pounded my head to drive out the memory of what I had seen, but still the red sky looked down on me, the sea of blood washed at my feet, and the thing in the coffin murmured.

I picked up my knife out of the sand. If I lived not another instant it would be preferable to living in the sight of Etash Wesa. What did I care of my promised freedom? What did I care of strange wars between wizards? What did I care, even if the world would be better off rid of Etash Wesa?

I did what I had to. I gouged out the eye Emdo had given me. If I had burst like a bubble then, it would have been a blessed escape.

I heard Emdo's voice for an instant: "No! Stop!" Then he was gone. The pain was real. The blood ran down my face. I gasped, and fell onto the sand, and lay there, panting, bleeding, waiting for the end to come.

I waited for a long time. The sun set and the stars came out. The salt tide went out and came back in again, nudging seaweed against my feet.

The rest is a muddle, a fever dream within a dream within a dream. I think someone found me. I remember walking along a road for a time. There was a bandage over my empty socket.

There were a few words, a song, a carriage wheel creaking and rustling through dry leaves. I think I lay for a day beneath the hot sun in the middle of a harvested field. A boy and several dogs came upon me, then ran away in fright when I sat up.

Somehow I came to Ai Hanlo, the real city, where the Guardian rules, where the bones of the Goddess lie in holy splendor at the core of Ai Hanlo Mountain. I remembered slowly——my mind was clouded, my thoughts like pale blossoms drifting to the surface——that my son was here, that he had come to serve the Religion. I went to the square of the mendicants, beneath the wall where the Guardian comes all draped in gold and silver to bless the crowds. I slept with the sick and the lame. Somebody stole my boots. So, barefoot, tattered, stinking, my face a running sore, I went to the gate of the inner city and demanded to see my son. But the soldiers laughed and sent me away. I begged, but they would not call for him.

But what is the begging of a dadar?

I prayed to whatever Forces or Powers there might be, to the remaining wisps of holiness that might linger over the bones of the Goddess, but what good are the prayers of a dadar?

What good? At the very end, when I sat in a doorway, very near to death, a gate opened and a procession of priests came out, and I saw a face I knew, and I pushed through the crowd with the last of my strength. I called my son's name and he stopped, and recognized me, and wept at my wretchedness. He took me to his rooms and comforted me, and later I told him that above all else I wanted to rejoin Tamda, his mother, my beloved, if she would have me, knowing me to be a dadar, without a soul, an uncertain thing.

"But Father," my son said, "consider what uncertain things all men are. What is a man, but a bubble in the foam, a speck of dust on the wind? Can any man know that his next breath will not be his last? Can he know how fortune will treat him, even tomorrow? What of the calamities that carry him off, or the diseases, or even that one, faint breath of damp midnight air which touches his old bones and makes an end to him? Then what? Do we walk a long road till at last we come to the paradise at the top of the world, there to hear forever the blessed music of the Singer? Or do we merely lie in the ground? You think these are strange words, coming from me? But the Goddess is dead, and the last remnants of her holiness quickly drain away. All things are uncertain. The world is uncertain. Will the sun rise tomorrow? Father, you are weeping. How can a mere projection, an empty thing like a skin filled with wind——how can such a thing weep? It may deceive itself, but not others. I see your tears. I know that you are more than a sudden, random, fleeting shape, as much as any man is. Yes, a man. If you were not always a man, I think you have become one over the years through your living and your love."

Which brings me back to weeping.

When at last I was able to travel from Ai Hanlo, my son went with me. We followed the way Tamda's wagon was said to have gone, asking after her in every town. She made a few coins singing, people said, or selling sketches or doing sleight of hand. She looked thin and worn, they said.

At last we found her at a crossroads. It had to be more than just chance. She leapt down from the wagon and ran to me. Again we all three wept.

Later she said to me, "We are always uncertain. If you fade away, so shall I, when we are old. It may be very sudden. How are you unlike any man in this? Stay with me. Let the days pass one at a time, and live them one at a time. You can love. How are you unlike any man in this?"

Which brings me back to weeping.

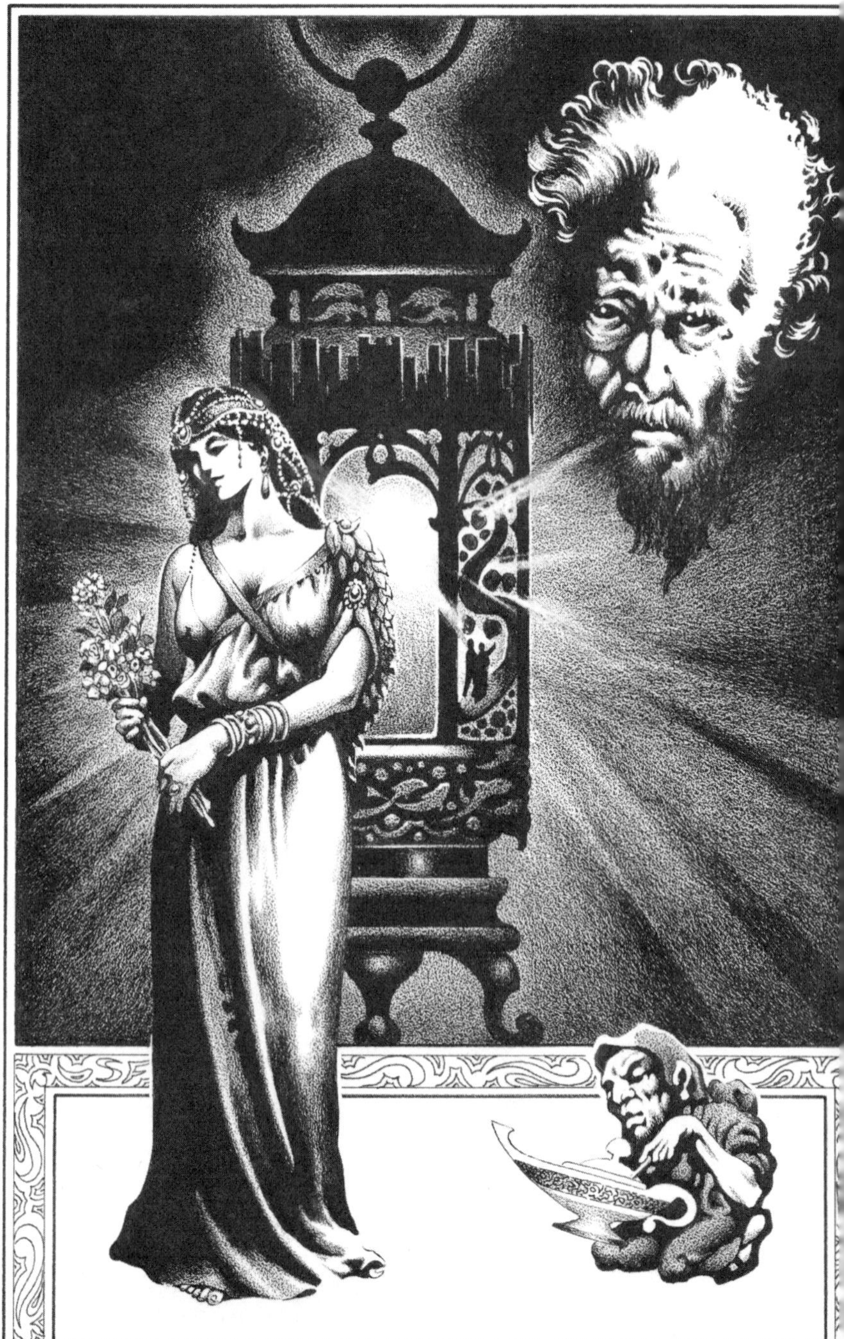

A LANTERN MAKER OF AI HANLO

In Zabortash, all men are magicians. The air is so thick with magic that you can catch a spirit or a spell with a net on any street corner. Women wear their hair short, lest they find ghosts tangled in it. Still, they find them in their hats.

In Zabortash, even the lantern makers work wonders: the present moon is not the first to shine upon the Earth. The old one went out when the Goddess died, but a Zabortashi lantern maker consulted with a magus, and was directed to that hidden stairway which leads into the sky. He hung his finest lantern in the darkness, in the night, that the stars might not grow over-proud of their brilliance, that men might know the duration of the month again.

In Zabortash, a land far to the south and filled with sluggish rivers, with swamps and steaming jungles, the air is so thick that in the darkness, in the night, the face of the moon ripples.

So it is said.

In Zabortash, further, for all that the folk are magicians, there are men who love their wives, who look on their children with pride when they are young and wistfulness when they are old enough to remind the parents what they were like in their youth.

In Zabortash, people know beauty and feel joy, and know and feel also hurt and hunger and sorrow.

So it is said.

In the time of the death of the Goddess, there dwelt a lantern maker in Zabortash named Talnaco Ramat who was skilled in his art. He was a young man, and wholly in love with the maiden Mirithemne, but she would not have him, being of a higher caste than he, and he would not be satisfied with any other. Therefore he labored long on a lantern of special design. He cut intricate shapes into the shell of it, making holes for light to shine through. The lantern was like a metal box, as tall as an outstretched hand, rectangular with a domed top and a metal ring hinged onto the dome to serve as a handle. At the outset, it was like any other lantern Talnaco Ramat might make, but he inlaid it with precious stones and plated it with gold. He carved schools of fish into it, swimming around the base, and those winged lizards called **kwisi**, which hop from branch to branch and are supposed to bring constancy and long life. He carved hills and villages, the winding river which is called Endless, and he fashioned the top half of the lantern into the shape of Ai Hanlo, the holiest of cities and center of the world, where the bones of the Goddess lie in blessed splendor. That city is built on a mountain; at the summit stands a golden dome, beneath which the Guardian of the Bones of the Goddess holds court. In this likeness was the dome of the lantern made, complete with tiny windows and ringed with battlements and towers.

Finally, Talnaco Ramat carved his own image and that of his beloved into the metal. He depicted the two of them walking hand in hand along the bank of the river, going up to the city.

Then he lit a candle inside the lantern and carried it into a darkened loft. Light streamed through the carven metal, and all his creations were outlined by it. As he watched, the river seemed to flow. The images were projected onto the walls and roof of the loft. Then he was not in the loft at all, but beside Mirithemne. All around them lizards hopped from branch to branch, wings buzzing, fleshy tails dangling.

Mirithemne smiled. The day was bright and clear. Rivermen sang as they poled a barge along. A great **drontha**, a warship of the Holy Empire, crawled against the current like a centipede on its banks of oars.

They came to the holy city, entering through the Sunrise Gate, mingling with the crowds. They passed through the square where mendicants waited below the wall that shut them out of the Guardian's palace. Once a week, he explained to Mirithemne, priests came to the top of that wall, and, holding aloft reliquaries containing splinters of the bones of the Goddess, blessed the people below. Miraculous cures still happened, but they were not as common as they had once been. The power of the Goddess was fading.

He led Mirithemne to a house at the end of a narrow lane. A wooden sign with a lantern painted on it hung over the door. He got out a key.

"This will be our home," he said.

He unlocked the door and went in, only to find himself alone in the loft, with the candle of the lantern sputtering out.

He was satisfied. The lantern was adequate.

That night, in the darkness, after the moon had set, he spoke a spell into the open door of the lantern and it filled with a light softer than candleflame, with vapors excited by the ardor of his love.

He climbed onto the roof of his shop and set the lantern down on a ledge. He spoke the name of his beloved three times, and he spoke other words. Then he gently pushed the lantern off the ledge.

It hung suspended in air, and drifted off like a lazy, glowing moth on a gentle breeze. He sat for a time, watching it disappear over the rooftops of the town.

But the next morning he found the lantern on his doorstep. Its light had gone out and its shell was tarnished. He knew then for a certainty that his suit was hopeless. A sorrow lodged in his heart, which never left him.

The sign was very clear.

So Talnaco Ramat transported himself to Ai Hanlo by some means which comes as easily to a Zaborman as breathing. The great distance was traversed, the tangled way made straight, dangers avoided, and the lantern maker come to the Sunrise Gate, dragging a two-wheeled cart filled with his belongings.

For a moment he had the idea that he would become rich here in Ai Hanlo, since the folk there had surely never seen anything as wondrous as a finely-wrought Zabortashi lantern.

He was wrong. There was no novelty. In fact, there are so many magicians in Zabortash that many of them go abroad in search of work. A number of them had settled in Ai Hanlo. Some of those made lanterns. He had to join a guild and pay a share of his earnings, but it was a comfort to be surrounded by men and women who spoke his own language. They found a place for him to live and work.

It was a house at the end of a narrow lane, with a wooden sign over the door.

He prospered in his new life and seemed to forget his old. In time he married a woman of the city called Kachelle, and she bore him three daughters, and, later, a son, whom he named Venda. His life passed peacefully as his family grew. He made lanterns of great complexity and beauty and sold them to nobles of the city, even to the Guardian himself. For all that, he was never too proud to turn out a simple oil lamp, or even to mold candlesticks.

So his years were filled. Then his daughters married, and went to live with their husbands. Later, his wife Kachelle died, and he had only Venda, his youngest, for company. He taught the boy every facet of his craft, all the secrets of magic that he knew. He knew only little spells and shallow magic — he was not a magus who could make the world tremble at his gaze — but to Venda it was impressive.

In time Venda married, and brought his wife to live with his father. As his sisters had done before him, he made his father a grandfather, and the house was filled with the shouts of children, and the sounds of their running feet, not to mention the clangor and crash when one of them blundered into a pile of lanterns.

All these children were of the city. They spoke without the accent of Zabortash, as did Venda's wife, who never seemed quite convinced that Zabortash was a real place, and that the stories about it were other than fables. Venda himself had never been there.

So Talnaco Ramat began to feel alone, a stranger once more in a strange country. For the first time in decades he began to long for his homeland and the places of his youth.

One day, while rummaging in the loft above his shop, he found something wrapped in an oily rag. He unwrapped it, and beheld the tarnished lantern he had made for Mirithemne, so long ago. He had forgotten about it all these years. Now memories flooded back.

Once again he saw himself on the rooftop, watching the lantern float above the town. He remembered the songs he had composed for Mirithemne, and the letters he had labored over with uncertain penmanship. He remembered the great fairs of Zabortash, where grand magi and lesser magicians and craftsmen of all sorts came together to conjoin their magic, that the Earth might continue to follow the sun through the universe now that the Goddess was dead, and not be lost in the darkness, in the night. There were wares displayed, feats performed. The high born women of the land were in attendance, among them Mirithemne. He smiled at her, and waved, and even spoke with her when she mingled with the crowd of common folk. She smiled back —— was it out of politeness, or something more?

Talnaco Ramat remembered what it is like to be young.

Therefore he took up the lantern and carefully polished it, until it shone as it had on the day of its completion. He oiled the hinges of its door.

He waited for evening with barely controlled excitement, speaking to his son and his son's family about trifling things, his mind far removed in time and space.

High up Ai Hanlo Mountain, a soldier blew a curving horn that hung from an arch, announcing that the sun had set.

Talnaco Ramat went out into the cool evening air, bearing the lantern. The dome of the Guardian's palace still glowed with the last light of day. He came to a courtyard he knew, which was filled with trees. It was the autumn of the year, and dead leaves rustled underfoot. He sat down on a stone bench and looked up at the dome, waiting for it to grow dark.

He was alone. The night was quiet, but for occasional distant noises of the city.

When the time came, he did not hesitate. He lit a candle and placed it inside the lantern with a steady hand, speaking as he did the most powerful spells he knew. The candle burned more brightly than it would have with mere flame. He closed the door of the lantern and at once the intricate carvings in the metal shell were outlined in fire. He set the lantern down on the bench and knelt before it, entranced by the shifting shapes. The glowing fishes swam in the air before his eyes. The Endless River flowed around him, its fiery waters splashing over the walls of the courtyard, swirling between the tree trunks. Everywhere, spirits of the air were suddenly visible in the magic light: glowing, stick-legged things wading in the earth like impossible herons; an immense serpent beneath the ground, engirdling the world, its gold and silver scales polished bright as mirrors. He saw turning at the world's core that great rose, half of fire, half of darkness, where dwell the Bright and Dark Powers, the fragments of the godhead.

He turned away from all this, drawing his awareness back into himself, into the courtyard. He concentrated on the lantern before him. It seemed to float in the air. The light grew brighter, brighter; the door opened and he was blinded.

When he could see again, he was by the side of the river called Endless, at a spot he knew well. Mirithemne was with him. He could not see her, but he sensed her presence. She was just beyond the periphery of his vision. He spoke; she did not answer; but he knew she heard.

He was still kneeling, as he had been in the courtyard. He got to his feet, expecting every joint to ache with the strain, but he found that, although he still wore the clothes he had as an old man, and his tools were still in the pockets of his apron, he was young again. He got up easily. He looked at his beard and saw that it was no longer white.

When he walked, he heard Mirithemne's footsteps beside him, but when he turned, she was not there. He continued walking. The sky was clear and the day warm.

He came to the mouth of a cave in the side of a hill which sloped down to meet the river. From within he heard a voice crying, "I am burning!"

He rushed inside, and there found an anchorite writhing on the floor of the cave. The man was dressed in rags. His beard and hair were matted with dirt. His skin was brown and wrinkled, like old leather, but there was no fire.

"I prayed for it. Long I prayed for it. Now I have it, and I am burning," the anchorite said, his voice frenzied.

"What have you prayed for? You don't seem to be burning," Talnaco said, puzzled. He turned to Mirithemne, sure that she would understand, but she was not there.

"I prayed," said the anchorite. "I prayed that a fragment of the Goddess would settle on me, that I might be made as holy as she. Oh, it was an arrogant wish! But now it is fulfilled, and I am burning with the spirit. Soon I will be completely consumed."

Before the lantern maker could reply, the other began to babble. He prophesied in tongues, but there was no one to understand his prophecies, except perhaps Mirithemne. He spoke the thousand names of the Goddess, first the common ones, then those known to sages, then those which only the greatest of Guardians may apprehend but dimly, and finally all the rest, which never before had been spoken.

Talnaco waited patiently while he was doing all this.

At last the holy man sat up, and stared at the lantern maker in a distracted way.

"You too are burning," he said.

"No, it's not like that at all."

The holy man fell down once more, writhing. He babbled. Then he was calm and lay with his eyes closed, as if he were sleeping. Slowly, with apparent deliberation, he spoke the name of Mirithemne.

Talnaco fled. For a time he lost his way in a dark forest, but still his beloved seemed to be with him. For days and nights he travelled, resting little. When he finally emerged from the forest, the river was before him again. Once more an imperial **drontha** crawled against the current on the legs of its oars. Once more the rivermen sang as they poled their barge.

He made his way to Ai Hanlo, entering through the Sunrise Gate. He followed streets he knew until he stood before his own door. The key was in the pocket of his apron. He went inside. The place was filled with dust and cobwebs. At once he set to work cleaning it, making it ready for the practice of his craft.

So again a young Zabortashi lantern maker established himself in Ai Hanlo. He labored long and hard, selling excellent lanterns to the best clients. In each lantern, somewhere among the intricacies of the design, he carved the image of Mirithemne, all the while sensing her nearness. She became more evident every day. He found his bed rumpled when he had not slept in it. His cupboard was left open when he had closed it. He heard footsteps. He heard shutters and doors opening and closing, but when he went to see, no one was there.

One day he found a woman's comb on a chair. There were long, yellow hairs in it. Mirithemne's hair was like that. Then he found her mirror, and when he looked into it, he saw someone staring over his shoulder.

He turned. The carpet on the floor moved slightly, but he was alone in the room.

At last, as he sat in his workshop in the upper room of the house, just below the loft, there were gentle footsteps on the stairway outside, followed by a light rapping at the door.

"Enter," he said.

The door opened slowly, but no one entered. He got up, and found Mirithemne's lantern on the threshold.

The sign was very clear.

Therefore Talnaco Ramat bore the lantern into a courtyard he knew. It was sunset, in the autumn of the year. High above the city, a soldier blew on a curving horn. The light of the golden dome faded, while the light of the lantern grew brighter.

The door of the lantern opened. His eyes were dazzled. He fell to his knees.

And when he could see again, Mirithemne stood before him, holding the lantern, as graceful and as beautiful as he had remembered her. She smiled at him, and, reaching down, took his hand in hers and lifted him to his feet. Then she danced to music he could not hear, her long dress whirling, the leaves whirling, the golden shapes projected by the lantern whirling over the walls, the trees, the ground, over Talnaco himself as she danced, the lantern in hand.

He could never imagine her more perfect than she was at that

moment.
  Later, she was in his arms and they spoke words of love. Later still he sat with his memories, and it seemed he had lived out his life with her, in the shop at the end of the narrow lane, in the city, and that he had grown old. Still Mirithemne was with him. He vaguely remembered how it had been otherwise, but he was not sure of it, and this troubled him.
  He vaguely remembered that he had a son called Venda. He was old. He was getting confused. He would ask Mirithemne.

  In the darkness, in the night, Venda made his way up a narrow, sloping street that ended in a stairway, climbed the stairway, and came to the wall which separates the lower, or outer part of Ai Hanlo from the inner city, where dwell the Guardian of the Bones of the Goddess, his priests, his courtiers, and his soldiers. Venda could not go beyond the wall, but he could open a certain door, and slide into an unlighted room no larger than a closet, closing the door behind him.
  He dropped a coin into a bowl and rang a bell. A window slid open in front of him. He could see nothing, but he heard a priest breathing.
  "The power of the Goddess fades like an echo in a cave," the priest said, "but perhaps enough lingers to comfort you."
  "I don't come for myself," Venda said, and he explained how he had watched his father go into a courtyard with an old lantern and vanish in a flash of light.
  The priest came out and went with him. He saw that the priest was very young, little more than a boy, and he wondered if he would be able to do anything. But he said nothing, out of respect. Then he realised that this was a certain Tamliade, something of a prodigy, already renowned for his visions.
  They came to the courtyard and found the lantern, still glowing brightly. The priest opened its door. The light was dazzling. For a time Venda saw nothing. For a time they seemed to walk on pathways of light, through forests of frozen fire.
  They found Talnaco Ramat sitting in the mouth of a cave, with the lantern before him, its door open, the light from within brilliant.
  "Father, return with us," Venda said.
  "Go away. I am with my beloved."
  Venda saw no one but himself, his father, and the priest, but before he could say anything, his father reached out and snapped the door of the lantern shut.
  The scene vanished, like a reflection in a pool shattered by a stone.

  They found themselves in the courtyard, standing before the lantern, which rested on the bench. Again the priest opened the little door, and the light was blinding. The priest led Venda by the hand. When he could see again, they were walking after his father, up the road to the Sunrise Gate of Ai Hanlo. His father hurried with long strides, bearing the lantern. Its door was open. The light was less brilliant than before.

"Father——"

"Sir," said the boy priest. "Come away."

Talnaco stopped suddenly and turned to the priest.

"What do you know of the ways of love, young man?"

"Why——why, nothing."

"Then you will not understand why I won't go with you."

"Father," said Venda softly.

Talnaco snapped the door of the lantern shut.

"If you want to get another priest, do so, but it won't do any good," the boy Tamliade said.

They stood in the courtyard, in the darkness, in the night.

"It's not that," Venda said. "What do we do now?"

"We merely follow him to where he is going. He has gone far already.

The priest opened the door of the lantern. The light was dim. It seemed to flow out, like the waters of the river, splashing over the ground and between the trees.

Again they stood by the riverbank. An imperial **drontha** went by. Boatmen poled a barge.

Venda followed the priest. They came to a cave, where lay the blackened, shrivelled corpse of an anchorite. They passed through the dark forest and eventually into Ai Hanlo, along a narrow street, until they came to the shop with the wooden sign over its door.

The door was unlocked. The two of them went quietly inside, then up the stairs until they stood before the door to Talnaco Ramat's workroom.

Venda rapped gently.

"Enter," came the voice from within. They entered, and saw Talnaco seated at his workbench, polishing a lantern. He looked older and more tired than Venda had ever seen him before.

"Father, you are in a dream."

His father smiled and said gently, "You are a true son. I am glad that you care about me."

"None of this is real," the priest said, gesturing with a sweep of his hand.

"Do you think I don't know that? I have lived out my life suspended in a single, golden moment of time. It doesn't make any difference. Mirithemne is with me."

He glanced at the empty air as if he were looking at someone.

"This thing you think is your beloved," the priest said, "is in truth some spirit or Power, some fragment of the Goddess which has entered your mind through the lantern, like a moth drawn to a random flame. It is without form or intelligence. Your longing gives it a certain semblance of a shape, but it loves you no more than do the wind and the rain."

"Perhaps I am in love with the mere memory of being in love. Perhaps... in my memory now, I remember two lives. In one my wife was called Kachelle, in the other Mirithemne. In both, I had a son, Venda. Both are in my memory now. How shall I weigh them and know which is the more true?"

Venda looked helplessly at the priest, whose face was expressionless.

"I am tired," said Talnaco Ramat. He rose, taking the lantern, and walked slowly out of the room. The light was very faint now. They followed him to the courtyard. By the time he set the lantern down on the bench, the light had gone out.

The priest snapped the metal door shut. Then he and Venda led Talnaco home. He was delirious with fever.

"He is burned by the spirit," the priest said. "There is little we can do."

They sat by Talnaco's bedside, as he lay dying. Venda wept. Toward the very end, the old man was lucid.

"Do not weep, son," he said. "I have known great happiness in both of my lives."

"Father, was there ever someone called Mirithemne, or did you imagine her?"

"She is real enough. She's probably old and ugly now. I don't think she ever knew my name."

Venda wept.

At the very end, his father said, "I have found the greatest treasure. It was worth the struggle."

Venda did not answer, but the priest leaned forward, and whispered, "What is it?"

"A smile. A touch. Whirling leaves. A single moment frozen in time."

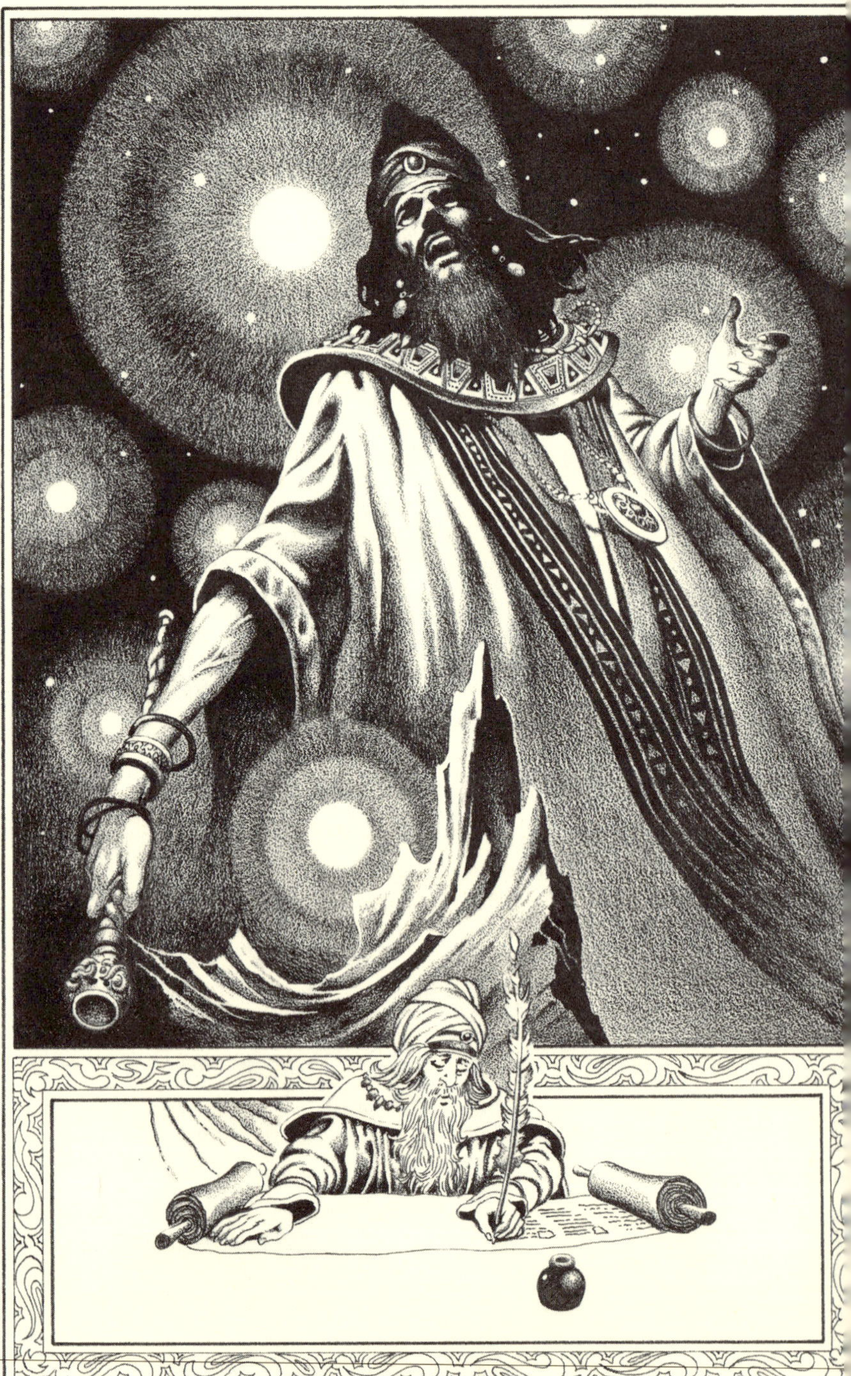

THE STORY OF OBBOK

There once was a poet named Obbok who lived in the court of the King of Rhoon. He had written thirteen books and was a poet in good standing, and on the third day of every week he would recite his poems before the King and his vassals and the ladies of the court. Each time his audience would applaud politely when he finished, and at banquets he was given a place of honor, as befitted a person of his high calling.

Now by the time Obbok was entering into old age his son began to show great promise at poetry also, and it was sure that he would succeed Obbok in the position. The young man's verses showed a proper regard for meter and rhyme, and treated those subjects poets usually write about in the manner they traditionally treat them. Thus he was exactly like his father in all matters of literature and content to travel the sure path that lay before him.

But Obbok was not satisfied, and between his appearances in court he dreamed. He dreamed of what it would be like to be a great poet, to have the power to move men with his words, to evoke laughter and sorrow and awe, to carry them to the very ends of the universe, to traverse eternity itself, from the Days Before Time to the Ending of All, to wrench the hearts and souls of his listeners with his songs.

He knew that the respect given him was borne more of ritual than appreciation. Often he would see the King's eyes wander as he recited, and the ladies would whisper among themselves, and the nobles tended to sneak out before he was finished. He wanted to put an end to this, to mean something to the people, to uplift them and contribute something to their lives.

So he sat down one day and considered the things that great poets write about, these being gods, nature, and wars, and he composed verses about them in his usual style, and delivered the verses at the appointed hour on the appointed day, and the King was as polite as ever. He thanked Obbok and praised his poetry in the customary manner, and when the poet left the throne room the men went on with their gaming and arguing, and the women continued their chatter, and servants were reminded of urgent tasks left undone. All was as before.

Sorrow came to the heart of Obbok, for he knew he would die soon and his body would be laid in the Hall of Bards along with his ancestors, and no one would remember him, and when his son died the same thing would happen, and the process would continue until the ending of his line.

He resolved then to pray to the gods, and thrice daily and

thrice nightly he climbed to the top of the Tower of Stillness and communed with them, yet nothing came of it and his next performance was like the one before, like all the ones of his lifetime and the lifetimes of his father and grandfather, no doubt also like all the times his son would read until he too passed from the lands of the living.

Many months passed and Obbok was greatly unhappy, until one day it was mentioned to him by a scribe that south of Rhoon and Lan and east and south of Dzim there was a mountain called Cloudcap, whereon dwelled a holy prophet named Amayar who spoke with the gods as if they were his kin, and was thus the possessor of great wisdom.

This news lifted the heart of Obbok and he arranged for an absence from court, and three days later he set out on his horse for Cloudcap, and the King and his nobles scarcely noticed that the poet was gone.

*   *   *

For three days and three nights Obbok rode southeast from the capital at Klor, and on the morning of the fourth day he crossed the river Xrum and entered into Lan. Two days later he was at the feet of the mountains which divided Lan from Dzim. He had to wait six days there until a caravan came along, for the mountains were infested with robbers, but finally one did come, and in the company of twenty Rhoonish tea merchants, he made the crossing. Four more days brought him to the southern frontiers of Dzim, again to mountains similarly haunted. This time there was no caravan, for no traders went into the seven wastes beyond, and Obbok crossed alone. He was not molested and he reached the Last Hall by evening, and early the next morning traded his horse for a camel and set out across the desert.

Five more days and nights passed and he stopped only briefly to rest and draw water from one of the few oases to be found in that region. He guided himself by the sun and stars, till finally he espied Cloudcap on the morning of the sixth day, standing tall above the world, caressed by the light of dawn.

Of the prophet Amayar he found no trace save for an old abandoned hovel which could have as easily belonged to a beggar or a thief. It was all but buried in the sand, its roof blown away, obviously uninhabited for many years. So it was that Obbok himself ascended the mountain to speak to the gods.

All that day he struggled up the precarious trail, till by evening there was no trail at all, and he inched his way over seamless rocks and up all but vertical cliffs. This was not work suited to an old man's muscles, and many times he was tempted to lie down and rest where he was, but he did not, for this was a sacred mountain from which blessings flowed and the lands spread out, and on its slopes no man could sleep. Such a thing would be a horrible sin in the face of the gods. Does a slave dare doze before a great king?

Dawn was just lighting the east when he reached the summit, and as the sun rose Obbok performed the proper rituals with earth and air and fire and metal, and he invoked the gods, that they might aid him in this hour of need. All that day and into the next night he called out to them, never pausing, his voice never silent.

Now Gheeznu, the god of poets, is a small and insignificant god in the eyes of the Great Ones, and he is not often involved in the important affairs of the universe. Thus it happened that he had nothing to do at the time that Obbok addressed him, and he decided to hear the old man's prayers. He peered down from his ivory seat in the Land Behind The Sky, looked down through the clouds and corporeal airs, and saw there on the summit of Cloudcap the tiny figure of Obbok the poet. And for reasons not known to theologians he granted Obbok's wish. Some say that he was moved by pity, while others claim he meant what came after as a moral lesson to make men content with their stations in life, although another school of thought holds the whole affair to be one of the mischievous pranks the gods often play upon men. But regardless of the motivations of the gods, which are only speculation, the results were definite and obvious.

Obbok's fire rose until it touched the sky and the tops of the flames vanished into the clouds overhanging the peak, and when it again receded and burned low and extinguished itself, lo! there was before the aging poet a wondrous scroll not even hot from the fire, engraved in nine and ninety languages, none of which could ever be deciphered by men. Obbok took up this scroll with great reverence. He wrapped it in his cloak lest his hands soil it, and hastily departed from that holy place, shouting thanks aloud to the gods as he did.

On his way back across the Seven Wastes he pondered over the writings, and as he rested in the Last Hall he gazed at the scroll often. Men saw it and recognized its nature and source, and Obbok was treated with great respect, as one touched by the divine.

In truth, though, nothing happened to Obbok until he returned to Klor and laid the scroll on a special stand which he commanded his apprentices to build. Exhausted then he retired to bed without trying any more to learn the meaning of the thing. And that night, as Time strode across the world and his hounds drove the day fleeing before them, the spirits of the gods came down between the stairs masked in dreams, and to them the scroll in Obbok's chamber shone like a bright beacon. They clustered about it and read thereon the instructions of Gheeznu. And thus wondrous things entered into the head of Obbok that night.

He saw all eternity as a continuous strip, past, present, future and end molding into one. He saw the primal screaming chaos which spawned the gods, and against which they battled in the days before Time. Revealed to him was the shaping of the world in the hands of the various deities, and the reigns of the Kings

Before Men, the driving into the sky of the immortal dragon which threatened to devour the world and still nibbles at the sun. He saw also the coming of Time from the mists of chaos, and he knew then how the brothers Time and Fate drove the world before them with sword and hammer and toppled Throramna, the Father of Cities, and smote also the ancient lords of Earth, toppling their corpses into the jaws of the jackal Death. The coming of man Obbok saw, and before the eyes of his dream, kingdoms rose and melted away like seasons before the onslaught of years. And from the Farthest East he saw the hounds of time come, unleashed by their master, howling after the lives of men. Gnath and Belhimra came and went. Even his own country died before a flood of savages from the south. He saw new continents arising, only to sink again beneath the seas, and he caught a glimpse of the war the gods fought over Aduil; he gazed in horror at the coming of the Lizard Earls, the return of chaos and the dimming of days, the final death of the world and the gods. And yet more was revealed, all the secret thoughts of men laid bare. He saw into their minds and hearts, discerned nobility, self-sacrifice, stupidity and cowardice, love of country, greed, treason, murder and love —— all the things which make men what they are. The veils were drawn back yet further and he saw into the hearts of the gods, and in them he saw the same things again, plus their contempt for all creatures lesser, their conceit and contempt for one another, and finally their fear of the One who is greater than the gods and keeps the universe in a bottle in his pocket.

At this point the gods cried out and the world trembled, for the spirits had shown too much, and the gods recalled them at once and sent the Sisters of Forgetting into Obbok's sleep. But it was too late, for Fate and Time, who are impervious to the gods, again strode over the world scattering the night before them, and the dreams of Obbok left him with the coming of morning.

And the gods were very much afraid, save for Gheeznu who seemed rather pleased with himself.

Great was the wonderment that seized the awakened Obbok. He roused his servants even though it was before the accustomed hour, and sent them scurrying to fetch all the pens, ink and writing parchments they could find. There was fire in his face that made them all fearful, and they went off at once. Soon a great pile of writing materials was in Obbok's chamber. Night and day he wrote, and wore out pens, and higher and higher grew the pile of pages. Cautiously his apprentices and servants approached him and laid out a meal before him, only to remove it again when they saw it was cold. They muttered among themselves, saying, "Surely the Master is possessed by a demon or devil," for Obbok had never previously taken writing too seriously and had only composed verses out of necessity or boredom. Now, of course, the heat of inspiration was in him, but the others did not understand, for they knew nothing of the true meaning of the mysterious scroll.

One day the King sent a messenger into the room of Obbok to summon the poet so that he might hear some of this new poetry that the whole castle was talking about. Yet the poet did not come, and the messenger spoke as if to one deaf, for Obbok did not speak or even slow his hand, and the messenger was moved with fear when he saw the look on the old man's face.

At this point the King grew angry and sent his guards to seize Obbok and bring him to the courtroom at once, for never before had anyone dared to ignore a royal command, and the King would have an explanation. The guards went, but when they came to lay their hands on the bard, Obbok **did** look up, although he paused not an instant from his writing, and the terrible glare frightened the guards, for they saw something in those eyes that was not of mortal Earth. They too turned and fled.

Then the King himself came to Obbok and the poet paused for the briefest of seconds and spoke a single word which gave reason for everything and caused the King to fall down on his knees and beg forgiveness for the interruption. That word was a god word, and it had come at the very end of the dream. It was never intended to be uttered by the mouths of men or heard by their ears.

The King withdrew, and all the castle was moved with fear and bewilderment at this new thing. All activities stopped. Everyone waited for Obbok to finish his work as they would await the sentence of a harsh judge, and the court soothsayer proclaimed a miracle of the first order, bidding all to go and purify themselves in the temple, then return and hear the wondrous revelation of Obbok.

And after fifteen days Obbok called out from his room and bade his servants lift him into bed. With failing voice he commanded them to bring food and water, and medicines, for he was exceedingly weary. These things were done and Obbok slept for two days after he had eaten, and none dared enter and read the manuscript while he slumbered.

Finally the poet roused himself and sent word to the King, informing him that he was ready. Nearly all the people of the castle came to hear him this time, every lord, every general, even the guards from the walls and the cooks from the kitchen. All stood in silence and complete attention was on Obbok, and the ladies did not whisper among themselves, and no one **dared** slip out.

Obbok came and recited his poem before them, and it was four thousand and nine stanzas in length.

* * *

There is some confusion as to what happened after that. No books tell of it, and the whole affair and especially the ending of it has been shrouded in great secrecy. The King died shortly afterwards, and it is only by piecing together the accounts of the various servants and courtiers who were **not** present at the recital that the tale is known at all. And yet no two of them have ever been able to agree on certain parts of it.

According to some, so terrible was the content of Obbok's poem that its words drove all who heard it mad, and for this reason none who heard it could tell any of it, and if asked they would only roll their eyes up to heaven and mutter something obscure, or else not respond at all. Great were the secrets revealed that day, all the things beyond the knowing of philosophers, and no one had the courage to understand it let alone repeat it. Fervently they begged the Sisters of Forgetting to slay them, but there was no relief. Many went out and slew themselves afterward.

And others claim that the King declared Obbok to be possessed by a devil, and he had him hanged from the highest tower. The poem was cast into the fire, according to this version, for none dared leave it around. It had the power to corrupt.

Yet others will tell you that it was Obbok who went mad, and after speaking the final verse he collapsed to the floor and whimpered like a child, begging gods and men to forgive him for what he had done. He was carried away and locked in a remote tower in a distant castle, for it would have been bad luck and poor form to allow a madman to wander about one's court.

And still others insist that while all were dazed by the effect of the poem, Obbok grabbed the manuscript and fled from the court, and not able to destroy his work, he hid it in a place from which it will issue forth on the last day, rendering men helpless with its words and bringing back Chaos, causing the final death of the universe. And those who tell the tale this way believe that Obbok still walks the world in the guise of a minstrel, and he sings only of simple things and pleasant happenings, of the birds of the air and the bees of the flowers and the coming of spring. Those that behold him see a sorrow beneath his calm and do not ask of it.

And finally there are some who swear by all that is holy that as soon as Obbok finished his poem, the floor was rent apart and a demon sprang up into the throne room, devouring Obbok and the manuscript in a single gulp, and thus the blasphemy and horror of it were removed from the lands of mortal man.

No one can be sure of any of these things now, for there is a new king in Klor, and Rhoon is troubled by wars and no one has time to bother with the past. Furthermore the King has been cautious and has decreed that anyone prying into the matter will be tortured to death by devices unimaginable, learned by wicked sorcerors from demons conjured for that purpose alone.

The son of Obbok dwells in the court now, and once every week he recites his new poems, all of which deal with the subject matter common to courtly verses and written in the classical manner. They are applauded out of courtesy, and the ladies whisper and giggle during the performances, and some of the men slip away unnoticed, and the poet is given a place of high esteem and privilege in the court, as befits one of his noble calling.

THE OUTCAST

Let us hear now of the heroes of old,
Of Constantine, the Christian king,
And Arthur, wielder of the wonder-sword.

Their flesh is dust; their bones are cold;
Their ghosts are gathered on lonely fens.

Let us tell the tales of brave warriors,
Of Hnaef, who held the hall,
And Aelfric, master of the sea-steeds.

Their flesh is dust; their bones are cold;
Their ghosts are gathered on lonely fens.

Now let us sing of poets, recall the songs
Of Caedmon, who wrought the words of man's beginning,
And Eothere, who warned the world of evil coming.

Their flesh is dust; their bones are cold;
Their ghosts are gathered on lonely fens.

My lord lies slain; his stead is burnt;
His thanes all fallen on the field;
His people cast into the dark earth-cave.

Their flesh is dust; their bones are cold;
Their ghosts are gathered on lonely fens.

Alone I have lived, to wend the ways of weary exile.
I sing of the past, when conquerors ruled the land.
There is no one to listen, none who knew the days that were.

Their flesh is dust; their bones are cold;
Their ghosts are gathered on lonely fens.

I know this: that all men shall die,
Their lives shorn short, their deeds soon done.
Soon lords and folk shall sink into sleep.
Soon great will be gone, soon lowly lost.
Soon shall my foemen fall before years.

Soon shall I be with my lord.

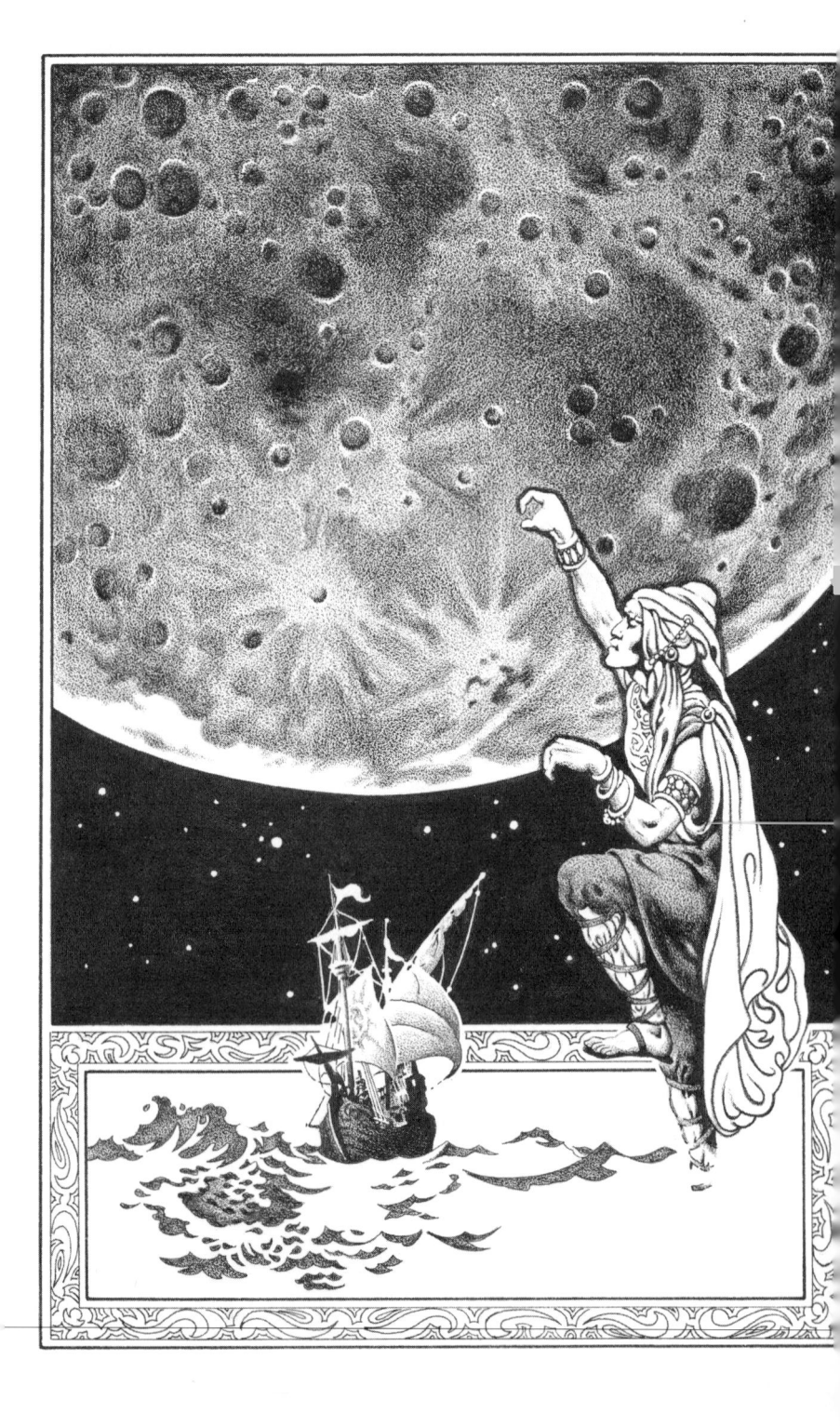

THE PRETENSES OF HINYAR

It was a hot and stuffy day in the Hall of the Thieves when the last story was told. The last one was as marvellous and as fine as any that preceded it, but when it was finished there were no more. The gong rang, indicating it was time for another tale; but all the storyteller could do was nod and whisper to the thief beside him: "There are no more."

And that thief turned to the fellow beside him and whispered that there were no more; and the third thief did likewise, as did the fourth and the fifth, until the message reached the ears of the Head Thief.

Then the Head Thief put down the bone on which he had been gnawing, picked his teeth with a stolen toothpick, ran his hands through his long and grimy beard, and after a long silence said:

"There must be a deed."

At this all the thieves trembled, for they knew that a deed requires a doer, and that any new tale would necessitate someone's performing some exceptionally perilous feat. Stories, it seems, are fun to listen to, but hellishly painful to partake in. This perhaps explains why so many of the heroes of myth and legend are dead: their stories did not have happy endings.

It was this fear of an unhappy ending that caused all the thieves to shake so, and they cowered all the more when the Head Thief called for the Pole Fetcher, a holder of an ancient and honorary position, whose sole function it was to fetch the Head Thief's story pole. And when the Pole Fetcher had returned with the object of his office, a long and light rod capable of reaching to the very ends of the Hall, every thief in the place went pale and held his breath.

Their leader then took his instrument and reached randomly into the crowd, touching someone on the head. When this was done everyone sighed with relief, save for the person who had been touched. He was as petrified as ever.

His fellows shrank back from him; and as the space cleared around him all could see that the hero of the new story would be Hinyar, son of Yan, who was called The Snitcherous and widely reputed to have the most nimble fingers in the world.

Not a bad choice, everyone except Hinyar agreed.

One cannot defy the tradition of the Order of Thieves. This Hinyar had known since the day he was born, so he stood silently in the middle of the room as the Head Thief consulted with the Elder Robbers and Master Highwaymen of many lands. At last they were finished, and the Head Thief turned and looked down at Hinyar and said:

"Your tale shall be one of the finest ever told. We have decided that you shall burgle Karakuna, the house of the gods."

At this a gasp spread through those assembled, and there were murmurs of blasphemy and worse. Only the Head Thief remained calm.

"Of course, the gods will not be there if you arrive on time," he said. "There is a certain time of year when the hours of darkness threaten to overtake entirely the hours of light, and it is then that the gods must go forth and fight this darkness so that light may grow again and spring may come. It is during this period that you shall steal the greatest treasure in the universe."

"And what is that treasure?" asked Hinyar.

"I haven't the slightest idea, but I'm sure you'll recognize it when you see it. Go now."

Hinyar went. He went at once from the Hall and down to the docks of the city of Kosh-Ni-Hye, and stealing a boat he propelled it over the sea by means of one of those spells known only to the very best of thieves.

He sailed south out of the Bay of Lyani, along the coasts of Rung and the other lands of that region, past the Isle of Fearful Thunder, and then west across the Middle Sea. Ten days later he came to the Isle of the Headless Men.

Now it was on a Tuesday that he arrived, and this was very significant. Know, O Reader, that the Isle of Headless Men is a barbarous place near the bottom of the world, far beyond any civilized lands, and the men there have no heads save for the One, which is passed from each ruling sovereign to his successor, thus illustrating the maxim that in the land of headless men the one-headed man is king.

The thing to remember about the Isle at the time I tell of is that there were two kings. They were twin brothers, named Thanos and Yanos; and they shared the head, each passing it to the other on alternate Tuesdays. When Hinyar got there all the inhabitants of the Isle were groping their way toward the royal palace, that they might be present at the ceremony, as was the custom. Since they had no heads, they could not have eyes, obviously, and were blind. Thus it was not hard at all for Hinyar to infiltrate their ranks.

He came to the palace at the crucial moment, when Yanos was handing the head over to Thanos. Now the reason this was an important time is that as Yanos removed the head from his shoulders he could no longer see, and Thanos would remain sightless until it was firmly in place on his. For the moment, the only person on the entire Isle who wasn't blind was Hinyar.

Taking advantage of this, he leapt up to the platform whereon the two kings stood, and intercepted the head as Yanos passed it to Thanos. It took them a few minutes to realize what had happened, and when they did there was nothing they could do except stamp their feet in rage, since they had no mouths and could not cry out. Hinyar was lord of them now, for in his hand he held the One Head, in which was implanted the One Eye (for the head resembled that of a cyclops) and from the nostrils of which dangled the One Nose Ring.

Hinyar kicked Yanos on the shins a number of times, communicating with him in the simple manner of these people who had no mouths and no ears. What he said might best be translated like this:

"I am Hinyar the thief. I have stolen your head. Tell me what I want to know about the house of the gods or I'll throw your head into the sea."

They had no choice but to tell him, and tell him they did. Being unnatural creatures, they often had contact with other unnatural creatures, and were thus wise in lore. By kicking him on the shins, they were able to tell him how he might come to Karakuna.

Bruised but satisfied, Hinyar returned the head to Yanos, first plucking out the eye and pocketing it. He had use for it later.

Yanos gave the head to Thanos, whose turn it was this week. Greedily the other put it on, and it was only then that Hinyar's even more foul trick was discovered.

The king howled, and his subjects jumped up and down in impotent fury; but since they could not see Hinyar, he was able to escape with ease.

Thus ended the first part of his journey. As soon as he was in his magic boat again and well out to sea, he removed his right eyeball and put it in his pocket, replacing it with the stolen one. It took a minute for the new one to get into focus; but when he was able to see out of it Hinyar found he had the witch-sight, and could view all manner of marvelous things which pass by ordinary men unnoticed. For the rest of his voyage he constantly saw monsters and chimeras swimming by, and the elves in their long white boats. Once he even caught a glimpse of that dread eater of dragons, the glimich; and when he did he turned away quickly. Furthermore, when one night a half-man, half-fish creature the length of a dozen longships passed under his craft, he knew he had just beheld Yognith, Lord of the Sea, one of the few lesser gods who does not belong to the company of Karakuna.

After ten days he turned north and sailed along the western coast of Yingol, past the City of Kluish and the barren lands beyond, until he came to a horrible wood without a name. And disembarking at this place, he carved certain powerful runes on the side of his boat that it might be invisible to men and demons alike, and then set out into the forest armed with his sword, his magic, and his wits.

After many encounters with assorted monsters, the actions of which were all so much alike as to render accounts of them tedious, he came to a ladder. Now, this ladder would have been invisible to all lacking the witch-sight, but to Hinyar it was an ordinary rope ladder hanging out of the sky and stretching up much higher than he could see, even with his wonderful new eye.

He knew then that he had come to the right place and that this was the ladder used by certain vermin to climb down from the cellars of the gods into the lands of man, where they might be feared as mighty beasts. He mounted at once and climbed.

And climbed.

And climbed.

By evening he seemed no closer to the top, even though the ground beneath him had faded to an indistinct blur. By midnight the stars flowed all around him and he looked down on the top of the moon, which no man had ever seen before.

Now occasionally certain abominations, most of which were the size of medium-length whales and possessed the bodies of scorpions and dragon-like wings, spied this morsel curiously suspended in air, and attempted to eat it. If they had had the witch-sight, they would have seen the ladder, but they didn't so the thief seemed to be lacking all support, and if any of the creatures had been intelligent they might have paused and marvelled at such a phenomenon. But it is not the nature of abominations to question the laws of physics, so they merely tried to devour him.

They never succeeded, however, because every time one would draw too close Hinyar would glare at it with his eye, and the creature would turn and streak away in terror.

After a while the fatigue of climbing began to tax the thief's muscles sorely, and he knew he could go no farther, so he tied his thief's sack to a rung of the ladder, climbed inside, ate of the provisions he had stored therein, and went to sleep. The next morning he awoke and climbed all day, stopping once more in a similar manner for lunch and a brief nap; but still by evening the end of the ladder was not in sight. He had long since stopped looking down, so he couldn't possibly have known that the sky below him looked exactly like the sky above him, and that the earth had passed from view entirely.

Thus he journeyed through the highest regions of the outer airs, past the sun and all the planets, past the great chain which holds all worldly things together, and out of the cosmos entirely.

It was then that forty-seven days and nights of climbing came to an end and he hit his head on something hard above him. Looking up, he saw a trapdoor floating in the air, as if not attached to anything.

Opening this door, he came to the cellar of the house of the gods.

His timing had been perfect, for not an hour before there had been a great rushing of winds throughout Karakuna, and all the gods had departed out a window that they might fight the forces of darkness and assure the coming of spring.

After Hinyar had pulled himself up into that place, he rested for a minute, then put on his black slippers of thievery and stood up to look around.

He was in the basement, obviously, for there were winebarrels everywhere. But this was not a mortal basement, and the sizes were somewhat increased, so that Hinyar seemed a mouse before the barrels as tall as small mountains. Even the stones in the floor were huge, many of them a hundred man-lengths across.

A stairway, which was so immense that its top could not be seen in the gloom, rose to one side of the room. The individual steps were higher than the tallest of men, but Hinyar managed to mount them, for his slippers gave him the power to leap from one to the other like a frog, until at last he arrived, somewhat winded, at the top.

He was now beneath a great doorway, the arch of which was lost in the vast heights above him. He crossed the kitchen (for this was the room he had come to), and after walking three miles he came to another doorway.

This one, unlike the other, had a door in it; and the door was closed, yet Hinyar had no difficulty crawling under it. It was only after he stood up on the other side that his difficulties started.

Two evil eyes swam in the darkness.

"Who is it that disturbs Etu, the beast of Lerad?" a voice boomed.

Before Hinyar could answer, a mountain of toad-like flesh burst upon him. He drew his sword and held his ground, waiting until the monster came very near. And when the monster had come very near he rushed forward and stabbed it twice on the big toe.

Howling in pain, the creature began to weep oceans of tears; and when the quantity of these tears was sufficient, it dissolved itself in them and was gone.

"Coward," said Hinyar.

After twenty more rooms, he came to a corridor; and at the beginning of this corridor there stood a sign, which read:

> BEYOND THIS PLACE ARE THE ROOMS
> AND TREASURE TROVES OF THE GODS,
> THE SAME ONES WHO PERPETUALLY DEFY
> EVIL AND UPHOLD THE UNIVERSE.
> [quiet please]

But Hinyar gave the sign not a second glance. The corridor was lined with doors, all of which were too big for a man the size of Hinyar to open, of course; but again his thief's slippers came to his aid, for he was able to walk up the vertical faces of the doors in the manner of a fly, that he might look through the keyholes and see what lay beyond.

Behind the first there was a mass of glittering things in

addition to a forge, an anvil, a hammer, and a bucket of water the diameter of Lake Ianos. This Hinyar knew to be the holding of Chiyanuil, the maker of stars, and these things to be the materials from which he wrought his works. Surely this was a great treasure, and it would have been easier and safer for Hinyar to have presented part of it to the Head Thief, but obedience is a very important thing among thieves, and he knew that this was not the greatest of all treasures, so he passed it by and went on to the second door.

And behind the second door there was a wide plain of fire, on which seven chariots drawn by dragons and driven by worms, raced endlessly about. Hinyar didn't know to whom these belonged, and he didn't care to know. He hoped that there was no treasure behind **that** portal.

Behind the third door a hundred maidens danced. Since they were at least a thousand feet tall, Hinyar would not have been able to steal them even if he had wanted to.

Behind the fourth was a queer little green monkey whose feet were made of ink. Even as Hinyar watched, this creature pranced across open sheets of parchment and wrote thirty-five odes, a dozen sonnets, a sestina, six ballads, and part of an epic. He passed this one up too.

Behind the fifth was all the money in the world. **All.** Yet still he did not stop, for he had heard somewhere that there are more things in life than money, and he was sure that the gods themselves would have less mundane tastes.

Behind the sixth was Etu, beast of Lerad, with an oversized bandage on his big toe. Hardly anyone's idea of a treasure.

Behind the seventh was a ship, from the sides of which sprang the wings of an eagle. Surely this would be a fine prize, and perhaps a good means of escape from this place, but it was not what he sought.

Behind the eighth was a phoenix reading a book. What strange knowledge might be possessed by that bird, and what immortal work of literature it might be reading, he knew not, and he did not attempt to discover. If it did indeed turn out to be the greatest treasure in the place, he could always come back for it.

So he went on and on, his slippers carrying him up the walls and doors without fail; and with few exceptions the treasures grew progressively more fabulous, until his mind scarcely could comprehend their vastness. Truly when something becomes that valuable, the whole concept of price is meaningless. But even if such a thing can be said, the treasures themselves paid no heed, and continued to grow greater and greater; and thus each time Hinyar knew he had not yet found the greatest of them all.

At last he came to a room whose door hung open. It was a very drab place, and there was nothing in it save for a match-box the size of a large trunk. Intrigued, he approached it.

"This is the greatest of all! This is the greatest of all!"

squeaked a bright red rabbit with the many-faceted eyes of a fly, as it scampered away.

Then Hinyar opened the box and held in his hands the greatest treasure in the universe. It was a parchment about ten feet square on which was written an epigram once muttered by an obscure philosopher, an epigram which contained all that ever need be said about the conditions of existence. Beyond doubt, it was a monumental piece of wisdom.

But Hinyar, alas, had never learned to read.

He was still cursing and pacing about, trying to figure out the meaning of all this, when again that enormous castle was filled with the force of a thousand gales, and the gods came home. They found Hinyar right where the rabbit had said he would be.

Were they angry with him? No, not at all. They laughed heartily as they towered over him, so that for a third time there was a great wind; but this time it was a wind of mirth. They picked him up and tossed him from hand to hand, as children might do with a ball; and some dipped him in their cups that his screams might flavor their wine. Many other things they did to him also, and many games they played with their new toy, but these were so terrible I dare not speak of them.

At last, when his novelty had worn off and all the gods were tired of him, Lerad, chief of the gods, tossed the thief over his shoulder and out a window.

Hinyar fell all the way back to earth, covering the distance it had taken him forty-seven days to climb in a little under three. He landed in a cornfield in northwestern Guaz and made a great hole in the ground. And to this day that hole is called Hinyar's hole; and folk from all over the world come to see it, while official persons conduct tours and unofficial persons sell refreshments and souvenirs.

As for the thieves, while they never found out all of what happened, they did learn a good deal through an oracle, and imagination filled in the rest; so they got a story and were satisfied for a time.

And when that tale was told the Head Thief sent for his Pole Fetcher, and another was made to do a deed.

But I shall not tell of that here.

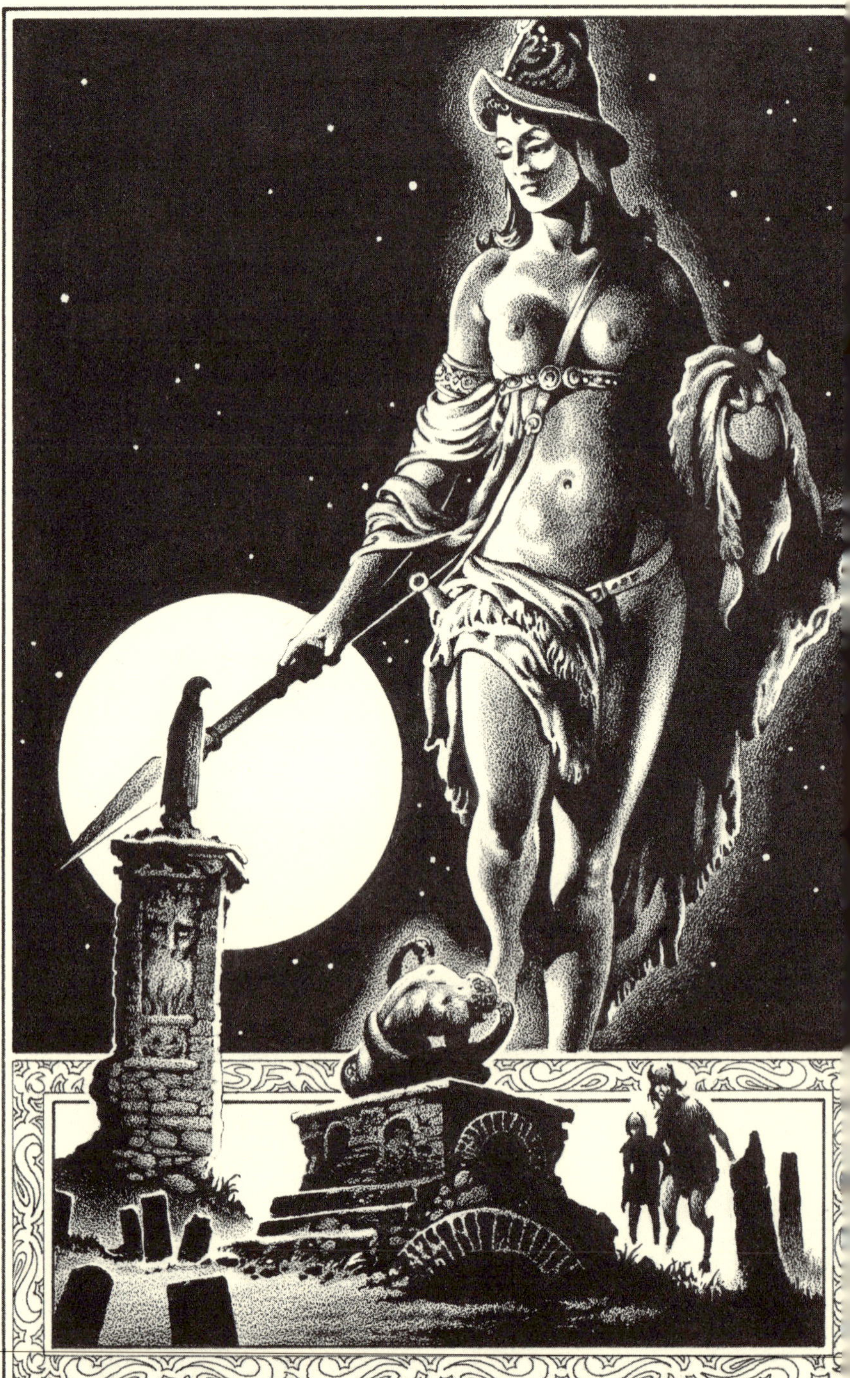

THE STORY OF THE BROWN MAN

When I was a boy, long ago, before the reign of the Emperor Constantine, my Uncle Septimius had an estate in the country about five days journey from Naples, and almost every summer my father and mother and I, along with some of our servants, would go there to visit. It is splendid country in that part of the world, with high rocky cliffs overlooking the sea, and green, crop-covered terraces dropping down to meet the waters. The servants would bear us endlessly past cultivated fields, through small forests and villages, along the eternal paved roads, until at last we would come to my uncle's villa and he would be there at the front gate with his wife and chief steward and some of his slaves, waiting to welcome us.

So it was for my sixth, seventh, eighth and ninth years. Often we would spend the entire season there. The air was fresh and free of the harmful humors that infest crowded towns, and the days were always bright and pleasant. There were many things to see and do, and it was a very exciting time for me.

This was not so in the evenings. Then I was bored, for it was in the evenings that my father and my uncle would sit on the porch watching the sun sink red and golden into the distant sea, and before the light grew too dim they would read from the books in my uncle's library, and talk of such people as Plato and Aristotle and Epicurus, who I assumed were philosophers or something equally tedious.

Now when this was going on my mother played the harp in another part of the house, and my aunt and the ladies of the household would gather around her and listen, and sometimes sing. The result of these simultaneous doings was that I was supremely bored, for at that age I had no interest whatsoever in the classics, and scarcely any more in music, save for the simple songs I sang to myself. Since there were no boys of my age on the estate except for slaves, and I knew it would be demeaning for one of my rank to associate with them, I felt very lonely on those long summer evenings.

I remember how it was on one particular evening, during the second week of our stay, that I wandered away from the grounds unnoticed. I walked across the courtyard and out the gate, then over the fields. I stopped for a time to watch the slaves as they labored to finish up their tasks in the fading light, but in a short while I grew tired of that too, and moved on. At length, when the house was out of sight over the top of a rolling hill, and the plowed fields were behind me, I passed through a copse of trees and came to an ancient and deserted graveyard filled with marble tombs covered with vines and moss. I wandered among them looking at the inscriptions, and it was then that I met the Brown Man.

I had stopped before a particularly large and fine sarcophagus, the stones of which had turned green with age, and on it were carved the images of two maidens holding hands. I ran my fingers over the two—were there twins buried here?—and said aloud, "I wonder what that means."

And very much to my surprise a voice said, "I can tell you if you like."

I turned and beheld the Brown Man emerging from behind a monument. He had obviously been watching me for a few minutes at least. I named him "The Brown Man" to myself at once, because he was darker than most people, though not black like the African slaves my uncle owned. In all he was a very strange person. He wore no clothes at all and was very hairy. His legs were covered with thick fur, and the hair on the top of his head stuck out wildly, like that of a savage. I suppose I was too young to be afraid of him. Or perhaps the tone of his voice put me at ease. In any case I did not run from him.

"Who are you?" I asked.

"My people have no names." He stepped fully into view and it was then that I noticed the strangest of the many strange things about him—his feet. He didn't have toes like a normal man; he had hooves. Round, shiny hooves, like those of a cow. Cloven in the middle.

I gaped at this wondrous thing, but he acted as if nothing were out of the ordinary. He crouched before the two carven ladies, and as he did I noticed that he had a tuft of hair above his rear forming a short tail. He pointed to the tomb image.

"These are the sisters Sleep and Death," he said. "They are the daughters of Oblivion and they rule this place."

"How do you know?"

"Why——why, I can read the inscriptions. Can't a boy of your age read yet?" He laughed, and whatever fear I might have had of him vanished with the sound.

"I am learning letters a little. I'm trying to read, but it's hard." That was a lie. In truth I was resisting all efforts to educate me with the determination of a spearman in a phalanx facing an onslaught of the enemy. My tutors were two eunuchs named Arcadius and Gallus, and I found both of them to be terrible bores. My parents often scolded me for refusing to cooperate with them. I did not yet know even simple Latin, let alone the Greek that marks a man as civilized. The Brown Man was the first would-be teacher I ever listened to.

"Well," he said. "I shall have to explain all these to you."

"All of them?"

"All if you wish."

"Some now, and we'll save some for later." Already I was envisioning a series of nightly meetings.

"So be it then," he said, and took me by the hand. He led me deeper and deeper into the graveyard, and if I should have felt any superstitious dread at being in a place of death I did not. His presence was reassuring.

Here and there we would stop before some monument and he would explain the motif on it. We came to one featuring a soldier, and the soldier was falling over, an arrow in his foot.

"That is Achilles. The owner of this grave reminds others of their mortality." Then he told me of Achilles and how he died.

We came to another grave, and around its four sides were a man, a lady, and a lot of pigs.

"Ulysses and Circe. The swine are his crew after she had bewitched them."

And another, with soldiers, a burning city, and a large horse.

"Aeneas fleeing Troy, coming to found Rome." Briefly the Brown Man told me of the origins of our country.

And another.

"This one shows Adonis, who has died, but shall rise again."

And so we went on among the marble tombs, until the evening was done and darkness was upon us. Then once I turned around and the Brown Man was with me, and I turned again and he was not. I returned to my uncle's house and found that I had not been missed. My father and uncle had moved inside and by the light of candles and braziers they still pored over the books, and my mother and the ladies no longer played upon the harp, but merely talked softly among themselves. An hour or two passed and everyone retired.

That summer was like no other that I had known. Often I was bored in the days for the first time, for daytime activities had paled in the face of expectations of the evening, and as soon as I could I would slip away after the last meal of the day and go to meet my new friend. I should have been at my lessons then, but I escaped this by a simple method. I told Gallus that I was studying Greek with Arcadius, and I told Arcadius that I was studying Latin with Gallus. The two of them never found out that I had deceived them. They may have been scholars but they were not really smart at all. Perhaps eunuchdom does that to a man.

Each evening I would run across the fields with great eagerness and in no time at all I would be at the graveyard and the Brown Man would be waiting, and he would show me all the secrets of the place, and also at times he would take me to the sacred groves in the forest nearby, and sit with me there and tell stories of the ancient heroes. I loved him, and he taught me much, but his manner was not at all that of a teacher. He spoke with enthusiasm and excitement, as if he had witnessed and been involved in the things he had read in a book.

And he worked magic for me. At first he did only illusions, but then greater things. Once he turned me into a worm, so that I might know the ways of living things beneath the earth, and again into a rabbit, to learn of things on the earth, and a fish to learn of the things in the sea, and finally a bird, that I might soar and see all the world from the air above. And he said to me that I would someday be a great magician, if I followed the true way. But as he said this his face grew long, and his voice melancholy.

"I fear you are one of the last. All these things must perish soon."

"What? What shall perish?"

"The old ways, and even the old gods. People don't honor them anymore. In time they shall all be swept away."

"But I shall honor the gods! I promise!"

"Then try and remember all the things I have told you. Maintain a light in the dark times ahead."

"I shall! I shall!" I tried to draw him out of his gloom. It hurt me to see him unhappy.

"Then I shall do you a great honor. I shall show you the gods. Would you like to see them?"

"**See the gods**?" This was incredible, impossible. No one can see the gods unless **they** show themselves to him.

The Brown Man smiled once more. "Come," he said, and he took me by the hand, and by some subtle motion we left the earth and began to fly through the air. My body seemed as light as a cloud. There was no sensation of motion, no weight. I never looked down, never saw the fields and sea dwindling below us, but I knew that I was flying. The setting red sun grew brighter and brighter before me, until it was yellow and white as in midday. It grew and grew until it filled the sky, and yet I felt no heat and no pain. The sun filled all with blinding light, and yet still higher we rose into the very face of it and I forgot all things, even the Brown Man beside me. I was alone in the glory and the light.

And I saw the gods. In the midst of the sun, faint, barely visible, radiant even against the fire-filled sky, I saw them talking among themselves. They stood tall and majestic and their speech came in whispers, like wind and the rustling of leaves. I knew not a word, for their speech was the language of Olympus. They seemed oblivious to all things around them. Not once did they look up into the heavens or down at the earth. They were sufficient of themselves.

Then, before I knew it, I was again on the earth, by the brook in the middle of the wood. At first I could see nothing in my bedazzlement, but at last sight returned and I perceived that the Brown Man was gone. The sun had set and it was night, the moon staring down between the branches of the trees.

It was not many days afterwards that the stranger came. He arrived suddenly in the middle of the night. My uncle arose and came to the gate and greeted him, clasping his hand like an old friend he had dearly wanted to see. I observed all from my window above —— I had been unable to sleep that night, my mind awash with marvels —— and I saw at once that the newcomer was not a Roman gentleman. He wore no toga, and even in the darkness I could tell that his clothing was ragged and dirty. Also his face sprouted a thick and matted beard, which he did not shave in the manner of a Roman, even after he had been with us for several days.

Still, my uncle seemed to honor him highly. Often they conversed in hushed voices and I overheard little. The stranger's Latin was stilted, often broken, and his accent strange.

No more did my father and my uncle sit on the porch at the end of each day discussing the old writings. No more did the ladies sing to the tune of the harp. Instead all gathered around the newcomer and listened to what he had to say. They revered him and called him "Teacher" although I never knew what he taught, since it was apparently deemed unfit for the ears of little boys. In any case this strange one occupied the adults more intently than ever, and it was easier for me to slip away and meet the Brown Man, so I never questioned my good fortune very closely.

But then there was a night near the very end of summer, only a few days before we were to leave for the city, when I returned to the house to find a company of soldiers at the door. There were about twenty of them, mounted, and an officer with a red cape and a plume led them. I hid among the bushes and observed all that went on.

The officer was insisting to my father that something was true. My father said it wasn't. The soldiers snickered. My father and the officer argued, and Uncle Septimius came and argued also. The officer commanded his men to dismount and search the house, and they did, and everyone watched them fearfully. When nothing was found they rode away without another word. Masters and servants alike watched them with ashen faces as they vanished down the road. My uncle and father went inside immediately after the soldiers had gone, and I also went in, fearing that something was terribly, terribly wrong.

I remember the scene in the main hall of the house clearly in every detail, even after so long a time. The hall itself was wide with a floor of pink marble. A table and a set of lion-footed chairs of white marble stood in the center by an indoor fountain. Great pillars held up the roof and cast long shadows over the room, which the coal-filled braziers and flaming torches failed to dispel. Tapestries on the walls billowed with a breeze entering through upper windows.

My uncle and my parents were seated at the table with the one they called the Teacher, and they all started in alarm when I entered the room.

"It's only me," I said.

My father said nothing, but rose and bolted the door. He then took me by the hand and led me to the table.

The stranger spoke. There was fear in his voice.

"They know I'm here. I cannot stay any longer."

"Yes, and they will be back," said Uncle Septimius.

"It's time then," said my father. He spoke the words almost as if passing sentence. He too knew fear, as did I then. A boy looks to his father for all things, and when his father is afraid he knows there is no protection. "There is something you must learn," he said.

Then the Teacher spoke again, and droned on about many strange things that I did not understand. Some of them sounded like the stories the Brown Man had told me, about a god who died and was born again, but in so many ways everything was stern and drab and different. Names I had never heard before, ideas completely strange. I admitted my confusion and the Teacher forced a smile.

"When you are older you shall understand these things. But there is no time now for further explanations." He glanced at the others and they nodded. I was taken over to the fountain and told to kneel. The Teacher took water in his hands and poured it over my head, while chanting some words. I assumed it was magic of some sort, although it was not as impressive as the magic of the Brown Man.

"Now you shall have eternal life. No one who has not been thus baptised can live forever." With that the stranger turned and departed. I never saw him again.

After he had gone I asked my father, "Am I really immortal now, because of that water?"

"Yes, your soul is. It is a wonderful thing."

"And we can make other people immortal, just by doing that?"

He saw my meaning. "We can. The Teacher wants us to. Have you a friend you want to baptise?"

"Yes."

"Tell me about him." There was genuine eagerness in my father's voice.

So I started to tell him about the Brown Man. I only started because he never let me tell much. I told of our first meeting and began to describe the odd features of my friend, and as soon as I mentioned his wondrous, bestial feet, my father grew angry.

"Don't say such things! You have seen a devil! Everything he told you is wicked! The old gods are false!"

"But——but I saw the old gods! He showed them to me."

My father would not listen to me. In fury he took up a rod and beat me until his rage was spent and he stalked off. I ran to my room and huddled in a corner, filled with pain and fear, unable to comprehend how I had offended, how my father could not have loved the Brown Man as I did. How could he say that the old gods were false? Had he not taken me to public sacrifices? How could he deny them now? I was terrified at the very idea, fearful that a wrath-filled Jupiter might strike us all down with thunderbolts for saying such things.

Once again a day dragged wearily to its conclusion, and each hour seemed like three. Arcadius came and tried to make me recite the forms of the Greek verbs, but I could not keep my mind on it and after a while he screamed at me in his shrill eunuch's voice, wrung his hands, and left. I watched all day as Apollo drove his chariot across the sky. Never before, it seemed, had his steeds run so slowly.

Still, evening did come at last, and with supper served and finished, I managed to evade my watchful father and steal away. I ran across the fields, mind racing faster than feet, filled with countless questions I would ask of my friend. Yet I was afraid as I went, afraid that he would be angry at me for telling about him, afraid he would take revenge on my father for insulting the gods, afraid of many things.

Breathlessly, I passed through the trees and into the graveyard. Already shadows stretched long before the tombs and the sunward faces of the marble glowed red with the light of the dying day.

The Brown Man was there. I greeted him, but he drew away from me. He did not seem glad to see me, as he always had been before.

"Is something the matter?"

He let out a loud wail. "No! No! All is lost!"

"Please! Tell me what is wrong?"

He turned from me, as if the sight of me filled him with horror. "You are of the new god! You are of the new god!" He turned and fled.

"Wait! Come back!" I ran after him.

He did not look behind him as he went, faster and faster, out of the graveyard, over rolling fields. His howls of despair echoed from the hills. I pressed after him with all my strength until that strength had gone and my breath came in labored pants, and my feet felt like stone weights, and the distance between me and the Brown Man grew. I fell over rocks, slid down hillsides, until my clothing was ragged and my sandals were gone, but soiled and barefoot I continued after him in vain. I could not catch him, and when the last rays of sunset faded he was a speck before me, and the darkness swallowed him up and I fell to the ground and wept.

It was nearly dawn by the time I got back to the villa. Father and the servants had been out looking for me, and when I was found I got another beating. This time I was locked in a cellar room so that I would not run away, and Arcadius and Gallus were sent in to see to my studies. There can be no torture greater than being locked in a room with those two!

A few days later we left the estate and returned to the city. We never visited again. Something happened to my uncle, but I was never told what. I stayed in the city for the rest of my childhood, and eventually I learned what I had to learn, but never again did I dream wondrous dreams or see the gods. The old stories seemed again only lifeless stories. The Brown Man came to me no more, and it was only much later that I understand what had happened.

THE LAST OF THE SHADOW TITANS

The island stood up in the purple twilight, thundering, its legs massive as mountains, its torso blotting out the sky. The head of the creature, misshapen in silhouette against the sunset, **was** the island as mariners saw it. The head alone remained above the waves all day, as the huge body crouched in the sea, sand and stones and driftwood encrusting its enormous face. Now it stood raging, water pouring from the crevices of its dark flesh. Waves foamed and broke around its knees.

Oineras the Knight Inquisitor beheld all this from a small boat. Even he, the most hardened of all the servants of the Nine Gods, was filled with amazement and terror.

The boat rocked in the rough water. He clung to the gunwales. Kadmion, his apprentice, struggled at the oars.

"Keep at it, boy. Don't look."

But Kadmion looked.

"Boy! I told you——do you need blinders?"

It was too late. The boy saw the giant-thing with an island for a head standing tall against the sky, hurling thunderbolts from either hand until the horizons flickered in reply. The whole earth trembled. The thing conversed with gods other than the Nine known to the righteous.

Kadmion screamed, let go of the oars, and fell to the bottom of the boat, writhing, his hands over his ears, his arms blocking his tightly shut eyes.

"Master! Save us! I hear it thinking! It is filling me up! It ——"

*   *   *

Vedatis, last of the Shadow Titans, sent forth a dream into the world. In distant lands, men and women of vision fell down in ecstasy. Closer at hand, Kadmion perceived it clearly.

The boy shared the memory of the Titan and knew, as if it had been his own life, a tale as old as time. He saw the Nine Gods, newly born, walking through the fields of Heaven. They came to a rising of the land and there beheld the first sunrise. Then they turned, and saw their own shadows cast upon the fields, flowing like dark rivers into the void of Unbeing, which lay beyond the rim of Heaven.

Kadmion knew all this, as vividly as if he had been there, and he felt the terror of the Gods when their shadows drew strength from the Unbeing, and sprang up, and defied them. These were the Shadow Titans, the equal and opposite manifestations of the

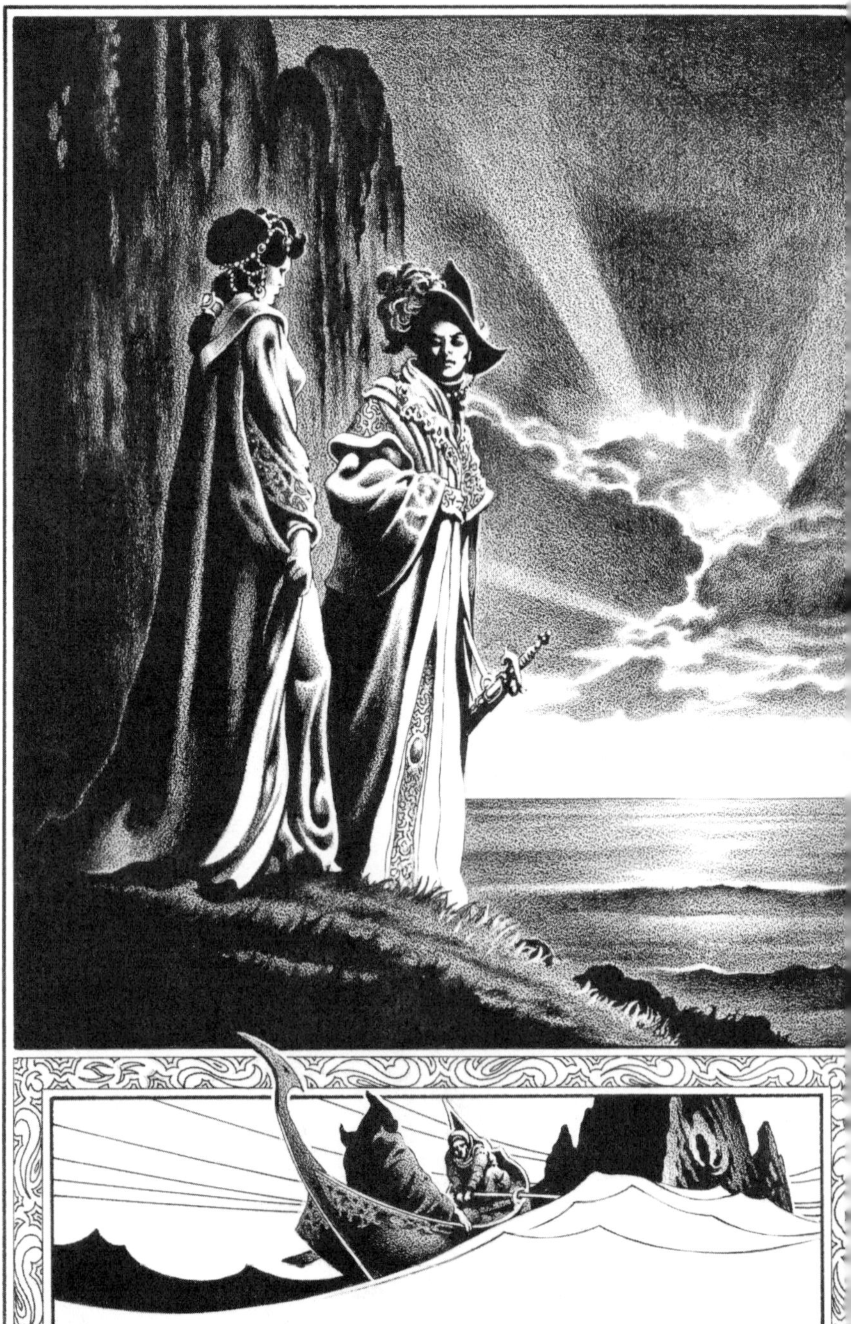

Gods, the sowers of wild discord and darkness amidst the purity and order and brilliant light of the Gods. There was a Titan of Fire, and one of Earthquakes, and Sedengul, the Master of Wind and Snow, and Aradvas, the Lord of Lust, and also Vedatis, the Titan of Dreams.

The Titans fled from the Gods, shrieking, laughing, trailing the darkness of the night sky behind them like a banner. The Gods pursued, separating the light from the darkness, and the Earth was made, and covered over with lands and seas, with beasts and men. Then the shadows of the Titans fell upon the Earth and changed it beyond the understanding of the Gods. Seas raged. Beasts slew one another. Men dreamed the dreams Vedatis sent them, and knew strangeness and beauty and terror and death.

So the Gods spoke to the worthiest of men, and filled them with their spirit, and sent them forth to battle the Shadow Titans. Many were afraid. Many more were enraptured by the dreams Vedatis send them, and strayed from their mission. But, in the end, those heroes of the first generation of mankind killed eight of the nine Titans, as the Gods had commanded them. But the world did not return to purity and order and light. It remained mostly as it had been, for Vedatis escaped.

Vedatis was the most elusive of the Titans, and had never entered the battle directly. Instead, to protect his brothers, he reached out and touched the minds of men, giving them visions, saying, **"Now that you have seen the great Dream, which is a vast ocean on which your world floats, now that you know, truly, what it is to be alive, to dream, how can you ever put all this aside?"**

But the sternest of men prevailed. Vedatis fled, disguising himself as a whale, as a whirling storm, as a swarm of bees, as a sound in the night, and, finally, when he had not the strength to flee further, as an island.

All this filled the mind of Kadmion, and he fell down screaming. It touched the mind of Oineras but lightly. He dismissed it as an idle fancy. Oineras never dreamed.

But he knew the tale. The heroes of old told it to their sons, and they to theirs, and so on through the generations of mankind. Many fell away, ensnared by the dreams of Vedatis, but those who remained, who remembered their ancient mission, became the Knights Inquisitor.

There were not many left. However, there would soon cease to be any need for them.

For Oineras knew the **ending** of the tale.

Oineras had come, at last, to kill Vedatis, the Titan of Dreams.

* * *

The boat pitched wildly, turning from its course. A wave broke over the side. Oineras lurched forward to grab the oars before they slipped from the oarlocks. He sat there awkwardly, holding the oars, regarding his apprentice.

It occurred to him with some exasperation that while Kadmion possessed sufficient piety in his own way to become a Knight Inquisitor, and this was a rare thing in this decadent age, the boy otherwise left a great deal to be desired.

He prodded him with his foot, splashing.

"Get up, you fool!"

Kadmion screamed, then fell silent, then began to weep softly. "It is so beautiful," he said. "The dream. I am lost in it. I can't find my way back. I——"

Oineras made to kick him in the ribs, but he controlled himself. A Knight Inquisitor is always controlled, he reminded himself, serene in his faith.

He pulled the oars into the boat, then lifted the boy up.

"Get up," he said gently. "Do not be afraid. Remember that we are servants of the Nine. They are with us."

Half-conscious, fumbling, the boy sat, and with his master's help got the oars back where they belonged. More water slopped into the boat. The boy began to row, mechanically, like one in a trance.

"What did you see?" Oineras asked.

"I cannot say. Some of it was about the Gods and the Titans. Some of it... I was in the dream, and I can't describe it..."

"Were you afraid?"

"Yes."

Oineras said nothing for a minute. Then he smiled very slightly.

"You are my bloodhound, Kadmion. You are leading me to my prey."

The boy turned the boat's bow into the waves. He rowed vigorously now. He did not look over his shoulder. Oineras removed the ornate, peaked cap of his office and bailed with it.

"Think of it, my boy," he said. "In a short while your dreams will end. Then the purity of the Nine will fill you, and you'll want nothing. This is what we believe. In the meantime, your suffering serves the cause of righteousness. Be brave. Be a hero. You can, you know. You can."

Oineras looked up once and saw dark clouds close like a curtain over the stupendous figure of the Titan. Lightning flashed beneath the low, dark ceiling of the storm. White-ridged waves ranged before them, blocking the island from view.

* * *

They dragged their boat onto the beach in the driving rain. Surf thundered on the rocky coastline. Water hissed on sand. Pebbles rattled. They hid the boat far from the water's edge, among some boulders, then set out for the island's interior.

"Master? What if it stands up again? Won't we fall off?"

"A true servant of the Nine has no fear. Just follow me. Bring my bag."

Kadmion followed, carrying his master's cloth satchel. They climbed sweeping curves of stone. It seemed to Kadmion that the wind blowing through the crevices was shouting **No, no, no** half in anger, half in fear. It seemed. Oineras paid it no heed.

They passed between two mountains with enormous faces carven into them, blank faces, like almost featureless masks. The mouths of both gaped. From one came thunder, from the other, mist.

Beyond the mountains was a plain, wholly desolate.

"Does anyone live here?" Kadmion asked, almost forgetting where he was, thinking of the island as an island.

"There may be corrupt and depraved men, who have strayed far from the truth of the Nine Gods, and have been transformed strangely by Vedatis, that they might be better servants to him. Such as they might live here, but no righteous man."

Oineras was reciting, as he did every day when instructing his pupil. Kadmion found the familiar, firm tone comforting.

Still wind howled across the land. The curves of stone were like a sea-storm frozen in place.

The ground trembled.

After a time, a light appeared, flickering in the darkness. As they neared it, it steadied.

"It is one of the eyes of the Shadow Titan," Oineras said. "Let us prepare ourselves."

In a place where the land dipped and folded over itself, forming a shallow cave with a ledge above it, the two of them knelt before the bag Kadmion carried. Oineras opened it and took out a bottle of ointment made from the tears of the Nine Gods. He and Kadmion stripped, shivering in the cold wind, and anointed themselves. Then they put on long white robes, pulling white hoods over their heads. Finally, with special rite, they donned masks of gold wrought into simple, identical faces.

Kadmion paused before putting his on. He recognized the face. It had been carven on the mountains.

"These masks, these robes," whispered Oineras, "are the garb of the unholy priests of the Titan. Yes, there are such. They call themselves Brothers of the Dream. We will probably meet some before our mission is over. Now hurry. Put it on."

The boy obeyed.

In the bottom of the bag was a sharpened stake of **eru** wood, which is sacred to the Gods. It is an **eru** tree which forms the axle of the world. The stake had been hardened in holy fire for ten days and nights. Kadmion knew. He had labored hard over it. Now Oineras hid it beneath his robe.

All was in readiness. After a prayer to the Nine Gods, they set out toward the light, which was the eye of the Titan.

* * *

"It looks like a window to me," said Kadmion.

"That is only an illusion, but for now it will be convenient to think of it as a window."

It was the window of an inn, situated in the middle of a tiny village. There were no more than a dozen tumbledown houses, all of them dark and silent. Everyone seemed to be at the inn, singing a raucous hymn to gods other than the proper Nine, to shapes which rise out of the darkness of the Dream to beguile men.

Oineras knocked on the door. Rainwater ran from his sleeve. Kadmion's teeth chattered as his drenched robe clung to his back.

The door swung inward to the Knight Inquisitor's touch, and the two of them entered a wide room lit by a roaring hearth fire.

The hymn ceased. There were twenty people in the room, perhaps men, perhaps women, all dressed in hooded white robes and nearly featureless golden masks.

For a time, no one spoke. Flames crackled. Rain rattled on the windows. Kadmion looked longingly toward the fire, still shivering in his wet robe. But he stood by his master.

"Who are you?" demanded one of the many. "You are not of the body of Vedatis, our Father."

"You are not of the Dream," said another.

"Truly we **are** of **his** dreams," said Oineras. "We have wandered long in the dark spaces between the worlds, until Vedatis summoned us into wakefulness on this island. We have come to join you."

"This has never happened before."

"Vedatis turned in his sleep, and new visions come to him. For everything, there is a first time."

"And this is it," said Kadmion.

Oineras unobtrusively stepped on Kadmion's foot, hard.

"Then join us," said one.

They joined them in singing the blasphemous hymn. Oineras knew that the Gods would forgive him this means to so righteous an end. Kadmion merely did as the others did.

* * *

Vedatis, dreaming the dreams of a corrupted world, trembled. Crouching in the cold sea, he was aware of something moving across his face, like an animate coal burning his stone flesh.

He opened his eyes, and every window in the village blazed with light. Mountains were tipped with fire. He spoke with his many mouths, where the wind touched caves and craters and ravines and gave him a voice. But he could not find his enemy.

His dreams were troubled. He turned in his sleep.

In the houses, timbers creaked. Tiles fell from rooftops, pottery from shelves.

* * *

There was a feast of meat and fruit and wine, all served from a bowl that never neared empty. Each of the company carefully raised a golden mask a little while eating, so that faces were still concealed.

Kadmion heard muted voices, the tinkling of bells, leather creaking, faint music. He looked up and saw phantoms step from the shadows in the corners of the room: kings, warriors, priests and priestesses of past ages. Their costumes were beautiful and strange, their faces very pale. Their procession circled the table, and the walls of the inn behind them shifted as the phantoms moved, and it seemed that the table and diners were no longer inside a building at all, but on a mountaintop, beneath a clear night sky filled with stars. There were faces visible behind the stars, like giants staring through dark glass into the universe: the dim incomprehensible visages of the forbidden Gods of the great Dream.

The boy wondered if anyone else could see this. Oineras sat still. He made no sign. The others went on with their meal.

Then the sky rippled like a reflection on water when a stone is cast in, and the scene changed. They were in the great hall of a castle. It changed again: the deck of a great barge, all hung with black drapery, afloat on a fog-bound sea.

And further: a green meadow on a spring day, beneath a bright sky scattered with white streamers of cloud. He knew the meadow. It was near his home. He recognized a tree he had once climbed. A company of people were coming toward him over the grass, festive, laughing. He knew them all. They were people from his own village. His parents were there, whom he had not seen in four years, since he was ten and was sent to be the apprentice of the Knight Inquisitor.

He wanted to call out to them. He wanted to join them. He started to rise from the table.

Then the feast was done, and all of the company raised their hands, and the walls of the inn were as before. Kadmion sat down. As the many watched, two carried a large mirror into the room and stood it before the table. All turned so they could see. The room was still, and silent but for the rain, the wind, and the crackling flames.

They watched, as an image formed in the mirror, at first something huge and misshapen, like the half-finished work of a mad sculptor, and then, as the features slowly diminished and straightened, one dressed in a white robe and wearing a golden mask.

"Hail Vedatis, our Father," said the many, sliding from their chairs, kneeling.

"Rise," the thing said, extending its hand out from the glass, into the air.

They rose, and this manifestation of the Shadow Titan told them the secrets of the Gods of the Dream and also of the Nine, and the histories of the aeons before ever those Nine walked the fields of Heaven. Vedatis lived outside of time, and could see the past and future even as a man turns his head to the left and to the right.

He spoke of what was to come.

"A long tale is coming to an end," he said. "A quest is almost complete. For one, there is only resignation, a sinking into a final sleep without dreams. One is very old, very tired. One senses the ending very near at hand. For another, the tale does not end. It is only beginning. For this other there is, perhaps, a revelation."

For a second time, if only for an instant, the Knight Inquisitor was afraid, sure that he had been discovered, but the remark seemed to pass along with numerous other prophecies. He and the boy were not molested.

* * *

In the end, the image vanished, the mirror was carried away. Once more the walls rippled like water, and the humble inn was transformed into a vast palace of white marble. Richly-liveried servants, all wearing golden masks, conducted each of the company to chambers for the night.

Oineras and Kadmion stayed together. They were put in a single chamber draped with something like silk, but cold and rigid to the touch, like tapestries of ice. The shape of everything was uncertain. Whenever either of them gazed upon a certain spot, then looked away, then gazed again, a wall or a corner or a bedpost would be fashioned differently.

There was a single bed, covered with tattered blankets. The tatters waved gently, like the limbs of a sea anemone. Oineras took out the **eru** stake, touched it to the bed, and the blankets became mere cloth.

He directed Kadmion to lie down. Reluctantly, the boy did. Oineras knelt beside him, stake in hand.

"Now sleep, and spy out the defenses of our enemy. When you come to the very center of the Titan's dreams — we are in a labyrinth, very near to the center now — the truth and the weakness of the Titan will be revealed. It will be like a door, through which we enter in to find the evil one before us. Go. Go before me."

He laid the stake on the bed next to Kadmion.

The boy slept.

* * *

Vedatis felt his strength draining into the ocean around him. The burning sensation was remote now, like something felt by someone else. He was tired. His legs were weak. He knew he would never rise again. He felt the waves wearing at the shoreline, reducing it to sand.

Still he dreamed his dreams and sent them forth, into the minds of men, but he could not concentrate, and they were brief, fragmentary things, half-glimpsed, like the wings of bats fluttering in the dark.

* * *

Kadmion saw a peacock with flaming, jeweled feathers soaring into the sky, scattering jewels, which became the stars. The bird itself became the moon, pure white, without feature.

In the darkness, beneath the star-filled sky, he recalled idle fancies from his childhood.

Once, when he was very small, he had imagined that he had heard voices outside his window at night, urging him to come out into the forest beyond the meadow, to hear strange songs, to see wondrous things.

"How far is it?" he asked. "How long do I have to go?"

"Forever and ever," said the voices.

Now he walked through the forest, and it seemed forever. Trees stood in black silhouette. The clearings were filled with delicate silver. The forest was alive. Always, just ahead of him, beyond the next great stand of trees, the voices called to him.

"Forever and ever. Into the Dream."

He followed——

She was there, by his side. There was a girl he had known in a city where he and Oineras had dwelt for a year. That was much later. He had not heard the voices then. But now he heard them, and she was with him. Usually, she paid little attention to him. But sometimes she had laughed when he tried to tell a joke —— laughed with him, not at him as everyone else did, but **with** him —— or paused to listen when he played upon a pipe. He had never been in love. His master had not allowed him time for that. He wondered what it would be like. Maybe later. He was not very old yet.

Now he walked with her, hand in hand, through the forest in the pale moonlight, until they came to a hilltop he knew, where the trees ended and they could look for miles, toward the sea, where the moon shone silver on the waves. The two of them stood for a long time, imagining strange lands beyond the horizon, telling each other tales of kings and queens and wizards in golden palaces.

He could see the palaces clearly now.

Then he heard a voice calling him. He couldn't make out what it said. He looked up, and saw that the moon had a face on it. For an instant, it was his master's face, but then it became another, a wild face, more beautiful and terrible than anything he could imagine.

He screamed and turned away, and found that he was falling slowly through a forest of delicate glass, spinning through the treetops, sending showers of shards whirling in his wake. He was not afraid. There was no pain. He felt only an intense longing, as if he had almost beheld something more wondrous than anything in the world, but had lost sight of it before understanding what it was.

He was alone, in the darkness, falling, and the whole forest began to disintegrate at his passage.

* * *

With the very last of his fading strength, knowing that the great Death had settled on him and that the Dream was finished,

Vedatis the Shadow Titan stood up one more time.

His body did not come with him. It fell away like a heavy cloak.

He walked upon the shore of the sea, and the waves broke against his legs.

He thundered in the marble palace, in the darkness, and lightning flickered in the great halls.

He came to a door. He felt his enemies within, like a hot coal burning on his face. He wrenched the door from its hinges; the whole wall exploded into dust. Cracks spread through the floor and ceiling. Pillars fell. Corridors folded in on themselves in clouds of debris.

* * *

Kadmion woke to the sound of thunder. He blinked. The room was dark and filled with dust. His master hauled him up out of the bed, as the floor shook, as a huge beam fell from the ceiling with a thud and a shower of stone, crushing the bed.

The ice tapestries were melting, shattering. The walls caved in from every side.

Then Oineras held up the stake of **eru** wood and shouted the names of the Nine Gods, slowly, pronouncing each carefully. With each name, the sounds receded, the debris seemed to fall further off.

In the end they stood together, in silence, in a grey fog. Kadmion shivered in the cold.

"Did you see him?" Oineras whispered.

"Yes."

"Did he say anything?"

"I think so. But I couldn't understand it."

"That is just as well. If you had, he might have entrapped you."

"Where is he now?"

"Very near. Come. Maintain the courage of the righteous. Victory is ours."

Kadmion was not as confident as his master, but he followed him through the thick fog, across the lifeless, boulder-strewn land. Only a few feet away, his master was a grey silhouette, looking the part of the true holy warrior now, the Knight Inquisitor, treading carefully, tense, turning from side to side. He held the **eru** stake like a sword. To Kadmion, Oineras had never seemed more formidable than he did then, more inhuman, like a stalking shadow of death. At the same time he, Kadmion, less and less understood what they were doing here and why. He felt once more the intense longing for what he had glimpsed in his vision, and, more especially, for what he had not seen, for what remained just beyond the range of his perception.

Then he considered that these thoughts were sent to him by the Shadow Titan. They were the Titan's temptations, his snares.

He ran after Oineras, afraid, struggling to keep up. The Knight Inquisitor seemed to glide over the rocky ground, while he stumbled, bruised his shins, fell, got up, hurried on.

Oineras turned to him once, still grey, almost featureless in the fog, remote from all things solid and warm and breathing and real.

"Do not be afraid," he whispered in a voice like the wind between the stones. "Think on the Nine Gods and be comforted."

But he was not comforted. Still he hurried after his master. The only sounds were his own sounds, his breathing, the pebbles rattling at his footsteps. Oineras was a wisp of fog shaped like a man.

Then, very suddenly, but very subtly, his master was gone. He could no more define his disappearance than he could remember the instant of a random eyeblink. He was simply aware that he was alone.

He stopped walking. He didn't know what to do. Somehow, he didn't want to start shouting. The silence was a fearful thing, but the prospect of noise was worse, as if the fog were a living, sleeping monster all around him, which he did not want to awaken.

He merely sat down and waited, confused, afraid. If Oineras needed him, he would come for him. If not, he would wait until the Titan had been defeated elsewhere. He, Kadmion, didn't necessarily have to have any part in it. As an apprentice to the Knight Inquisitor, he knew he should, but just now he didn't think he would ever hold such an office.

Why? he asked himself. **Why?** He didn't know, about anything. He had just become the apprentice of Oineras somehow. His parents handed him over when he was too young to understand. He had just grown into the role. It was the only one he knew. He **was** his master's apprentice.

"**Kadmion**," came a voice, quite near at hand. It was utterly expressionless, like something partially apprehended in a dream, rather than heard.

He looked up and saw someone standing before him, veiled in fog, clad in a white robe with a hood, wearing a golden mask.

He got up, and ran to the other.

"Master?"

The other did not speak. He merely removed his mask, turning it sideways, out from his face as if he were opening a door.

For the merest instant, he saw the wild, terrible face of the Shadow Titan. Then there was a void, not merely an empty hood, but an infinite darkness.

"**Look, and wonder.**"

The darkness flowed out of the hood like heavy smoke, settling on the ground, spreading, until it stretched as far as Kadmion could see in three directions. Only behind him was there still uncovered ground.

The stranger collapsed into the heap of an empty robe, and the robe was gone, covered over.

Kadmion was standing on a cliff. The darkness became the night sky, filled with stars. The world merely **ended** a few feet from where he stood.

Then the revelation came to him, and he understood that the night sky was not the night sky, and the stars were not stars. He perceived the great Dream directly beneath the thin fabric of the world. He saw it as no one had ever seen it before, as a void from which men awaken into life with indescribable loss and mourning, to which they return, bewildered, afraid when finally unburdened of the flesh, having forgotten nearly all concerning that primal, blissful state.

It was all of these things, and more, and at times none of them. Kadmion's mind could not grasp, nor could words express, the magnitude of the great Dream.

It was clearly the Dream of Gods, of Titans, and not that of a fourteen-year-old boy who followed his master because he didn't know anything else to do. He was lost in it, obliterated, like a raindrop fallen into the raging sea.

But, clinging to one shred of consciousness, he understood clearly one thing: that he had no understanding, only vision. And he knew that his master had understanding, but lacked vision, any capacity to dream at all. That was the tragedy of the two of them. If they could have become one, if——

He saw all the world, and the spaces between the worlds, and he saw the things which repose in the memories of the Gods, both of the Nine and of others——

He was like one born blind, in the company of the blind, so that sight is unknown, inexpressible. Suddenly he could see——

"Kadmion! Young fool! What are you doing?"

——and was made blind again, darkness crashing——

Oineras held him by the shoulders. He screamed and struggled. He wept. The Dream was gone, like a picture in a glass window, smashed. There was only fog all around, the barren landscape, the cold air, the Knight Inquisitor holding him, looming over him.

He went limp, but Oineras held him up, and turned him to face the direction in which he had been staring. There was no cliff edge there now, no starry abyss, only the grey, rocky ground vanishing into a fog a short way off.

* * *

"Titan!" Oineras shouted.   His voice echoed back through the fog: "Titan-an-an-an..."

"Titan! Leave the boy alone! Come to me! Show me what you showed him."

"I, Vedatis, am here. Let go of me," the boy said.

The voice was like thunder. Oineras, startled, let go.

It wasn't Kadmion. The figure grew taller as Oineras watched, towering over him. Then it removed its mask, turning it to one side like an opening door.

There was only darkness, utter and absolute, without any memory of a transition into it.

* * *

The youth Oineras sat in the dark cell, deep inside the holy mountain, trembling with anticipation, with holy dread. For all the place was damp and cold, for all the earthen walls felt like ice, he was drenched with sweat. His heart raced.

It was his time of manhood. With ancient ritual, the priests of the town had led him, and all the young men and women, down the long tunnel to hide them from the sky and from spirits of the waking world, so that, on this night or succession of nights, the Gods would touch each of them, and bring them into adulthood, and, through dreams, give direction to their lives. It was one of the three great passages. He had been told this often. The other two were birth and death.

Oineras sat. He waited. He lost all sense of time. It seemed but an hour had passed when he began to hunger, when his tongue was swollen for want of drink. He stood up to lick the moisture from the ceiling, but gagged and fell down, fainting. Later, he awoke in the darkness, stiff and cold, with no memory of having dreamed. All the while he did not cry out. His voice would shatter his dreams before they came to him.

He remained silent. Again he fainted, or slept, and again awoke, without any memory of having dreamed. The Gods did not reveal themselves.

Then the thought came to him: was all of this his dream, this very lack of dreaming?

And he sat, attentive and still, trying to discern the meaning of this dream.

Nothing happened. He became sick from the foul water, and vomited and emptied his bowels. He woke and slept so many times that he could not remember how many.

Nothing happened.

At last there was a footstep. He opened his eyes, and saw a light floating in the darkness, some ways off. It was no different than the many ghost-images his blind eyes had seen.

Then, it was different. He closed his eyes, and it was gone. He opened them, and it was there again, burning steadily, coming closer.

The light illuminated the face of an old crone. She held a taper. Her face was painted with broad, alternating black and white stripes, as he knew a face to be painted when one has to deal with the unclean.

She looked on him with distaste.

"You still here? You're the only one. I knew it would be you. It figures."

She prodded him with a stick. He lurched to his feet, reaching to her for support. She stepped back. He fell in the mud.

Later, when he was stronger, he got up and followed her out of the holy mountain, into blinding daylight.

The priests and elders of the town were waiting for him.

"I have brought the **unvati**," the woman said. She threw down her taper and hurried away, leaning on the stick.

Unvati. He knew what that meant. Unseeing one. Failed one. One to whom the Gods will not speak. One who cannot dream.

The elders and the priests turned from him. Everyone he met in the streets somehow knew that he was **unvati** and hid their faces as he went by.

Weeping, he ran from the town. Then his sorrow became anger. He marched across the world. Time sped up for him, day and night passing like the flapping of black and white curtains in a breeze. He crossed many lands. He came to the hall of the Knights Inquisitor and became the greatest, the most zealous among them. He learned that those who had called him **unvati** were foul heretics, ones who had strayed far from the purity and light, from the true and only way revealed by the Nine Gods.

He travelled over the world, seeking the last of the Shadow Titans. He acquired an apprentice, Kadmion. Together they went, at last, to the island which was not an island, which was the head of the huge body of Vedatis, the Titan of Dreams.

He stood, in the fog, holding the boy Kadmion by the shoulders. Then Kadmion was not Kadmion, but Vedatis. He turned, towering over Oineras.

"**Behold**," said the Titan. "The Dream is revealed to you at last. Here it is. All of it."

Vedatis swung aside his mask. He had no face.

Then he was gone. There was only darkness. Oineras saw nothing. But he understood. At least he had understanding.

He wept.

* * *

Kadmion perceived the rest of the adventure but dimly.

For a few minutes, he stood beside his master in the fog. Then the sun rose, and the fog melted away. Oineras was still beside him, his mask gone.

Sunlight touched a mountain top. Kadmion looked up, pointed, and shouted, tugging on the Knight Inquisitor's arm. Light and shadow shifted over the mountain, and the color of stone and sand formed the face of an old man, staring down at them, the face of the Titan Vedatis.

The Titan sighed and a wind roared over the island.

Opposite this mountain was another. On it, the sunlight and the withdrawing fog revealed a huge golden mask.

These mountains were the two he and Oineras had passed between when they arrived. Now both of them were alive, the enormous mask glaring, hateful, the old man's face merely tired and sad.

Kadmion had the impression of a struggle. His eyes couldn't follow it all. Oineras loomed high as the mountains, shouting with wrath until the ground shook and avalanches came thundering down. Kadmion screamed an unheard warning when the mask on the mountainside opened its mouth and spewed out a river of fire. He felt the heat as it filled the valley. He fell down and covered his face, writhing to avoid the flames that somehow never touched him.

With a crash, with thunder, with the trembling of the world and the voice of the flames, fire and stone met and broke over Oineras, over Kadmion too, like the tide over a post stuck in the sand. Very, very faintly, more like the impression of a dream than anything actually seen, Kadmion was aware of Oineras standing in the midst of the fire, wrestling with the unleashed figure of the Titan, who had broken free of the mountain that held him. The Knight Inquisitor had become a giant, as huge as the Titan. He held aloft the **eru** stake, and the fire recoiled from him.

Kadmion, coughing, his eyes stung by the smoke, pummeled with raining stones and ash, watched what he could. Soon the enormous figures were hidden from view, and he saw only dark clouds moving before one another, lightning flickering among them.

The boy stood up and ran away a short distance.

Then he looked back. The clouds of smoke parted, and quite distinctly he saw the face of the Titan, again on the mountainside. He saw it come loose, like a tent cut from its supports, sliding down the cliff, rippling over the stones.

* * *

Much later, as the air began to clear, Kadmion walked through the smoking valleys. He called out his master's name.

"Over here, boy."

The voice was weak. Kadmion turned toward it. He found his master standing over the face of the Titan, which lay crumpled like a fallen tent. The hot stones burned through the flesh. In a place where it had burned away completely lay the Titan himself, faceless, his body shriveled and blackened and raw, embedded in stone like one lying in shallow water. He was still huge, at least fifteen feet from the crown of his head to where his thighs merged with the earth.

Vedatis was still alive. He twitched feebly. Kadmion felt a stirring in his mind. A faint memory of the Dream came to him.

Oineras walked across the face of the Titan. He was breathing hard, staggering. Kadmion thought his master would faint.

But he did not. Sheer determination drove him. The knight Inquisitor stood over the Titan, legs astride his neck. He held the **eru** stake high, then drove it through one of the bloody eye sockets, deep into the skull.

* * *

Vedatis the Shadow Titan, at the very last, beheld the Death which had come for him from beyond the worlds, which had settled into the form of Oineras the Knight Inquisitor. He saw it in the conventional form of death, which he had revealed to men in their dreams countless times: a skull-faced spectre, standing astride him, towering high, a stake of **eru** wood upraised. The skull-face became a tarnished golden mask, then a human face, soot-stained, sweaty, wild-eyed, hate-filled.

He reached out one last time into the mind of Oineras, found madness, opened the madness like a door, and touched the innermost region of that mind with the memory of the great Dream.

Then he only sought to escape from pain, to submerge himself in his past. He looked to one side, into the future. There was only darkness. He looked to the other, into the past, and saw his long and glorious life.

* * *

Kadmion felt the Dream die. Oineras, for the first time, also felt it.

Kadmion fainted. Oineras screamed.

Much later, when Kadmion awoke, Oineras said, "Now we must convert those we have liberated to the true worship of the Nine Gods." He said it with such hollowness that Kadmion did not even ask him if he believed what he was saying.

Later still, as they walked across the island beneath a clear sky, Kadmion said, "I understand now why he fought. He knew his end had come, and there was nothing he could do about it. But he wanted to survive just long enough to make us understand. To make us remember him."

"And the great Dream," said Oineras. "He wanted us to remember that."

"Yes. That's it."

Even as they walked, both of them felt the remaining echo of the Dream, like a fading shout in a cave.

* * *

The inn was partially standing. All the surrounding houses had been shaken down.

Oineras and Kadmion entered. The twenty masked ones were seated by the hearth, which was filled with ashes.

"He is dead," said one of the many.

"He is dead," said the Knight Inquisitor dully. "You are free now."

"We are not free," said one. "Nor are you. Nor shall you ever be."

They took their masks off and became individuals, old men and women, youths and maidens, one boy about Kadmion's age, all of them pale with memory, wide-eyed with the echo of the Dream.

Kadmion realized that he was still wearing his mask. He took it off. He wondered if his face, too, was transfigured.

The face of Oineras reminded him of the one on the mountain, old and tired and sad.

"We," said one of the women weakly, "were those special people who felt the Wonder most strongly. All of us were outcasts, for the people around us were afraid of this thing we felt so intensely; and in the end, each came in his own way to Vedatis, who was beloved of us all. Now that he is gone, we are nothing."

"Then I have won," said Oineras, once more without any conviction. "The Gods will destroy you."

Once more Kadmion did not have to ask his master if he believed what he was saying.

"Let them try," said the woman. "We are filled with the memory of the Dream, and the Dream touches even the minds of the Gods."

"We shall haunt the Gods," said a young man.

"And we," said Kadmion, gently taking his master by the hand and leading him toward the door, "are filled with the memory of the Dream also. We shall haunt the world."

There was a broken piece of the mirror on the floor. Kadmion passed it on the way out. He saw his reflection.

His face was transfigured with light.

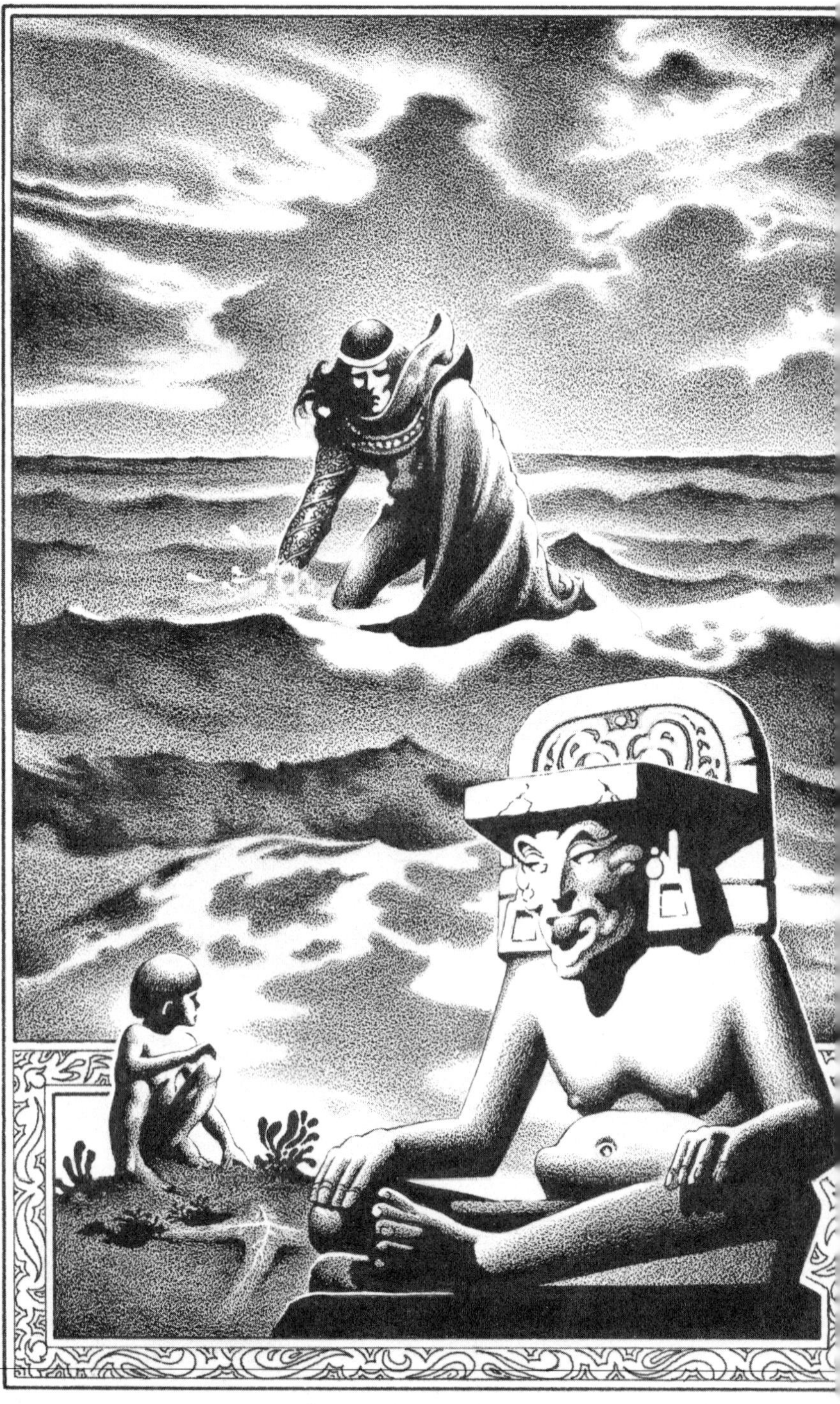

THE STRANGER FROM BAAL-AD-THEON

There were many gods on the island where I lived as a boy, a god of winds and of the storm, and a god of luck and another of ill-fortune, and a Father of Fishes. But foremost among them was Ornu, the god of the sea, on whom everyone's life depended. Ornu actually dwelt on the island, in the form of dozens of images carven among the rocks along the shore, each image dedicated by a different family. Because I was the youngest in my family, it was my task to take an offering out to the god every morning before sunrise. It was usually no more than a little cake that I carried in a wicker basket, but, whatever the weather or the season, I had to make my way in the dark, across the black, barnacle-crusted boulders at the water's edge to the alcove where the god waited.

If the tide were nearly in, it wouldn't be long before the sea accepted the sacrifice, but at other times I would have to remain for hours, driving away the gulls lest they steal the cake from Ornu's lap. In good weather, my father and my uncle Urred and my older brother Tal would go out in a boat to catch fish, but if my wait with the god had been long, I would not be able to go with them. At those times, after the cake had been washed away, I was expected to help the women and the other children of the village clean fish or mend nets or do whatever needed to be done, but often I would tarry along the beach for much of the day, gazing out into the grey distance beneath the almost perpetually overcast sky, or poking among the tide's leavings and trying to imagine what the world must be like beyond the little island that was my home.

Sometimes, very rarely, I would find strangely-shaped pieces of wood, or odd artifacts which were clearly not from the island. These were my treasures. I hoarded them in a niche between two boulders, and covered them over with sand and pebbles so no one else could find them. When I was alone, I would secretly take them out and examine them one by one, trying to decipher the coded message they contained from the great world beyond the sea. Once I even displayed them for Ornu, on a morning when the tide had been far out when I arrived. The sacrifice was not accepted until almost noon that day, and I sat for hours, hoping the god would explain the mystery to me, but he said nothing, and afterwards I felt foolish.

Even then, when I was so young, I knew that there had been a mistake. Some god had put a spirit too wild and too great inside the body of a little boy on a remote island which you could walk entirely around in half an hour.

* * *

It was in the autumn of the year when I was twelve and my brother was fourteen that Tal and I sat in the rain beside Ornu, shivering beneath our sealskin cloaks. He didn't want to be there. Mother had said, "There will be no fishing today because of the storm. Tal, go along and keep your brother company."

He scowled at me. "It's your fault. I'm colder'n Ornu's butt."

I gaped, shocked at his blasphemy.

"Come here," he said irritably, taking me by the arm and drawing me to him. We huddled together on the cold, wet stone, both cloaks wrapped around the two of us. I felt his ribs pressing into me as he breathed, but in a little while we were warmer. All around us, the rain hissed on the rocks and on the pebbly beach. The tide was higher than usual, the breakers sending great plumes of spray into the frigid air, then retreating into pools of quivering foam. Black clouds hung low over the sea.

There wasn't a gull in sight, and I am sure that Tal was thinking of deserting Ornu then. Even I considered it. But we both feared our father's anger, so there we stayed. The god sat impassively, water streaming down his weathered face as he spoke silently to the spirits of the winds.

Somehow the process seemed to go on forever. The storm never quite broke. The tide never came as high as I thought it would, and so it was by painfully slow degrees that the water advanced toward Ornu's lap. My brother and I began to talk of little things, the games we played when we were small, the stories our grandfather used to tell us before he died. We traded jokes we'd learned from the fishermen, and missed the point more often than not, but laughed at them nevertheless. Tal was embarrassed at having to confide even this much in his little brother. He fidgetted with the cloaks. He drew figures in the sand with his finger and watched as the rain and the spray erased them. Just then I felt closer to him than I had been for a long time. There had never been much between us. When we were very small we had experienced everything together, but we had parted early, he joining the prosaic world around him, me chasing after vague dreams and longings I didn't know how to express.

It was on that morning, right as the tide reached Ornu and the sacrificial cake was floating around between the god's knees, that we heard sobbing from further along the beach.

We both got up, Ornu forgotten in an instant, put our cloaks on, and scrambled over the rocks until we came to a broad, flat stretch of sand at the base of a cliff, the cold water swirling around our ankles.

There, crouched down and hugging the base of the cliff, was a man like no other I had seen before. He was not of the island.

His clothing was bright red and green and blue, of some smooth and shining material, ornamented with gold. I had never seen anyone dressed in anything but skins and rough wool, with carven bones for buttons. But this man wore a metal band around his grey and white-streaked hair like a crown. The water washed over his legs and feet, his brilliant cloak floating with each wave. He knelt weeping, wringing his hands. Jeweled rings gleamed on his fingers.

His voice was very loud, but it seemed a small sound amid the wind and the rain and the dull thundering of the breakers. Retreating waves trailed streams of clattering pebbles.

I reached out to take my brother's hand, but he lost his footing, caught hold of a boulder, and pulled away from me.

Then the man looked up, directly into my face. He did not seem to be aware of Tal at all. Even then I wondered if the two of them could see each other.

"I tried to find my way back," the stranger said, his words heavily accented. "I thought that with one more crossing I would come to Baal-ad-Theon, but no, I am **here** on this wretched island."

"B-bala——" I struggled to pronounce the unfamiliar word. "Is that your home?"

His whole body shook, not from cold, or even from obvious anger, but as if his spirit raged to get out. Then he suddenly seemed very weak, and I was afraid he would faint.

"It is more than my **home**," he said. "It is the place of dreams, of marvels and miracles, where all secrets are known and all mysteries made clear and all the more wonderful for the understanding of them. It is... I cannot fully say. Do you know nothing of Baal-ad-Theon?"

I shook my head.

He said sadly, "It is my doom, to wander until I reach a place where no one has even heard of Baal-ad-Theon. Throughout the world men sing of it, and prophets gaze upon Baal-ad-Theon in their visions, and great kings offer gold to philosophers who teach them how they might come to Baal-ad-Theon. But here, here—— no one has even heard of it!"

"I'm sorry."

He pointed his finger at me and spoke more intensely than before.

"No, you **do** know of it, child. You especially do know of it and long for it, even if you have not seen it and have never spoken its name. Look inside yourself and you will see that this is so. Then, let me tell you that Baal-ad-Theon is a place of gold near the Earth's rim, where the gods walk disguised as men. You can never know if any person you pass on the street, or the one reclining by you at the banquet table, is really a god, wearing human flesh like a heavy cloak. Oh, I should say nothing more and I could say so much more, I——"

He fell to weeping again and beat his forehead with his hands. I looked on helplessly.

Tal spoke up. "I'll —— I'll get Papa!" he shouted, already running.

I stood there in the rain, oblivious to the cold wind and the water splashing around my legs, while the stranger wept and babbled and spoke of Baal-ad-Theon. I did not understand most of what he said. When I tried to question him, he did not respond, but continued with his outcries.

After a while I climbed up onto a rock, out of the water, and sat watching him. Still he shouted and sobbed and thrashed about, kneeling or sitting back, or falling and rolling into the surf. Once a wave washed over him and covered him entirely. I stood up in alarm, but the wave receded, and he was there as before, grieving for the loss of Baal-ad-Theon.

I felt many things at once: pity for this very strange man so wracked by sorrow, and wonder at his arrival. It occurred to me that Ornu might have sent him to me, as a kind of answer, to reveal at last the secrets of the great world, which this man called Baal-ad-Theon. There was so much I wanted to ask him, but I could not while he wept as he did. I had waited all my life, and now the hardest part was waiting a little longer.

Suddenly I heard voices beyond the cliff. The stranger fell silent and looked up apprehensively. Then my father appeared atop the cliff, perhaps thirty feet above the beach. With him were Tal, my uncle Urred, and Naboin, a man who worked for my father.

"You, boy!" my father shouted, cupping his hands to be heard over the wind and waves. "What are you doing down there alone?"

"Alone?" I said too softly for him to hear. I looked then, and saw that the stranger was gone. I slid down from my rock and ran to the water's edge. A particularly strong wave came just then and knocked my feet out from under me. I got up on all fours and looked around frantically for the stranger, thinking he might have drowned himself in his despair.

"Get up here, you little fool! You'll catch your death!"

The stranger was gone. I saw only the rising and falling waves, and, farther out, the dark stones of a reef covered and uncovered so that they looked like a school of whales diving. Ragged, dark clouds trailed over the sea. The whole world was black and grey, without a trace of any bright color, of the brilliant clothing of the man from Baal-ad-Theon. Reluctantly, I got up and climbed to where the others waited.

"It's no weather for swimming," my father said jokingly. Then his manner hardened. "What did you see?"

Suddenly I didn't know. I couldn't say anything.

"I think it was a ghost," said Tal.

"No, I saw a man," I said.

"Let's get in out of the rain," Uncle Urred said. "If we get cold enough, who knows what we'll be seeing?"

Father led us back to the house. As the others went in, he took me aside and said, "The sea throws up phantoms sometimes.

That's what you saw. Don't tell your mother anything else."

Then he shrugged and went into the house. I stood in the rain for a moment, wondering. He seemed so confident that it had been only a phantom, but was he merely **wishing** it were one? He seemed afraid beneath his calm. It was a fantastic thing, for my father to be afraid both for me and of me.

* * *

My mother understood more than she outwardly seemed to. We all sat around the table at supper, before a warm fire, and I told a little of what I had seen, speaking no more than a few words. Tal told more.

"It was a ghost," he said. "Like a little cloud on the beach that didn't move with the wind."

"Yes, it was," I said quietly, but my mother's eyes met mine just then, and I knew she knew I didn't mean what I said.

Afterwards, she gave me a dry cloak and said, "Come with me." I put it on and followed her quietly out of the house.

The evening wind was sharp and cold, but the storm had broken, and the clouds fled before the wind. It was one of those rare times when the sky was revealed over our island, and I could see the first stars coming out between diminishing streamers of cloud.

We walked over to a ledge and faced the west, where the sun was already beneath the horizon, but still orange and red and gold spread on the heaving waves.

"It is a fine sunset," my mother said, "the finest ever. I think there is no better place to see sunsets than here. Their scarcity makes them all the finer."

But even as I looked, I saw in that sunset the faintest glimmering of the gold of Baal-ad-Theon.

We walked along the beach beneath the black cliffs and the darkening sky, and my mother pointed out how the shadows shifted among the great stones, and darkness seemed to pour out of the crevices and caves to form fantastic shapes.

"When I was a girl," she said, "we believed that there were giants here, and holy knights in armor forged by the gods, and they could only be seen in the twilight as they fought the giants. But I only saw the rocks and the shadows and heard the wind. Perhaps there are still giants here. Perhaps someone will see them again someday."

And again, I thought of the heroes of Baal-ad-Theon, some of whom were gods disguised as men. Their armor was more splendid than that of the knights who fought giants among the rocks.

She pointed to the stars and said, "Look. We can see the entire bowl of the sky. You can only do that here, on this island, at the center of things. I knew a man once who spent his whole life counting the stars and trying to understand their meaning. At the end he was very wise, but he did not understand the stars, nor had he finished counting."

And I thought of the spires of Baal-ad-Theon, which likewise cannot be counted.

We turned inland and came to a hill, the highest point on the island, and from where we stood the sea was like a great wheel with the island at the hub. Far away, against the sunset, a boat tossed in the rough water. Even from such a distance I could tell that the sail was patched and full of holes. A single man struggled at the oars.

"That would be Nadek, Kedwyn's son, hurrying home for his dinner."

Later, we came to a little valley behind the hill, the one place on the whole island where you couldn't see the ocean. The wind whistled over the rim of the valley like breath over the mouth of a jug, and we couldn't hear the surf. Mother pointed to a cave, into which I knew I would never go.

"I was afraid of this place when I was a girl," she said, "but when I became a woman I had to go into that cave in the spring and greet Ornu in a form which may not be described, by a name which may not be spoken. Soon you, too, with your father, will go to a place I cannot follow and partake of the mysteries."

When we came out of the valley the sunset had entirely faded, and the sky was clear. The faint white pathway of heaven stretched from horizon to horizon, and, indeed, the stars were more than ever could be counted.

When we got back to the house, she put her hand on my shoulder and said, "It's a great, fine world we live in. Sure, no one would want to leave it."

I said quietly, "Sure."

Then her voice broke, and she was barely holding back tears, and she said, "You're so young still. Yet you've been waiting a long time. Don't think I don't know. But you're not going away. It is only a fancy, something that will fade the way a dream does when you wake up."

But I did not answer her, and thought of Baal-ad-Theon as we went into the house.

And that night I dreamed of it, and saw it clearly for the first time in my life, and my whole life up to that point suddenly came into focus, its meaning and direction revealed.

I felt my spirit pass from my body. The flesh fell away like wet, heavy clothing. I hovered over my bed and looked down on myself, then drifted silently through the house. It was like walking on numb legs. I did not feel my footsteps. I made no sound as I went.

Naboin, the hired man, slept on a bench in the kitchen. He stirred in his sleep and made a sucking sound with his lips, as if he were trying to draw breath to speak, but the words would not come. Then he was suddenly awake, staring right at me. I froze in terror, but he did not see me, and a little while later I passed close by him and left the house.

The stranger was waiting for me on the beach. He was transfigured, his clothing burning with brilliant light, his face aglow like a lantern. He walked upon the surface of the water and colors splashed around him like the sunset.

He reached out his hand, and I saw that he held a ball of light, more brilliant than my eyes could look upon. I was dazzled, blinded, and yet I was drawn to him.

When I could see again, I too stood on the surface of the water, and he held me by the hand. He pointed, and I looked into the distance, and Baal-ad-Theon was there, almost transparent, its towers flickering like shapes of pale fire. And as I looked on it, my mind was filled, as if I had forgotten much and suddenly could remember. Then I, too, recalled Baal-ad-Theon and shared my companion's pain and loss.

I tried to speak, to tell him that I was an exile like him, only I had been born on this island. I wanted to tell him that I understood, to thank him for making me understand. But no words came. Bubbles of light floated from my mouth, and drifted up until the sky was filled with them, and all the world glowed with soft light.

A wave splashed against my legs, and the shock of the frigid water caused me to awaken.

* * *

I found myself in the dark attic loft where I slept with Tal. I sat up, shivering. A window was open at the other end of the loft. I made my way to it, crouching beneath the low ceiling, but before I closed it, I looked out and saw only grey. It was almost dawn, and the first traces of light spread through the clouds, which again covered the sky.

I closed the window and sat down there for a while, thinking. Then I got dressed and climbed down from the loft. In the kitchen, the hired man still slept. Beside him, on the table, was the basket containing the cake for Ornu. I took it and made my way silently from the house, into the darkness.

A short way from the house, I heard a footstep, and whirled around, terrified. It was Tal, still dressed in his nightgown.

"Where are **you** going?"

"To Ornu," I said, showing him the basket.

"It's too early. The tide's out. You'll have a long enough wait anyway." He yanked me back by the arm. I nearly dropped Ornu's cake. "Don't lie to me," he whispered in my ear.

I trembled then, in something like anger, but really a jumble of many emotions at once, and pulled free from him and began to run.

"Come and see! If you can!"

I glanced back once and saw that he'd gotten his slippers stuck in mud. He stooped to retrieve them, then gave up and ran after me, barefoot in the frigid air, holding his nightgown up like a skirt.

The stranger was waiting for me on the beach. His clothing did seem brighter than before, but his face was like any other. He took the basket from me and laid it on the sand. I looked into the dark recess where Ornu sat, and could just make out the smooth face of the god. I think I was waiting for the god to speak, to explain everything at last, but Ornu kept silent.

The man put both his hands on my shoulders and turned me away. His touch was solid and warm.

"Are you a ghost?"

He squeezed my shoulders harder, then turned me around and looked into my eyes.

"Do you think so?"

"No, I——"

He smiled. "I am not a ghost, then. Only a man."

"Why can't my brother see you?"

"I think your brother has already made up his mind about the world and what is in it. There is no such place as Baal-ad-Theon in his world. But there is in mine, and I think there is in yours."

He let go of me and we walked along the beach a ways among great masses of kelp thrown up by the tide. I told him what I had seen. He began to weep again, softly this time.

"I had hoped for this," he said, "and I had given up hoping."

Our footsteps crunched as we crossed a bed of mussels.

"I don't understand one thing," I said. "Why are you here?"

"I didn't come of my own will," he said in slow, measured tones, as if he were reciting. "I was cast out. All men dream of and long for Baal-ad-Theon, whatever the name they might know it by, and yet I was there and I was cast out. I came to this island because I was trying, one more time, to find my way back, and I failed. But I must tell you one further secret of Baal-ad-Theon. There is a single night —— when it comes, it comes; no one knows how its arrival is determined —— when the gods who walk as men in Baal-ad-Theon reveal themselves to one person only, and fill him with their spirit. This person, then, never dies, but he ceases to be who he was, and becomes the instrument and manifestation of the gods. Thus he is both infinitely blessed and annihilated. Now, on the night of a certain festival in Baal-ad-Theon, I came upon some revellers in a dark street. I took them for revellers, at least, by their fantastic costumes. As I approached, they played on horns and pipes and drums. But then they stopped playing and removed their masks, and I saw them as they truly were. They spoke to me in the language of the gods, which only the chosen one may understand. I understood clearly. Blinded by the light of their faces, and afraid, I fled. I wanted to remain myself. I did not want to be annihilated. I could not give myself to them. So I ran away. I remember crossing a square. Then I was no longer in Baal-ad-Theon, but in a place strange to me and inexpressibly drab and wretched. Since then I have travelled much, and everywhere is like that."

Just then Tal arrived. He ran up to me, shivering, hugging his sides, hopping as the mussel shells cut his feet.

"Who are you talking to?" he said, clearly frightened. "You're talking to the air. There's no one."

The stranger went on, as if there had been no interruption.

"Now the true question, my young friend, is not why I am here, but why you are. I think that you are the means by which I can finally end my exile. I think you can see Baal-ad-Theon clearly, and lead me there. Merely look across the sea, and when you behold Baal-ad-Theon, tell me. Then we will go there, you and I together."

He was weeping softly, and the tears gleamed on his cheeks.

"Stop!" Tal shouted. "Stop it! What are you doing?" He ran around in front of me, and for an instant the stranger's shape wavered and I could see my brother **through** him. Then I was hardly aware of Tal at all.

The sky lightened with the dawn. I searched the horizon for Baal-ad-Theon. We stood together, staring into the distance. Somewhere, far away, Tal was shouting something. But I saw only light. I was puzzled and anxious. More than anything else, I wanted to see Baal-ad-Theon. It would be absurd otherwise. My whole life had led up to this point. I understood everything. I was the exile who had lost my home before I was born. Soon I would look upon it for the first time.

But I only saw the light of the sun.

The stranger grabbed my shoulders again and held me tightly. He shook me a little, and pleaded, weeping, barely able to control his voice. "Tell me that you see it. Tell me. **Please.**"

And I was afraid, both of him and for him, and I lied.

"Yes, I see it."

"Then come."

He took me by the hand and we walked across the wet sand toward the water, among the shells and stones and kelp, and when we came to the water's edge I did not feel the cold touch of the ocean, and the waves did not foam over my shoes. Instead, we were on a kind of road. It stretched before me until it was lost in the glare of the morning sun.

My brother was shouting. I looked back once and saw him jumping up and down in the surf, waving his arms, a little stick figure doing a funny dance. A stray thought came to me: he must be cold, out there all wet in his nightgown.

"I'll get Papa!" he cried.

Then I could neither see him nor hear him.

* * *

We did not come to Baal-ad-Theon. Perhaps it is because I lied. I went through a long period of remorse for this, and repentance. Always the stranger remained at my side. Sometimes his name was Surezin, which means "exile," and sometimes it was Ead, which means "nobly born," and sometimes Musan-Tyrennir, "The Singer Who Does Not Hear." I had many names too, and sometimes I had none at all.

We sang of Baal-ad-Theon and told tales of it, in hovels, at crossroads, in royal courts. I came to see and remember it more clearly, I think, than did my companion. He depended on me for the remembrance, and when we were alone he begged me to tell him of Baal-ad-Theon and of the wonders there.

When I was still young, it was the wonders that fascinated me, but then I came to appreciate the beauty of Baal-ad-Theon, and the infinite perfection of the place and all who dwelt there. Later still, I hungered for knowledge, for the unravelling of all secrets in Baal-ad-Theon, where the wise men know everything, having been instructed by those rare individuals who have seen the gods directly and have been filled with their spirit. And as my youth passed away, I began to understand that I had not yet attained the perfection of my own soul, and this was why I could not come to Baal-ad-Theon.

In the course of all this my companion became quite mad. Often he would babble and address the air, and at other times he would fall silent, and when I would question him, it became apparent that he had forgotten his name, his life, and even Baal-ad-Theon. Then he would remember again, and weep, and beg me to tell him of the wonders. It was always the wonders. He became a child as I became a man.

Through many years we walked through many lands. We came near to the world's rim, to a city which shone golden in the dawn and in the sunset, but left it, for it was not Baal-ad-Theon. From the country of the centaurs we were banished for spreading discontent. Magicians invoked us, and we were manifested in many places.

Once we came by the shore of the sea, on a cold day beneath a dark sky. Piles of kelp lay beneath a cliff of black stone.

"You silly fool," I said. "Can't you see that Baal-ad-Theon is all around you, wherever you go?"

I sat down on a boulder to rest, and he sat at my feet, his head in my lap. He wept and I comforted him, speaking softly as I ran my fingers through his sparse white hair.

"In Baal-ad-Theon there is a fountain, and when people grow very old and weary, they immerse themselves in it, and are turned into silver-scaled fish, and they drift lazily in the warm water, entirely at peace as they gaze up at the frantic world."

THE BERMUDA TRIANGLE EXPLAINED

"It's battleshipping out there again," said Spanish Joe, and that's how it was.

Our ship went down in a storm south of Singapore, or maybe it was west of Sumatra. "Abandon ship!" yelled the Captain, so we did, and we never saw the Captain again. Six of us made it to the lifeboat——me, Jones, Yuan Li, Spanish Joe, Big Jim McGrath, and Charlie the Lookout. We drifted for days and days in the tropic sun (the weather having cleared up almost at once) without food or fresh water, while sharks circled all around, licking their chops. Then Charlie went crazy and did what every sailor knows not to do. He took a long, deep gulp of seawater before anyone could stop him. An hour later we threw his body overboard, and for a while, maybe five minutes, the sharks were satisfied. The rest of us dropped unconscious into the bottom of the boat one by one. I was the last, and right before I went under I looked around and saw the clear, cloudless sky in all directions, the calm and unspotted sea in all directions, and the circular horizon where the two met. I felt very small and alone. That was all.

When we awoke we had been rescued. I was inside a long, bare cabin with many doors, but oddly, no portholes. Around me in bunks were the others, still asleep. I didn't want to wake them so I tiptoed out of the cabin through one of the doors, and came out on deck.

We were aboard a schooner. Two huge sails hung limply on the masts. The sea was calm, with a few fluffy white clouds hanging over it near the horizon. There didn't seem to be anybody about.

"Hello!"

No answer.

"Ahoy there!"

Utter silence.

I walked the full length of the deck and saw that the vessel was old but well kept up, newly painted, neatly scrubbed, all in the apparent absence of a crew. There wasn't even anyone at the wheel. A rope tied from the wheel to a railing held us on course. Unable to make any sense of this, and perhaps wondering if we had been picked up by the **Mary Celeste**, I went back to the cabin and found the others up and around. They too had been outside, which was odd, since I hadn't seen them or heard them.

"Oh there you are," said Spanish Joe. "Ain't this really

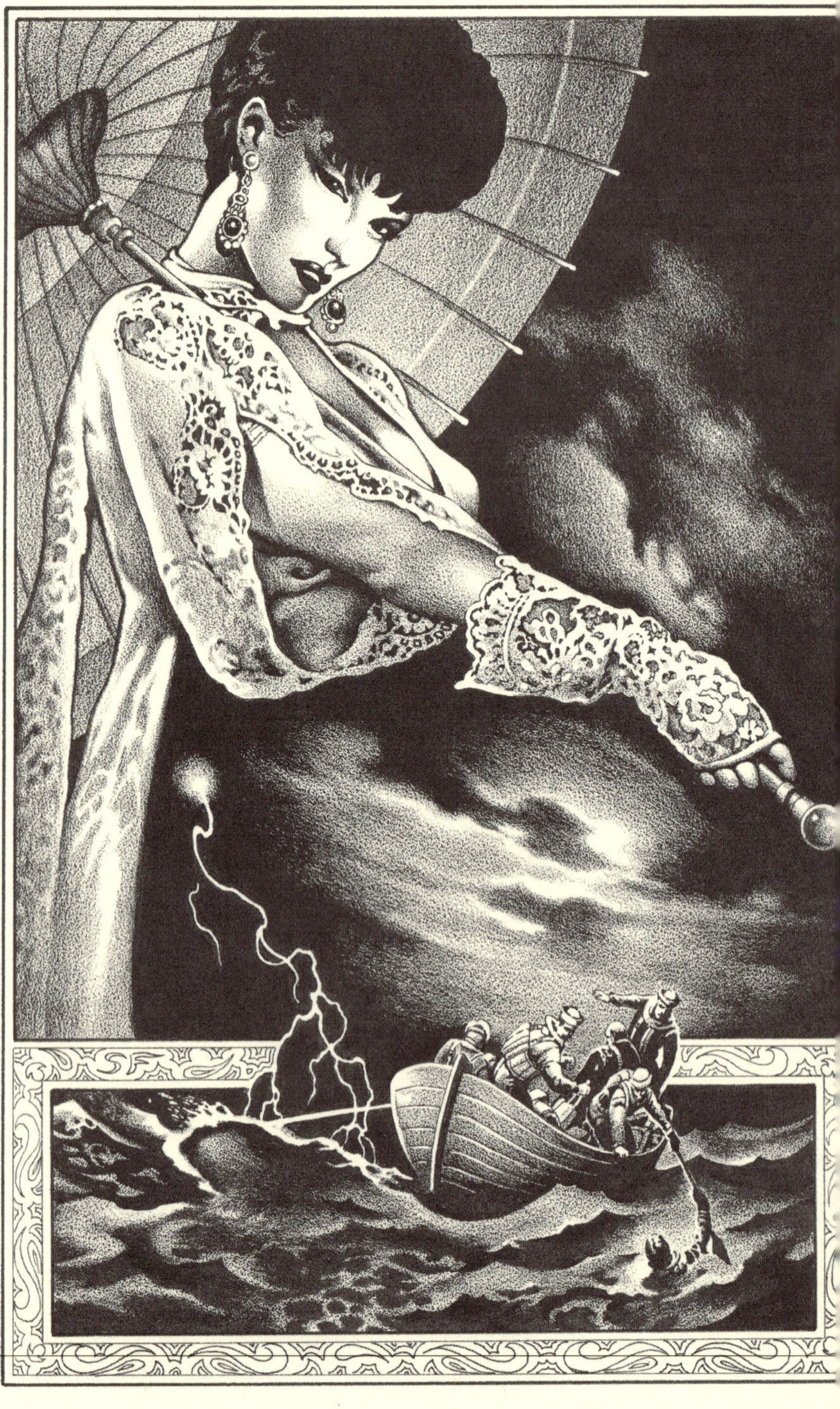

something?"

"Isn't what really something?"

"This barge. I never been on anything this big before."

"Stop kidding me, Joe. You've been on things bigger than schooners before."

To my complete bewilderment, he broke out laughing.

"Hey, that's good! Here we are on a goddam ocean liner with four fuckin' stacks —— four stacks! —— and you think it's a schooner! That's rich." He went on cackling to himself.

"Aw, it wasn't that funny," said Jones after a minute or two. "Your calling a tramp steamer a schooner. He's crazy, I'm sure. Who saw any four stacks?"

"What the hell's this about steamers?" Big Jim cut in. "We're on a Chinese junk."

"You're all crazy, you guys." This was Yuan Li. "I know battleship when I see battleship."

"When you see **what**?"

"Battleship."

"A junk!"

"Tramp!"

"Motherfuckin' **Queen Mary**!"

We argued and argued, and nearly got to blows, when I managed to calm everybody for a minute and get their attention.

"Why don't we all go out and see?" I suggested.

So we did, and were all the more confused. I led them out the door I had used, and there we were, on the schooner. The others were astounded. Spanish Joe cussed. Jones crossed himself. Yuan Li muttered something about Big Buddha being angry.

"Now wait a minute!" said McGrath, and he ran back inside, and opened another door. "Come and look at this!" We did, and there we were on a tramp steamer. The cabin looked different from the outside this time. I didn't know what to make of it. All I could say was "Jesus..." and trail off.

We checked all the other doors, and found in turn the junk, the battleship of Manila Bay vintage, and the luxury liner, each one of them as real as the last one.

"Are we all dead or what?" asked Jones when we were through.

"Damned if I know," I said. "I don't feel dead, and this deck is solid." I stamped it to make sure.

"Maybe we're all in the boat still, and we're dreaming this. Huh?"

I pinched his ass hard. He let out a yell.

"Still think you're dreaming?"

"Well no, but then you explain it. Where is everybody? What is this? Who fished us out of the drink?"

That was something everybody could agree on. Each version of our rescue ship was equally deserted.

"Let's look around," said Spanish Joe, and we bumped and jostled all at once through the low doorway, and emerged once again on the deck of the mammoth liner. Above us, smoke was belching out of all four smokestacks.

"She's under full steam," I said. "There has to be somebody in the boiler room."

"Right. Let's go."

We never got to the boiler room, or even below deck at all, because we met the lady in the white dress on the open deck by one of the tennis courts. She was leaning over the railing watching the waves. In one hand a parasol twirled.

She looked up when we got close, and I could see that she was old enough to look mature but young enough not to be dumpy, finely dressed and made up, and genuinely pretty. Of course to the five of us, who had been at sea for weeks, she was outright beautiful.

"Ah good morning, gentlemen. Isn't it wonderful?"

All of us looked sheepish and waited for somebody else to speak, and then I said, "Isn't what wonderful, Ma'am?"

"The sea. Oh, the sea. The vast and bottomless ocean which has been the same since oldest olden times. It's so **mysterious**."

"Yes Ma'am, I guess it is. I never thought about it much. Look, I'm Patrick O'Conner, the second mate of the **Try It Once**, which was a freighter that got sunk a week ago. We're all from there, and we're really grateful to you for rescuing us, but we want to ask a few questions."

"What questions?"

"Like what kind of ship is this and are we all seeing things," Jones blurted out.

"No, you are **not** seeing things, and as for this ship, well I guess you could say it's a composite of every vessel that vanished mysteriously for the last few thousand years. I was responsible for most of them."

Jones knew when he was being fed a line, or at least he thought he did. He slipped into that sarcastic way of his, and forgot all his manners, what little he had of them.

"And who might you be then?"

"My name is Lilith Circe McSiren, and I own this ship. I've sailed it everywhere."

"Gee, you ever been to the Bermuda Triangle?"

"Young man, I **am** the Bermuda Triangle."

That was that. She told us that dinner would be served in our cabin shortly, so we said good day and went back. As soon as we were out of hearing range everybody talked at once.

"I still can't believe it," said Spanish Joe. "We're dreaming."

"Naw," said Jones. "She's just some eccentric millionaire type. A... a... what the hell's the word? A philathropist. That's it. A philanthropist."

"I afraid," said Yuan Li. "This ain't natural."

"Well something is funny around here, I admit that," I said, "but don't talk about spooks till you see one."

"Sure is a funny name she got."

Dinner was served in the cabin like she said, and what a dinner it was! The cook was the only thing supernatural on this boat. The lady wheeled everything in on a cart by herself. No porters, no other crew members helped her. She came in alone, out of what seemed to be a tanker in rough weather. I caught a glimpse of a metal railing, some coils of rope, and a grey, whitecapped sea beyond. Cold air blasted in, but then the door was shut and the lady served us steaks on silver platters. Yes, steaks, as thick as deck planks, and cooked just right with seasoning, and there was wine and vegetables, and everything you'd expect in a high class restaurant. We all dug in and the lady just stood there watching us.

"Won't you be having some, Miss?" said Spanish Joe.

"I've already eaten."

"Well look," mumbled Big Jim McGrath through a mouthful of meat. "Why don't you just have a little bit of something? It don't seem polite for us to eat and you just stand there." Grease ran down his unshaven chin.

"Oh that's all right. I'll step outside till you're done." She did, and the sky was clear, and it was the ocean liner again. I blinked. Maybe it was all a mirage, except the meal that is. Certainly we didn't gorge ourselves and belch on any mirage.

The lady came back as soon as we were done, almost to the exact second the last bite was down, as if she'd been watching through a peephole. She took the plates and put them on the cart again, and pushed it out onto the deck (still the ocean liner). Then she returned and said, "Oh Mr. Jones, will you come up to my cabin with me?" And she gave us the wink that every seaman knows, and it surprised me to see it coming from so dignified a lady. She went out and Jones leapt up and shouted "Hoo-hah!" and rubbed his crotch expectantly, and ran out after her. The ocean liner had become something wooden, but not the junk or the schooner, and the sky was a little overcast.

All subsequent comments boiled down to one made by Yuan Li: "That **lucky** bastard!"

Jones came back maybe two hours later, and as soon as I saw him I knew something was wrong. I'd sailed with him for four years, and I knew damn well what he always looked like after a good lay. He would be smiling and quiet, contentedly replaying it again and again in his mind. But he wasn't that way at all this time. He just sat down on his bunk and stared at the wall. He didn't seem to care about anything. He looked incredibly bored.

"Well? What happened?" I asked.

"She sucked my soul out," he said slowly, and without any emotion.

"Aw," Spanish Joe sneered, "What ya really mean is the little boy got too excited and came in his pants."

"No. She took my soul. That's why she picked us up, and why she didn't eat anything. She subsists entirely on the souls of men."

"Bullshit."

"Really she did. I don't have a soul anymore."

"Jesus, that sounds terrible," said McGrath.

"Hey," said Yuan Li. "If you don't got no soul no more, how come you not upset about it?"

"**Because** I don't have one. That's just it. I don't feel a thing." Jones yawned. He gazed away from us, then stretched out on the bunk.

"Then we gotta get outta here, and fast."

"I couldn't care less," said Jones. "It's kinda comfortable."

The rest of the day he was no better. He wouldn't speak unless spoken to, and even then his answers were short and he yawned between sentences and seemed to forget what the question was. He wouldn't tell us any more about what had happened to him. The lady ate his soul. That was all. Jim got mad at him, but he didn't care. When Jim made a fist and said, "I'm gonna bust your head off!" Jones just looked up at him and said, "I guess you are." We just couldn't get him excited. When Spanish Joe went through his store of jokes and told a few that would peel the paint off a garbage scow, and had the rest of us laughing and rolling on the floor, Jones just turned over and began to snore after a while.

That evening we went out for a breath of fresh air on the battleship, and wandered all around the cramped turrets and things. Jones didn't come with us. He couldn't be bothered. We climbed up in the crow's nest and watched the stars come out.

Yuan Li looked up at the sky.

"You know, I never seen them stars before."

"He's right," said Big Jim. "I don't recognise any of the constellations."

"It figures," I said.

"Then where in Hell are we?"

"Oh Christ, don't ask."

When we got back to the cabin supper was ready for us. The lady was there with the wheeled tray again, and the silver platters, and everything. Jones was already munching away, oblivious to everyone around him. He didn't seem to care for the food, but it was the best I ever had. Gourmet stuff. Pheasant, stuffed lobster. I read the label on the wine bottle and it was Chateau something, 1748. A good year, I'm sure. The best.

When we were done the lady again took the dirty dishes away, and she turned to Spanish Joe and said, "Mr. Alvarez, may I have the pleasure of your company this night?"

She left, and right before Joe got up to follow her, he turned to Jones.

"Soul-sucker my ass. She's gonna suck somethin' **else**!"

But when he came back he was the same as Jones, bland, bored, and empty-eyed. The rest of us were a little afraid.

"What was it like?" I asked.
"A Roman galley, only there wasn't anybody at the oars."
"What happened?"
He seemed a little distracted, unable to focus his thoughts.
"Oh nothing much. She sucked out my soul. That's all."
"Oh really?" said Jones. His voice was a low monotone, like Joe's.
"Yes really. I don't suppose it matters much."
"No it doesn't." Jones didn't bother to cover his yawn.

I was horrified. It seemed to be true, but I had to be sure. There was only one way.

"Hey Joe, it's a dull night. Why don't you tell us about that Hong Kong whore?" That was his favorite story. We'd all heard it a million times, gloriously embellished.

"The what? Oh I'm terribly sorry. I seem to have forgotten the details."

I was sure.

The next morning at breakfast it was the same thing all over again. We had french toast with jam, and a genuine French snail omelette, more of that incredible wine, and lots of other things. I'd never tasted anything like it.

"Mr. McGrath," she said as she took out the dishes, "will you come with me?" Right before he left he leaned over and whispered into my ear, "I ain't gonna let her even **touch** me till I find out what's going on." I had hope for a while, but then he came back and was just like Jones and Spanish Joe. The ship had been an aircraft carrier without planes, and she'd done it right in the middle of the flight deck, but more than that he would not say. Yuan Li and I tried our best to get him to tell more, but all was in vain. The others didn't care, of course. They had no souls.

That's how it was. The situation was hopeless, and we went out all the doors and explored all the ships and didn't find a clue, or a crew. Even the boiler room of the liner was deserted, despite the smoke coming out of the smokestacks. Finally, when lunch was served Yuan Li went to his fate stoically and with great dignity, so there wasn't much of an outward change when he came back. All I could tell was that he looked limp inside and out, like a threadbare rag. He wouldn't say anything except, "It was a bark, with four masts all white," and he only said that once. He sat very still and contemplated nothing.

I don't know why she fed us so well. Maybe there's some connection between the fullness of a man's stomach and the richness of his soul. Maybe she was just being nice. I don't know.

In any case, that evening, at exactly the same hour she had come the night before, the lady showed up again, and through the door I saw a high and wooden gunwhale, and there was rain coming down, and overhead masts and rigging creaked.

The tray had another deluxe meal for the five of us. Swordfish steak, like they serve to millionaires, not something out of a ship's galley. And more wine, and caviar, and shrimp cocktails, and vegetables, soup, five courses in all.

She didn't have to wink or invite me this time, now that I was the only one left with a soul. There was no need for show. She took me firmly by the arm and said, "Come along," and leaving the dishes where they were she led me out onto what had to be Cleopatra's barge, only it was bucking up and down in a North Atlantic gale. She turned to me and smiled, and maybe there was a hint of sharp fangs and maybe there wasn't, but an idea came to me and I was desperate enough to try it.

"Wait!" I shouted over the wind. "I forgot to brush my teeth. I can't kiss a lady without brushing my teeth first. Would you excuse me for a minute?"

She hadn't been expecting that, but she only smiled and let go of my arm and said, "Be quick about it."

I ran back to the cabin, which this time was covered over with gold on the outside, and tripped over Spanish Joe who had been sitting in the doorway. He didn't stir. I cursed and none of the others moved more than a department store dummy. I tore open the other doors and saw the decks of the ocean liner once again, and a carrack like Columbus had, and a Viking longship (with a cabin?) and finally, to my great relief, a simple fishing sloop. I went out on the deck and looked around, afraid that the lady might be there, waiting, and I saw that I was alone, then cut loose the ship's dingy and got in and rowed as fast as I could until I was alone with the sea and sky, still unable to believe that I had gotten away. I kept going for a day and a night until I spied land, and then a port I knew. Don't ask me how, but it was Liverpool, England.

I tied the boat to the wharf and climbed up on the planks, cautiously at first, testing the solidness of the wood I was standing on. Then I ran into the street and kept going. It was real. I almost kissed the first person I met, and the first telephone pole, and the first fire hydrant. The relief I felt was as if a ten ton weight had been removed from my shoulders.

Silly me. The first odd thing, which I should have noticed but didn't, was that no one ever questioned me about the loss of the freighter. It is the lot of sole survivors of shipwrecks to be dragged before boards of inquiry and examined, cross examined, and all but dissected, but nothing happened to me, even when I hitch-hiked to London and got a job with the import firm run by the Captain's third cousin. He had ships, but I refused to sail anymore, so he put me to work in a warehouse cataloguing boxes. I lived in London for three months, looking fearfully over my shoulder for the first, quite nervous for the second, and finally at ease for the third.

I remained calm and safe until one evening when I went into a pub with some friends. The night wore on over beers until I looked at my watch and realised that I had to get up at seven the next morning. The pub had three doors.

"Well mates, I have to be going," I said, and walked out one of them.

And found myself in Quebec, on the boardwalk above the river, just beneath the Chateau Frontenac.

I reeled back like a man who notices at the last second he's about to step on a cobra. I looked around in horror, completely taken by surprise, disoriented, and I knew the feeling a drug user experiences when he thinks that his strange dream has been over for a long time, only to find that **it is still going on,** and all his subsequent life has been part of it.

I whirled around and ran back through the doorway, into the dark but no longer cosy English pub, across the room and out another door.

This time I couldn't identify the city, but it looked South American.

Again I went back inside and was in London, and seeing my distress the bartender said, "Is there anything I can do for you sir?"

"**No!**" I yelled as I desperately, hopelessly opened the last door.

Peking. I was sure it was Peking. I had seen this square before on newsreels. Over by the Gate of Heavenly Peace, the entrance of the old imperial palace, a gang of Red Guards were doing calisthenics.

I ventured a short way out onto the pavement, and then I saw someone coming toward me who didn't look at all Chinese, even though she was wearing baggy green overalls and a cap with a red star on it like everyone else.

Her voice was all too familiar. She called out in classic pidgin English, "Ah so, venerable comrade O'Conner, dearie, we meet again at last."

I had nothing to say, but still I mumbled, "But how? You couldn't——the ships——"

"You underestimate me if you think ships are **all** I can do. In truth I'm **much** more versatile——"

I should have believed her and realised that escape was impossible, but somehow my soul seemed more precious than it ever had before. I ran from her, threw open the door of the first building I came to, and went through as if leaping a hurdle.

I didn't arrive in a city this time, but **elsewhere.** I was in open country under a night sky, and before me an ashen hill sloped down to the shore of a thick, gelatinous ocean. Over the horizon in what must have been the west, two large crescent moons hung. In the east a sun was beginning to rise, and it was blue. The air was heavy and difficult to breathe.

"I'm **much** more versatile!" giggled Lilith Circe McSiren as she came through after me.

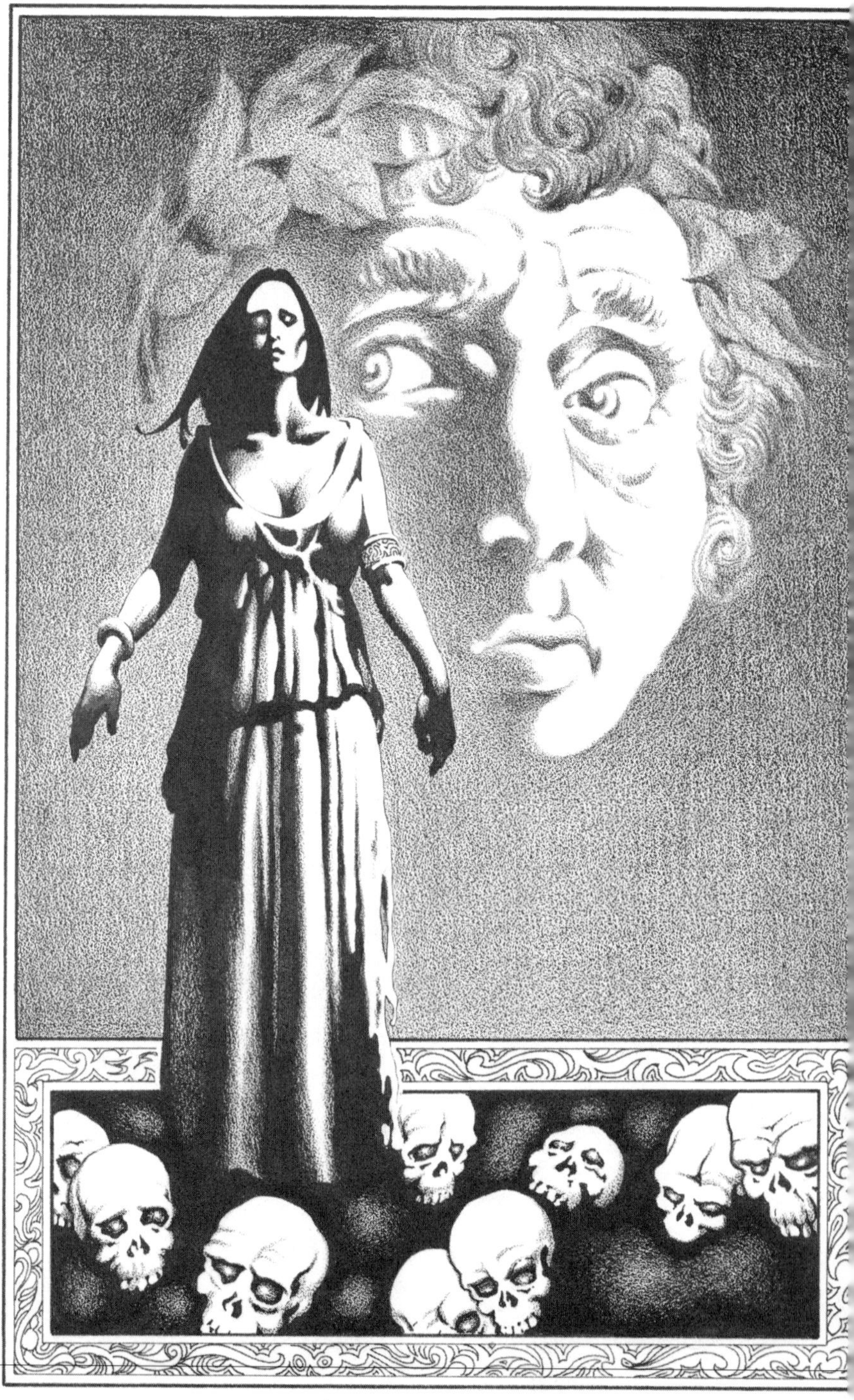

THE ADVENTURE IN THE HOUSE OF PHAON

24 June, 3rd Year of the Divine Antoninus

To T. Calvisius Valens, Greetings.

You inform me, my dear Titus, that you are composing a biography of my uncle, Vestricius Spurinna. This is indeed a noble project, and I thank the gods that so capable a writer as yourself has undertaken it, for now I am confident that my uncle's memory will be preserved in a manner worthy of him. He was one of the most interesting men of our age. I say this, not merely because I was his favorite nephew, but because I knew him, I think, better than anyone else still living. I at least caught a glimpse of the complexities of his mind, and I hope that I can provide you with much useful information. If there is anything you need to know, merely ask, and the doors of the Underworld will be opened, and the past will come to life again. (If you will forgive my presumption!)

Spurinna's public deeds are well known. I doubt I can tell you anything you don't already know about the offices held, the tasks he undertook, and the like. There are many others to praise him there.

I think you should know something of his whimsical side, too. He got a great deal of pleasure out of telling the story of the "Feast of Gaius." It seems that he had arranged for a sumptuous dinner party to be held at his house, and he only invited people whose first name was Gaius. Since he lacked that **praenomen** himself, he did not attend. Imagine the confusion when Gaius Vettius, who was acting as host, introduced everybody in the most intimate way: "Gaius, I would like you to meet Gaius. And Gaius, this is Gaius, and Gaius, Gaius, and... oh, yes! Let us not forget Gaius!"

Later in the evening, one of the servants, a Greek named Apollodorus (in fact **all** the servants were Greeks named Apollodorus, for all some had to be re-named for the occasion), entered with a parchment on a golden tray. It was bound with ribbons and sealed most impressively. There could be no doubt that it was a communication from someone of the utmost importance.

The servant got everyone's attention, then pretended to puzzle over a tag dangling from a ribbon. There was a breathless pause.

"It's a message for Gaius," he said.

But all this happened before you or I were born. I remember my uncle very much as the wonderful old man Pliny the Younger describes in his letters, still vigorous at seventy-five, taking long walks and rides and throwing a ball for half an hour every day to keep fit. Everything Pliny says is true: his sight and hearing were unimpaired at that age, and he lived modestly, though elegantly, surrounded by the best company, studying the best literature, and, indeed, writing some of the best Greek and Latin lyrics to be found anywhere.

Pliny cites him as an ideal, his old age something we all have to look forward to, when the years bring nothing but wisdom, and, after long labors are completed, the days bring nothing but rest.

This is a pleasing picture, but it is not complete. Spurinna, as I have said, was a man of uncommon complexity. While his old age was serene, it wasn't uneventful. This is what I am writing to tell you about. This is what you won't find in other sources.

It was in the early summer that I came to my uncle's house. I had just concluded some particularly tiresome business in Rome, and was looking forward to a few days of relaxation and pleasant company. His estate was not far from the city, just beyond the sixth milestone.

I found him walking with a few friends along a wooded path. A reader walked with them, reading aloud from Vergil's **Eclogues**. My uncle seemed deep in thought, but when he saw me he paused, raised his hand, and the whole company stopped. The reader fell silent.

"No, no," he said to the reader. "Continue."

Spurinna took me by the arm and we walked with the others, listening, but I could tell that his mind was not on the poetry, nor on the beautiful day that was already more than half gone. Sunlight slanted through the trees. We went in silence, but for the reader's voice.

Later, when we had followed the curving path back to the house, and the reader had been dismissed, he took me aside.

"Do you remember Gaius Fannius?" he asked in a low voice.

"Only a little," I said. "When I was a boy, I remember, he came to our house and read from a tragedy he'd written. I'm afraid I didn't like it at the time. I snuck out."

"Actually, it was rather good. I have so many memories of him. He was a dear friend. Did you know? He was the only person who agreed with me that there are too many people named Gaius. Funny how we think of such trivial things at such a time as this."

"Is he not... well?"

"He died ten days ago. I want you to come with me to his house. His widowed daughter, Fannia, is there alone now, but for the servants."

I wanted to ask him if it was appropriate for me to come along and console the daughter of someone I had hardly known, but he seemed to anticipate my question.

"I want you to accompany me because there's something you ought to see. And I may need your help."

He wouldn't tell me more. He was steadfastly mysterious about it.

* * *

We walked to the house of the late Fannius. I offered my carriage, but Spurinna refused. He wanted the exercise, he said, and he wanted to think. Being out in the woods helped him think. He lent me travelling clothes, a broad-brimmed hat to keep off the sun — although there was little sun left — and a cloak. We turned from the path and made our way through the trees, following a way he seemed to know. For all he was forty-five years my senior, I was hard-pressed to keep up with him.

Still he would not say more about what we were to see and do. He discoursed on nature. He asked about my family. He explained his new theory of the aesthetics of Greek painting. I think he used words as a shield, to hide behind when he wanted to be alone with his thoughts.

The woods thinned out, and we came to a field, and stood for a moment looking down a slope at the estate of Fannius. The main road curved near the house, and a path led up to the front door. In back there was a walled garden, badly overgrown with weeds and vines. Still, it was a lovely scene, the sun low above the hills opposite us, the first hint of twilight spreading like a mist over the fields, a few sheep grazing in the distance. But I felt a certain disquiet.

Fannia met us at the door. She was still dressed in her black mourning gown, and she wore a veil turned back over her hair. She was a year or two older than me, and in other circumstances might have been beautiful. She looked drawn and haggard, too pale for health. She probably hadn't slept in days.

"I am glad you've come," she said quietly to Spurinna. Then I was introduced. It was an awkward moment. I tried to express sympathy without seeming boorish. She didn't seem to be listening to anything I said.

She led us through the entrance hall, into a courtyard which, like the back garden, was beginning to get overgrown with weeds, then into an inner hall. There the shrine of the household gods was prominently displayed. The remains of several sacrifices had not been cleared away. There too was an open cabinet containing the death masks of members of the family. One of them was new.

As yet we had encountered no servants. When Fannia clapped her hands, only two men appeared. Still, for all her adversity, she was determined to play the hostess, and bade these two tight-lipped fellows convey us to the bath. We hurried through it. Later, she joined us for a quite adequate dinner, served by the same two. She said little throughout, and I didn't want to press her. The awkwardness of our first encounter returned. I looked to my uncle for help, but he was caught up in his own thoughts.

By now it was dusk. Fannia became nervous, even, I think, afraid. She sent one of the servants away, then rose from her couch.

"I'm sorry I can't stay here any longer. I have to be going."

"Yes, yes," said Spurinna in a soothing tone. "You can go to my house. The servants know you. You'll be welcome." I could tell from his expression that he knew what was going on, but wasn't ready to tell me.

Fannia came over to me. I got up.

"I'm glad to have met you, sir." She was nearly hysterical. I felt helpless. I didn't know what to say.

Just then the servant who had been sent away came back with a book satchel, which he handed to Spurinna. My uncle opened it and looked in. There were three scrolls inside.

"I hope they'll... help you," Fannia said.

"Lady, your litter is ready," the servant said.

She turned and hurried away, the two servants trailing.

"Farewell," my uncle said, raising his hand. She didn't look back.

"Uncle," I said, somewhat alarmed. "Is it safe for her to be on the road at night? Why does she have to go? This is most extraordinary."

Again he hid behind small talk. I paced back and forth, wringing my hands, as angry with him as I ever got. Still my uncle was reclining at the table. He babbled on about how the wine was imported from Spain and very exotic.

"Please! I don't care about the stupid wine!"

"Very well then. Quintus, do you believe in ghosts?"

I stopped in mid-stride. "What?"

"You wanted me to explain. Now that we are alone, I think I can. Do you believe in ghosts?"

"I suppose so. Why?"

"They've a new hobby of mine. No, it is more than that. It is a serious business. I am quite sure there are such things. Only I've never had a chance to see one before."

"You're not making sense."

"Sit down. Drink." He handed me a goblet of wine. I sat and drank. "The house is haunted," he said.

"The gods protect us then," I said slowly.

"You don't believe me. But you will soon. Fannia came to believe a few days after her father died. There were sounds. Things were seen. Her servants were so afraid she had to let them sleep outside the house. She wasn't very clear on the details, but she insisted that her father was **still here.**"

"Is he?" I glanced up idly at a mural. It showed Aeneas in Hades with the Sybil, standing before the gates of horn and ivory, through which true and false visions come into the world. Just then I wondered which gate was open. I didn't know what was real and what wasn't. I wondered if my uncle might have gone mad in his old age, but from his manner, I doubted it. The façade of his frivolity was gone. He was all grim purpose now.

"Quite possibly he is still here. But there is more." He sat up, swung his legs around, and put the book satchel in his lap. He opened it, and handed me a scroll. "Here, read this. This is the reason Fannius died."

With considerable trepidation, I began to read, but after a few minutes I was more puzzled than ever. It was a history of the reign of Nero, with an emphasis on the scandals and murders.

"I don't understand. What has this to do with——?"

"Fannius told his daughter something important in the last hour of his life. He showed her this book he was writing —— it is incomplete —— and said that he had had three dreams on three successive nights. Each time it seemed that he had fallen asleep at his desk, and awakened in the middle of the night, only to find Nero himself sitting on the couch with him, **reading his book.** On the first night, he read the first volume, on the second, the second, on the third, the third, which is the last. It was then that he got up and said to Fannius, 'There will be no more.'"

"So, was his dream more than a dream?"

"I don't know. But it was clear enough that he would not live to complete the fourth volume. And, sure enough, he didn't."

"Uncle... what are we doing here?"

"I think Fannia is right," he said. "Her father has returned. I think he wants to finish his book. He can't, of course, but he won't give up. **His** father was executed for treason under Nero, and he told me once that he would never be content until he had detailed all the tyrant's crimes for the world to see. I'm sure he meant it. If he isn't helped, he'll walk here forever."

"Helped?"

"He needs to be laid to rest."

* * *

We retired to Fannius' study. Darkness came on. Spurinna sat on the very couch where the dead man had lain when the spirit of Nero visited him. I wandered about in the uncertain light, sipping wine, glancing through Fannius' books. Everything was as it had been when he died. Writing materials were on his desk, and parchments, old books, and papyrus lay about in untidy heaps, his notes and research materials, I assumed.

I tried to think. I was frightened. Who wouldn't be? But I was also excited. This was an adventure we were setting out on. And I had confidence in my uncle. When he was serious like this, when the heroic core of his being was visible —— I do not exaggerate —— I would have followed him like a soldier after a general, into the very chamber of the gorgons.

If I could control my own fear, I too was eager to see a ghost. I wanted reassurance. I wanted to know that we continue after death, that the good are rewarded and the wicked punished. I wanted to ask the ghost all about these things. Otherwise... what can I say? Life is a meaningless horror. I am no philosopher who can find serenity in day-to-day things, without hope for the future.

My uncle sat reading Spurinna's unfinished history. I gathered from his occasional remarks that it was finely polished, but ghastly stuff. I couldn't concentrate enough to read any of it myself. Yet Spurinna read calmly, as if the two of us were merely spending a quiet evening in the library. To the superficial eye, he might have seemed oblivious to his surroundings. But I knew better. I admired his quiet courage.

It was nearly midnight when he put down the third volume and whispered, "Listen!"

I replaced the curious sculpture I had been examining——Indian, I think —— on a shelf and stood absolutely still. I didn't hear anything. I whispered back, "What is it?"

"Quiet!"

I sat down beside him. Now I did hear something, far away, from the depths of the house —— music, very faint, very delicate lyre music. There was something terribly sad in the sound.

"I thought we were alone in the house."

"We **are**..."

The music grew louder, even more melancholy. Its source seemed to be moving slowly, as if the player were strolling through the house. My heart was touched. It was the most beautiful thing I had ever heard, as if Orpheus had returned to Earth. I wept as I heard it. Spurinna was ashen-faced.

Still the player approached. I looked at the two open doors on either side of the study. The music seemed to be coming from every side. Then there was a footstep, and a figure stood in the right doorway, completely in shadow. I could only discern the outline of a heavy-set figure in a loose robe, arm and hand moving rhythmically as the lyre played.

I stood up, took a lamp from the writing desk, and approached the stranger.

"Who are you?" I whispered. "You are not Gaius Fannius."

The music stopped. The silence was stunning.

"No," came a soft, almost girlish voice. "I come through the gate of ivory, to bring beautiful dreams into the world."

Then the figure in the doorway was gone.

I turned lamely to Spurinna.

"It wasn't Fannius."

He made a gesture, like a schoolmaster dealing with an idiot.

"No, it **wasn't**." He covered his face in his hands and sighed. "No, it wasn't Fannius."

From his tone, I could tell that he was worried about more than my stupidity. I think he was afraid. But I desperately needed to believe that his courage would not break, that he would know what to do.

* * *

We waited for an hour in silence. I was too ashamed to say anything. I longed for the apparition or spirit or whatever it had been to come back, so at least I wouldn't have wrecked everything.

The two of us sat side by side, reading Fannius' book. It was everything my uncle had said it was. The crimes of Nero shocked and appalled me, but I felt a certain fascination with his character, as Fannius obviously had. At times I could almost pity him. Here was a child born into a world of treachery and horror and sudden death. His father had been a brute, his mother a venomous she-serpent. In the terror of those times, no one even remotely connected with the imperial house could ever know if he would live out the year. There were so many plots, accusations, orders to die. It was like a race. Some men fell behind quickly, generations before Nero, burdened by virtue, leaving the evil ones to overtake one another. Therefore it was only natural that his mother, the Younger Agrippina, the only surviving sister of the beast Caligula, who had known only terror and depravity all **her** life, from the time her own parents were murdered, should bring into her bed the freedman Pallas, the greatest scoundrel of the age. Pallas helped Agrippina murder his master, her husband, Claudius. Then she murdered Pallas and Nero murdered her. The dreary procession went on, as it had for generations. Nero had never known anything else, growing up alone, surrounded by flatterers who had daggers for him, he knew, if fortune should turn in favor of someone else. He was shaped by his environment, like clay in a sculptor's hands. He became one of the beasts, like the rest. But then, how could I convince myself he had not known what he was doing? His cruelties went on and on. He took to vice naturally, easily. He never once stopped to say, "No."

Spurinna put his hand on my arm. I carefully rolled the book into my lap.

"Listen, and be **quiet** this time."

I listened. The spirit was returning. Again, the intensely beautiful music grew louder. Again, the dark shape stood in the doorway, gently strumming the lyre. This time I didn't move, and the stranger came slowly into the room. I think the figure was a solid black at first, like a walking statue of black marble, but as the shadows shifted it assumed a more human aspect.

A man about my own age stood before us, barefoot in a loose white gown, playing a lyre. He was of average height, heavy, with spindly legs. His face was pasty, made up perhaps, and his blond curls were heavily scented.

"Jupiter preserve us!" I gasped under my breath. I drew back. Spurinna sat rigid, eyes wide, as astonished as I.

I didn't have to ask who this was. It was Nero. I was face to face with the tyrant. I wanted to stand up, to shout him away with accusations of matricide and murder. Here was the man who had once lighted a garden party with human torches, prisoners wrapped in oil-soaked skins, tied to stakes. He dined and recited poetry as they screamed. Here he was, and he had charmed us both with the very music of the heavenly Muses. He might as well have been a siren. We couldn't break away from him. I was revolted, at the same time entranced.

He played on. It seemed forever.

* * *

Then the performance suddenly stopped.

"Monster," a voice said.

Nero let out a little shriek and dropped his instrument. It struck the floor with a resonating clang.

"**Monster.**"

There was someone else in the doorway, definitely all black, like walking stone, shuffling into the room.

"**Monster.**"

Nero drew away, whimpering.

"**Monster.**"

The thing neared us, and, in the flickering light and shadow of our feeble lamps, became more human, a dark, long-haired woman, double-chinned and very pregnant. She too wore a loose white robe, only hers was soaked with blood down the front.

"Please," Nero sobbed. "I didn't mean to do it. I was angry. You made me angry. You **always** made me angry..."

"You didn't think of **our child.**"

"Poppea," Spurinna whispered to me.

Yes, of course. Nero's wife. He murdered another for her, then, when she scolded him for coming home late one night, he kicked her in the belly, in her swollen, pregnant belly. She bled to death.

"**Monster. Unnatural son.**" It was another voice.

A third apparition came through the doorway, a grim, hatchet-faced older woman, her fine gown ripped, dripping with seawater, the whole front of her body slit open. She came gliding across the floor, dripping brine and blood.

"I told the soldiers to rip out the womb that bore such a creature as you."

Nero screamed. He fell to the floor, knocking over the writing desk. Pens scattered.

"**Monster,** do you remember me?" This was a girl's voice. She stood in the doorway, dressed in a bridal gown. "Monster, who remembers Octavia, of whom it is said her wedding to you was her funeral? Do you? Every day that I lived with you, I died a little more. I was resigned for it. I had no hope. I never did."

"**Monster,** you made me the Prince of Youth. I never got to be king. You stole that from me." It was a boy, his face bloated. "What about Britannicus, your dear step-brother? What about me?"

Nero got up. "Leave me alone! Leave me alone!" he shouted. He tripped over his lyre, fell with a thud, got to his hands and knees, and scurried for the left door, whimpering and sobbing, his fat buttocks quivering, while his wives and mother and brother stood over him, screaming, "Monster, monster!"

He looked like an enormous swine, squealing on its way to

slaughter.

He got to the left doorway, then scrambled away.

A man about fifty wearing a senatorial toga came in with a mincing step.

"My dear boy, **monster**," he said. "Don't think you can get away from me. I made you what you are. And you made me... what I am." He held out his arms, which were slashed from wrist to elbow, pouring blood.

"Pallas," my uncle whispered.

"Can this keep on?" I asked.

"Be quiet. Don't do anything until I say——"

"Oh, get up, **monster**," said yet another newcomer, prodding Nero with a slipper set with pearls. "You're most inelegant that way."

On and on they came, all Nero's victims, bleeding as they were when they died, or torn apart by beasts, or hideously burned. Some my uncle could identify, some not. They chased Nero around the room, surrounding him. He knelt in their midst, shrieking, tearing his hair, babbling, "Forgive me. Forgive. Please. Who will be my friend? Do I have any friends? I never had any——"

"But we are **all** your friends," said Pallas, snickering. "We all love you more than we can say."

All this while the spirits were oblivious to the two mortals present. We sat still and watched. Spurinna put his hand on mine.

"Now, stay with me," he whispered. "I will need you more than ever. We can't let this continue."

I wondered helplessly what he proposed to do.

A general in full battle gear pushed his way through the crowd, his sword drawn.

"**Monster**, Corbulo saved your filthy empire time and time again. He did what you commanded always. He struck at the enemies of Rome. He does it still."

He ripped Nero's gown off. Naked, quivering, streaming with sweat, the emperor did indeed resemble some enormous animal. Corbulo grabbed him by the hair, yanked him to his feet, then rammed his sword in just below the hanging belly, above the groin. He ripped up with the blade, then sideways. Nero screamed all the more. His guts fell on the floor in a heap, and streaming blood poured out in impossible quantities, covering the whole floor of the library, washing over the writing table, the lyre, splashing around the feet of the assembled multitude. There were wriggling things in it, like huge worms with human faces, screaming in the agonies of his numberless victims. He lay writhing, splashing, and a flame roared out of his wound, became a winged Fury with a burning whip, striking him again and again. The crowd shouted and danced around him, knee-deep in blood, swimming in it.

I felt I was drowning. I had to get out. Spurinna pulled on my hand and shouted, "No! Stay here!" But I broke away and clawed my way through the crowd, gasping like a drowning man, as the room filled with blood. I was floating, swimming, and I poured out of the room in a great torrent of blood. I found myself in the atrium. I stumbled against the display of death masks, scattering them. The house shook with thunder. Lightning dazzled me. I ran, screaming, hurled by winds, until I came to a door. Then I was outside and the rain was an almost solid barrier against me. I pushed on, into the forest, in abject panic. This is my great shame. I abandoned Spurinna when he most needed me. I didn't even think of him. I didn't think at all, but ran and ran, straining for breath, while the trees moaned and swayed above me, while rain came down like an avalanche of stones, and lightning blinded me with fire, before I was tearing my way through thorns, blinded again by darkness.

I came to a path, from there to a crossroads.

A lady stood there, clad all in black, her gown flapping in the wind. She wore a silver crown. Huge black dogs licked her hands.

She pointed. I saw a light in the distance and ran toward it across a muddy, open field. Lightning flashed again, making it bright as day. I could see for miles. Then, in the darkness, I splashed to the edge of a thicket. The smaller light came from within. I seemed to struggle through the underbrush for hours, until I came upon a clearing. There, three eyeless women sat around a fire. One of them was spinning. Another weighed the thread between the blades of a pair of scissors.

"Sisters, I have Spurinna," she said.

"**No!**" I grabbed a stick and ran at them. The fire winked out, and I was striking about madly in the darkness. Then, terrified with some apprehension of what I had done, I backed away, forced my way back into the open field, and ran toward the house. I **wanted** to get back now, to help my uncle.

I couldn't find my way in the dark, in the wind and rain. Again, time seemed to slow down. Hours and hours seemed to pass. At last I stumbled and fell onto a road. I lay still for a minute, the rain washing over my face. There was more thunder, then hoofbeats, and four horsemen were upon me. I cried out and rolled from their path. The lead horse reared up, and a cloak fell away from the rider's face.

"**Hail Caesar!**" someone shouted from the far side of the road.

I got up and ran after the horsemen. They dismounted at the end of a path and hurried up to the house, the fat one in the cloak assisted by the others. Halfway there, they left the path and made their way through the underbrush to the wall of the garden. The others held vines aside while the fat one squirmed through a hole that had been dug under the wall. He looked like an immense rat or weasel then.

When he was through, the others exchanged glances and ran away into the woods.

I caught an outcropping and climbed over the wall, dropping into tall weeds.

I heard his voice from inside the house. "Phaon? Where are

you? Have you also deserted your emperor?"

I found Nero, exhausted, mud-splattered, barefoot, clad only in a loose gown, lying on a couch. He looked up wearily as I approached.

"Is that my good Phaon?"

When he saw that it wasn't, he stumbled from the room. I followed him through the house, until we came to Fannius' study.

* * *

The rain had stopped. The grey light of dawn shone faintly through the windows. One of the lamps was still lit. Otherwise the room was littered with broken furniture and scattered papers.

Spurinna stood there, waiting. I saw Nero come to him and fall to his knees.

"Where is Phaon, my loyal follower?"

"He is not here," Spurinna said gently. "But I will help you."

"Yes, yes, help me." Nero took out a dagger and handed it to my uncle, cringing. He tore open his gown, exposing his throat. "Help me!"

Spurinna leaned over him, dagger in hand. Nero began to cry, like a small, frightened child.

"Who will be my friend?" he said.

"I will be your friend," my uncle said. "I will help you escape. But for once, you must be strong. You must not be afraid, just this once."

I watched this from the doorway, like a disembodied spirit. It was remote and fantastic to me, like the tableau of a dream. Spurinna held the dagger to the emperor's throat, and Nero grabbed his wrists, driving the blade in. Then, at the last instant he seemed to lose courage, and Spurinna pushed it in the rest of the way, moving the dagger from side to side, cutting both of the great blood vessels in the neck.

Nero fell back, and sat for a moment, bleeding. He picked up his lyre, strummed, and said, "What an artist the world is losing."

The lyre fell from his fingers.

A long time later, Spurinna and I stood alone in the room.

* * *

"I understand some of this now," my uncle said, rummaging through the scattered papers."

"I don't."

"Look at these." He held up a handful. "Fannius had these for his research, of course. They're letters to Nero from Phaon. Phaon lived here. He owned this house before Gaius Fannius did."

"So I gather. But who was Phaon?"

"A Greek freedman. One of Nero's creatures. At the very end, Nero sought shelter in the house of Phaon. **Here. Nero died here.**"

"And now he has died again."

"In a way. He is at rest."

"Uncle? Did you do the right thing?"

Spurinna rose and walked wearily out of the house. I followed. "I don't know," he said. "I don't want to see any more ghosts." Much later, he burned Fannius' book.

* * *

And so you can see, my dear Titus, why I must tell you this story, even though it reflects on me the shame of cowardice. But I am but an ordinary man, and was afraid. My uncle was more. That is why I am still in awe of him. He had not expected what happened. He had come to help the daughter of a friend, and perhaps make an exciting discovery. He was prepared to interview the ghost of Gaius Fannius, nothing more. But when this extraordinary circumstance was upon him, he remained steadfast. He knew what to do. At the very end, he showed wisdom.

Yes, it was wisdom. I came to understand that after a time.

I did not see my uncle for several months afterwards. I was afraid of the memories. When I finally did, he seemed older, tired, as if our adventure had burned his spirit, searing some of the life out of him. Perhaps it was merely age, catching up with him at last. I don't know.

His mind was as sharp as ever as I dined with him, however, his conversation brilliant, but he ate little. Afterwards, he could not sit up with me for very long, so his servants carried him to bed and I remained with him for a while. I was finally able to discuss our experience. It was as if a great weight had been lifted from my soul. I told him all I had seen and heard that night. Indeed, as I had suspected, his adventure had been quite different.

"I think that when the great ones die," he said, "when the great ghosts are without rest, the past and present, time, and the mind itself become unfixed, all of them. If you will forgive an old man's babbling, this is my latest theory. I think they swirl around, like different colors of paint stirred in a pot."

"Uncle, I have been thinking... ever since... I never understood...."

"Yes? Come to the point. You never could, you know."

"I want to know. I want to be sure. **Did you do the right thing**?"

"I think so."

"But Nero **was** a monster. He deserved all that. You showed him mercy."

"What good would his continued suffering have done? The people he murdered can't be brought back. It's all over. Besides..."

He sighed and lay back on his pillow, his eyes closed. For a moment I was alarmed. Then I saw that he was breathing normally, and I thought he had gone to sleep. It was only after a pause of several minutes that he spoke again.

"... besides, Fannia needed the house back."

* * *

That is all there is to tell. It is a strange tale, and a complex one, but I think the meaning is clear. I hope you can use it in your book, Titus, my friend. You and I and your readers can then hope to emulate my uncle's virtues.

And so, farewell in the favor of the gods,

Q. Attius Tiro

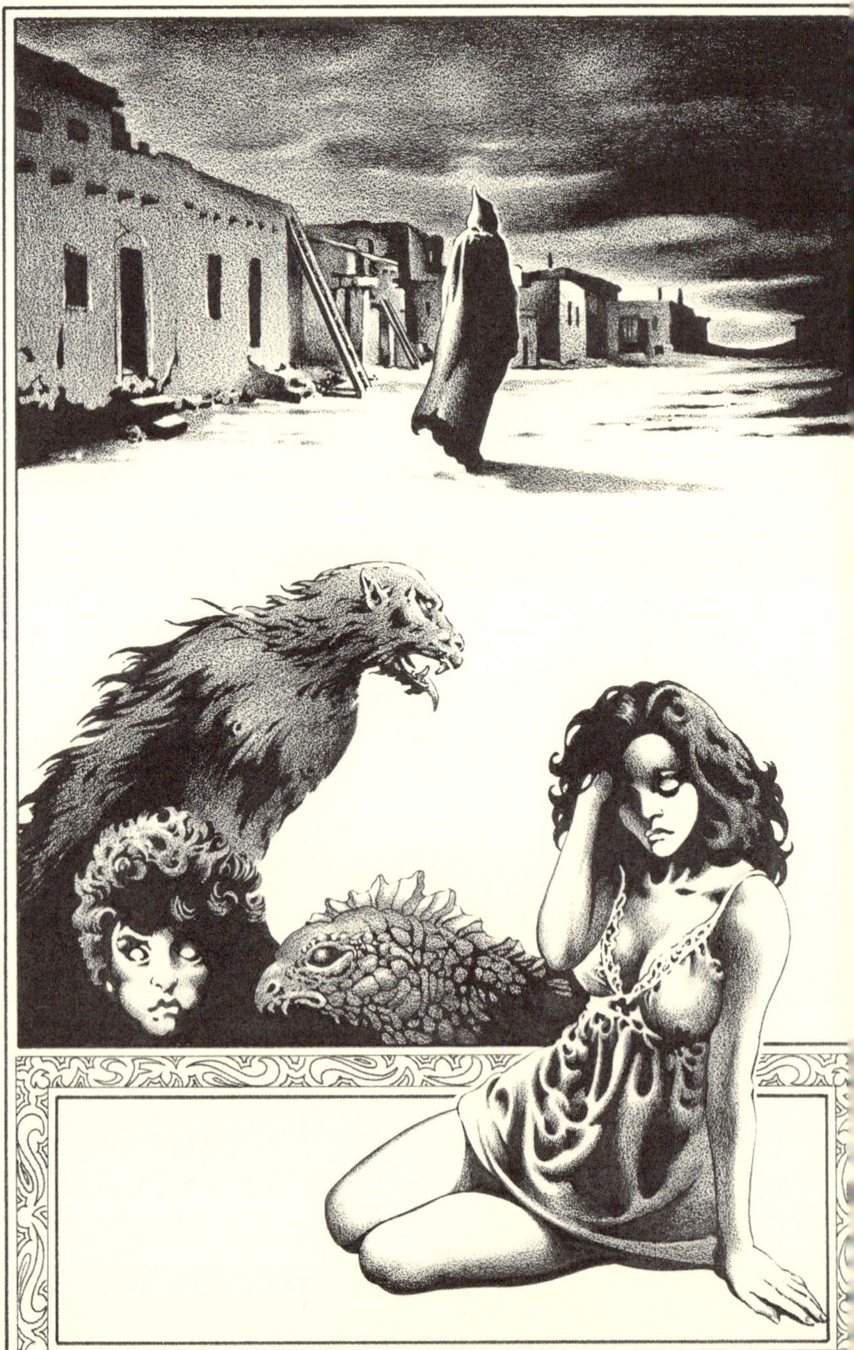

THE LAST CHILD OF MASFERIGON

written with JOHN GREGORY BETANCOURT

Throughout the long summer day, the guards on the walls of the city watched the storyteller's approach. At noon he was a dark speck on the horizon. Dust rose as he walked on the barren plain. In the evening he was a black, ragged shape against the sunset. Still a column of dust followed him. Flocks of sheep scattered at his passage. At night they lost sight of him. He walked among the squat mud buildings beyond the city's walls.

He came to a small gate left open for late travelers. Somehow, by the look on his face, the sentry there knew he was not as other storytellers. Unchallenged, the stranger passed by. He walked through the dark maze of buildings, but no hands were raised, no alarms given.

Shortly before midnight he came to a great square. He sat by a fountain in its middle. He looked at the drab, stone buildings, at the hundreds of gaudily-dressed people wandering about on this night of festival, and he knew there was almost always a celebration in this idle city. Lit by torches was a great arch commemorating the past glories of the place. It was built of black stone. The figures carved on its sides were squat and ugly, like toads.

Children pointed at the ragged stranger. Parents hushed them. Then a crowd gathered and the square was thick with people, with torches, with shadows.

When there was silence, he began his tale.

* * *

Masferigon did not create the Earth. He was a bemused elder relative of Shon Atasha, who did. But when the creation was done, the elder god walked over the lands. He swam in the oceans and made love to Aeldach, the Mother of Waters. It was not improper that he should love a river. That was the way of things, near to the beginning of time. She followed him wherever he went, her tributaries and streams watering the soil. Where he walked, forests grew, and great grasslands, and all the magical beasts Shon Atasha had created came down to the water's edge to drink.

One night Masferigon slept between two hills. The Mother of Waters circled around him, and the brown hillsides were green, the air thick with the smell of flowers. Night birds sang.

Content as he was, the god dreamed of the valley in which he rested. In his dream he saw it as the most beautiful of all the places on Earth, where winter was unknown and fruit always ripe on the vine.

The god slept with his hands closed, his fingers curled. As he dreamed, he opened his left hand, and the animals were there, large and small, stately, delicate, colored like nothing else that lived on the Earth. They scattered among the trees and underbrush of the valley.

Then Masferigon dreamed of men, more perfect of mind and body than any others, and he opened his right hand, releasing a man and a women, the first two of his children.

In the morning he rose and went out of the valley, following his beloved river.

Centuries passed. The offspring of the first couple grew numerous. They dwelt in perfect harmony with themselves, with the animals of the valley. The greater beasts did not prey upon the lesser, nor did men kill them in return.

The valley drifted through the years like a delicate ship, all the parts perfectly in place, yet with no hand to guide it.

Still the children of Masferigon multiplied, and in every generation there were those who asked, "What is beyond the valley?"

The answer was always the same: "Places less beautiful than this, and people less happy than ourselves, for they were not created by Masferigon."

Then there was born among them one whose spirit could not rest. He was not like the others. He had a name, but it is unworthy of mention.

This one was filled with pride, not simple curiosity. He wanted to know what was beyond the valley so he would be greater than his fellows. He did not ask what was out there, nor did he announce his intentions. He simply went.

Many years later, when he came back, he did not have to tell anyone where he had been. They knew by the look on his face and the strange clothing he wore.

He was filled with indignation and shame.

"We are not like other people," he said. "We are barbarians. We are little better than the animals that graze."

"How are we different?" the elders of the valley asked.

"They are mighty. They are hardened by winter. They wear the skins of beasts they have slain, even as I do now. They do not live as we do."

"How do they live?" the elders asked.

"They build great cities. They tear up the fields and sow their crops. They herd animals into pens and slaughter them. They do not regard their neighbors as we do."

"How do they regard them?"

"As potential slaves. As prey. As foes. Therefore they make war on them."

Later, the one who had been outside the valley killed the elders and made himself king.

More years passed, and the valley was transformed. Trees were cut down. Sharp plows tore up the meadows. The magical beasts of Masferigon's dreams were slaughtered, their skins made into garments, whose wearers were very proud.

A city was built, first of wood, then of stone. From out of the gates an army marched, to conquer and subdue other nations. And they were victorious more often than not.

By this time Masferigon had gotten over his romance with the river. Perhaps they had quarreled. Perhaps they had merely grown apart. In any case, the god had long since returned to Theshemna, the palace of gods in the sky, whose windows are lighted with lanterns that blend among the stars.

In an idle hour Masferigon gazed out one of those windows. He looked down on the Earth and wondered what had become of his valley. He swept down from the heavens like a falling shadow, then strode across the land.

He walked a long time to get there. The city in the valley had become the capital of a vast empire. Its roads girdled the world. Nights echoed with the tread of its tireless army.

He drifted through that great city in a wisp of fog. He saw how the people fought among themselves, how they murdered, how they amused themselves with cruel games. He looked in vain for the two hills between which he had slept. They were covered over now, bristling with battlements.

In the darkness he floated through a window, into a great hall. There he met the Emperor, who had blood on his hands from sacrificing a child. He was planning future wars by what her entrails revealed.

Masferigon appeared to him as an old man. His face glowed like a paper lantern.

"Do you not know me?" he asked.

The Emperor scowled. "You are a god. What of it? I have conquered the worshippers of many gods. I worship the greatest god of all, which is the spirit of this city, the god of might and glory."

Masferigon listened. He heard the voices of revellers in the city, and the shouts of the evening watch, repeating that all was well and the army victorious. The only other thing that moved among the rooftops was the wind. There was no spirit in the city. It was a dead place.

"Do you not remember this valley as it once was? Was it not beautiful then?"

The Emperor laughed. He threw a sacrificial dagger at the god, who vanished. Later, when he asked the soothsayers what this apparition portended, they told him the downfall of a city.

High above, drifting in a cloud, Masferigon wept. Then he was angry. Then, firm in his resolve, he lowered himself from the cloud and walked through the night again. Where his footsteps touched, where his tears fell, the ground trembled.

He sought out the Mother of Waters for consolation, but she was covered with warships, and ran thick with blood and the ashes of burning cities.

In his despair, the terrible despair and anger of a god, he came to a dark place, and opened the secret doors of the Earth, releasing all those evil things which Shon Atasha the creator had shut away. They gathered around him and even he grew pale with fear at their nearness.

"Go," he said, "and drink of the souls of that doomed city. You will find them to your liking."

They flew and hopped and slithered. They drifted like a foul mist. They entered the dreams of the people of the city, and the night was filled with shrieks of terror, with cries of madness, as fathers smothered their children, as husbands strangled their wives. The dark spirits crouched in corners, on windowsills, on bedposts. They drank deep. They feasted on souls.

In the morning they returned to Masferigon, like dogs to their master.

"Do any remain alive?" he asked.

"Yes, but we are sated." They looked up at him, their eyes dull.

"Return when you are hungry again."

The following night they fell upon the dazed survivors in the dark streets, upon the refugees in the roads. Screams filled the night.

"Do any remain?" he asked them, when they gathered in a cavern to hide from the sunrise.

"There is only the Emperor, whose magic is powerful. He sleeps alone in a locked room. He does not dream."

Masferigon went with them on the third night. He raised up the sacrificed child from her grave. He caused her to walk, naked, mud-smeared, her entrails hanging out, to the Emperor's golden door. She pounded on it with her fists.

"Great Lord," she cried with her dead voice. "Open the door. I have come to foretell the future."

The Emperor opened his door. He saw the corpse standing there, and beyond, in the darkness, thousands of hideous leering faces. Among them stood Masferigon.

"Do you not know me?" the god asked him.

The Emperor screamed.

Later, Masferigon wandered alone through the empty city. He wept. He began to regret what he had done. He wished he might find some survivor to instruct, to start again on the way to contentment. He prayed to the other gods, to Shon Atasha, the most powerful of all.

His prayer was answered. He was moved to search every house

until, at last, he found two boys locked in a foul shed. They were twin brothers, hidden away because their parents thought them idiots. Indeed, one had no mind left. He had never dreamed as other people do. Therefore the dark spirits had not recognized him, and had spared him.

He stood in the sunlight, his mouth slack, his eyes rolling. Masferigon changed him into a kind of animal and set him to guard the empty city forever.

The other brother was filled with visions. He saw so many things that when he tried to speak of them, his words came out in a confused babble. His dreams were so beautiful that even the dark spirits had drawn away from him.

He stood in the sunlight, blinking, his face filled with rapture. He recognized Masferigon. He had dreamed of the valley, even as the god had.

Masferigon straightened the boy's speech, and sent him out into the world as a storyteller, to describe the beauty of the valley and tell how it had been lost.

Then the god lay down in the empty city, sleeping a sleep close to death. He did not dream, but merely waited, as he waits now, for the last age of mankind, when his valley will be as it once was.

* * *

His tale done, the storyteller waited while a few copper coins were tossed on his cloak. The crowd began to drift away.

"Is this all my story is worth?" he asked in a quiet voice.

There was a moment of silence. Then a couple more coins clinked in front of him.

"We like stories of heroes and great battles," one man said. "Tell us one of those and maybe some silver will fall, if the tale is well-wrought."

"No," said the storyteller. "I only know one tale. I have told it. I leave it with you as a warning."

Then he was gone in the blinking of an eye, like a burst bubble. A woman cried out in alarm, but was hushed. The people stood still and silent for a long time.

The storyteller and his cloak had vanished. All that remained were the copper coins, dark against the pavement.

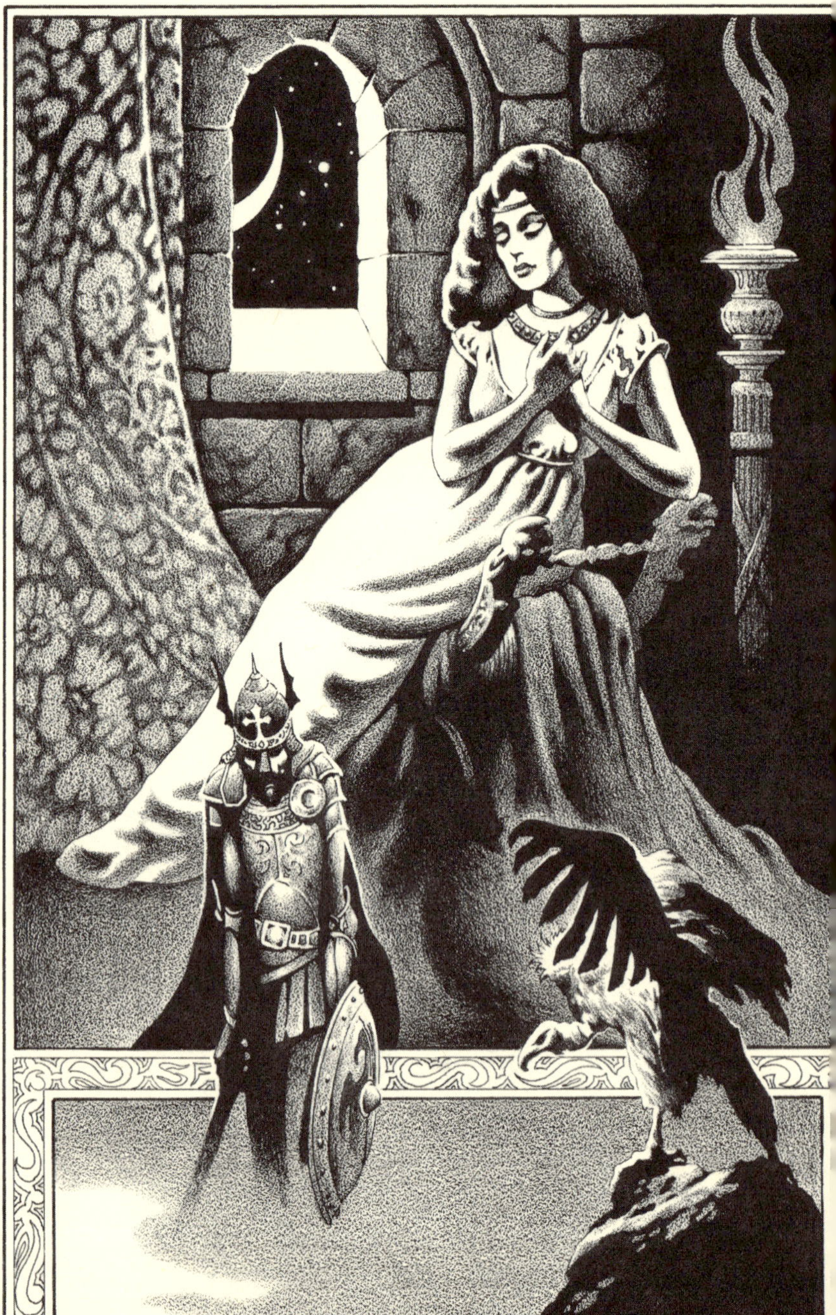

A VISION OF REMBATHENE

It is late at night, the feasting long over. Guttering torchlights swim in a haze of stale incense. The ghosts of ancient heroes, like shadows, stir in the corners, behind the limp hanging draperies and begin to move about as darkness creeps upon the exhausted court.

Amidst the revellers the King raises his head, and looks wearily over all. The Queen by his side whispers something into his ear, and he calls out to one on whom his eyes have come to rest, saying, "Tell me now of the cities of your dreams, that I too may behold them when I sleep."

The storyteller replies, "Of which, O King?"

"Of Rembathene."

"Ah Rembathene! Rembathene! Of all the cities revealed to me thou art the fairest! Rembathene, thy towers catch the dawn glow before even the mountain peaks the gods have wrought. Ah glorious Rembathene, a diamond with a thousand thousand facets, not built, but grown like some strange tree from that single pebble called The Soul of the Earth. Rembathene, all the Worlds envied thee!"

It was in Rembathene that Anahai the young king sat, on a throne of the East Wind carven, of night air frozen into a solid thing by magic and ancient rite, and shaped in secret beneath a broad moon of old, when they who first conceived Rembathene came out of the East armed with the sword. On this seat of his forebears he sat, brooding for the first time in the six months of his reign, the days of which before had dawned on nothing but peace and contentment, the enemies of his people having been subdued long before the birth of any man yet alive. Perhaps it was the very grace of his reign, and the splendor of his realm, that had brought him woe, for a pestilence had descended upon Rembathene, of the sort that a petty god sends when he is jealous.

By these signs was it known: First, a chill, such as one might feel when a window is left open in the evening, then a fever following, very slight, still not cause for alarm. But after that the suffering was swift and terrible. The afflicted one would awaken one morning covered with sores and welts, as if he had been flogged; blood would stream from every pore, and from his nose and ears; and he would go mad. In the end the flesh would decay while yet animate, and that which had once been a man would claw putrid chunks from itself as long as hands remained, and only after long hours of howling and writhing find relief at last in death. When a person was so stricken, all those around him would flee, for touch, or even nearness to such a one, would mean contamination, and a similar fate within days. So the people of Rembathene and the lands around fled in all directions, into the city and out of it, from villages and towns into the fields, and from the fields into villages and towns. They trampled the crops they had planted. They clogged the roads. Many were crushed in the great arch of Rembathene which had been built for triumphant armies. And all this was to no avail, for when one of their number screamed and fell they could only turn in another direction, often back the way they had come. The subtlety of the plague was that in any crowd there were always a few who were already infected but did not know it yet, so that Doom walked always as a silent companion among the refugees.

This young King, who knew himself to be the father of his people, who was willing to supplicate whatever god was angered and to sacrifice himself if need be, who had never truly proven to the people by effort that he was their king, listened helplessly to the reports brought to him, and watched much from his high windows. He felt in his heart the misery of the citizens of Rembathene.

He asked first of his Physician, "What cause?"

And the Physician answered, "Lord, it is not known. Many and marvellous are the secrets of creation, and marvel enough would it be if a cure were to come to us, or some mitigation of our suffering. To know the cause is to ask too much."

He turned then to his Master of Leechcraft, saying, "Has your art been tried, to draw out the evil humors?"

"Aye, Majesty, and there are fewer of my brothers than there were before."

And to his Magician he said, "And magic?"

"Magic has been tried, O King, and there are today fewer magicians in the land than there are physicians or leeches."

Anahai ran his fingers nervously through his beard——it was not much, for his years were few —— and the learned men stood impotent and afraid before him, and silence ruled in the room, until one spoke whose voice had not been heard before, an ancient who was not learned but wise, who had given up his name because he was so holy. All faced this revered one as he rose from where he had been seated, his black robe draped over him like a shroud, his polished ebony staff glistening like a living serpent.

"Most noble King," said he, "the cause of Rembathene's sorrow is not an imbalance of earthly humors, or a magical curse laid on the land by some enemy, or even the anger of a god, but this: beyond the world's rim there sits a Guardian with the Book of Earth in his lap, and this Guardian has fallen asleep with the Book open in his lap to the page of Rembathene; while he sleeps the spirit Nemesis has crept close, whispering 'Death, death, death' into the book."

"Then the Guardian must be awakened. How can this be done? What god shall I pray to?"

"There is one god only who can help you, one who is greater than all the gods of Earth. The God of Mysteries alone has power over the rim and beyond."

"He is not one to whom I sacrifice each day," said the King, puzzled. "Tell me of this god."

"Lord, there is little to say, for little is known. He resides in his tower, apart from the other gods, who are to him as ants to a great beast. He brushes them aside with a wave of his hand. His name cannot be known. His face cannot be seen. Perhaps he is not a god at all, but Fate or Chance, or some other force not yet imagined, for his ways are mysterious and hidden from men."

"But how was he carven then, for surely his image was carven?"

The nameless man paused, then looked at the others about him and said, "This is a secret only the King may know."

The physician, the leech, the magician, and all the others were sent away, even the two massive eunuchs who stood perpetually on either side of the throne. Then when they were alone, the holy one continued.

"Know, O King, that of old a carver in Rembathene was touched by a madness, and his slaves took him to the top of the highest tower in the city, and they gave him his tools, and stone to work with, and they drew a curtain around him. For a month he carved, as the moon waxed and waned, and when the moon was gone he shrieked horribly, and staggered out, his face ashen and wide, and when his slaves beheld him they knew their duty, and slew him. They touched not the curtain, and none shall, until the ending of time, when one shall tear it back, look on the face of the God of Mysteries, and bring non-existence to all things."

"But if we cannot see his face, how can we know his nature? Is he cruel or kind? We cannot know if he mocks us."

"Even so, O King, for his ways are hidden from men."

"Still I must go to him. Where is his tower?"

"From a distance, it is seen by many. Close by, by a very few. Its base I touched for the first time in the fiftieth year of my contemplation, and I have gone there many times since. I can take another with me, for I have gained this strength.

At sunset, when the way he was to walk had been purified as far as ordinary men could follow it, King Anahai went with his guide through the streets of Rembathene, until they took a turn no others could take, and the city grew dim around them. They came at last to a tower glimpsed often by travellers who look back on Rembathene against the western sky, but seldom discerned by anyone else, and the King alone entered. He climbed a stairway of a hundred spirals, looking out windows at each turn, and saw the dark and quiet rooftops sink away below him: saw the sun burning low and golden, the purple on the horizon; and at last, when he neared the top, the stars appeared, seemingly below and round him, as if he had left the earth altogether.

He came finally to a room at the top of the tower, which the old man had described to him, wherein resided the god he sought. It was dark in there, dimly lit by tapers and without windows. The air was heavy with incense and dust and the stench of slaughtered offerings, making the place very holy. At the far end lay the crumbling skeleton of the mad carver, whose remains had never been touched, and beyond them was a curtain.

The King prostrated himself before the curtain, but presented no sacrifice, for when a ruler seeks rescue for his people from a god, the only thing he may offer is himself. Thus he rose empty handed to his knees and spoke humbly to the god, telling how the folk of his country had suffered, and begging that some cure to the disease be revealed.

Whatever was behind the curtain remained still. Anahai remained on his knees for many hours until his legs were numb, and still no answer came. He wanted very much to leave, but dared not, fearing the anger of the god, and hoping that the god was only thinking, and about to speak. Also he knew that if he were to leave, and return to his people without some solution, there would be no hope at all, and he would have failed in his duty. Kings who fail, he had always been taught, are seen in the corner of the eye as dim shapes which vanish when gazed upon directly. They are phantoms, wisps of smoke, sounds in the forest when no ear listens, unworthy to walk either on the earth or under the earth in the land of the dead.

The musty air made his eyes and his whole body heavy. He first sat back on his ankles, then brought his feet out from under him after a while and sat cross-legged. Later he slumped to the floor, asleep.

A dream came to him. He saw himself asleep in the tower, on the floor before the black curtain. Suddenly a wind blew the drape back, against the god, and there was a hint of an outline, a form hunched and powerful, and a face not at all like that of a man. The figure on the floor screamed and thrashed about, yet there was no sound, and the spirit of Anahai, oddly detached and floating in the air overhead, knew that there was cause for terror, yet felt nothing. The body did not wake, and the dream continued. The lips of the idol moved and formed words silently, and in silence the body of the King got up and left the room. The spirit followed it down the hundred turns of the stair, into the city over which a heavy mist had fallen, through streets of looming, grey shapes, and out into the fields. Leagues passed, and at last a forest rose ahead, drenched in the fog so that the trees stood like dim Titans in the night. Led by a will not his own the King's body and awareness walked among them for a long way, somehow sure of the path no eye could make out.

Suddenly something before him moved, a shadow detaching itself from the general gloom to become a man.

"You!" cried the King. "Who are you?" As he spoke he awoke, and heard his voice echoing down the towers, "areyouareyouareyou..."

He was disoriented for a moment, but then he knew that the god had answered. He prostrated himself once more, in thanksgiving this time, before the curtain which was unruffled, and behind which no shape was visible, and he left the room. He looked out the first window he came to and saw that there was indeed a mist over the city, as he had dreamed, lapping against the towers like the silent waves of some magically conjured sea.

It was still the middle of the night. He was met in the darkness at the door of the tower by the holy man without a name, and with him he went through the faint, strangely turning streets until they emerged onto the pavement on which all men may walk. They went wordlessly back to the palace, where the King was met by his physician, his leech, and his wizard.

"Majesty, is it well?"

"I am sent to another place."

"Then go as a king must go, resplendent in your robes, with crown on your head and sword at your side, riding your finest stallion, with a troop of royal guards at your back."

And he did all these things, and rode out of the main gate of Rembathene, called the Mouth of the City, with his cavalry behind him, and his magician, his leech, and his physician at his side. Also with him was the old man of mystical learning, who spoke to the king in strange signs, and in whispers none of the others could hear.

When they were more than a mile beyond the town, the mist had swallowed all the towers. Anahai turned to the horsemen and said, "I need you no longer," and sent them away, and the old man nodded.

After another mile he sent away the three who had advised him, saying to them also, "I need you no longer."

And when he came to the end of the wood he had seen in his dream he said to the wise man, "I need you no more either. From here I must go alone."

The one holy, beyond naming, smiled. The King paused a second, unsure of himself, and spoke once more.

"Know you to whom I am sent, or what price shall be asked?"

"No one knows that, save He who will not reveal it. He may have no price, or the world may be his price. He may jest and give forth nothing."

"Then goodbye," the King said, and he dismounted, handed the reins of his horse to the other, and walked into the forest. His purple cloak, his red leggings, and his golden armor and crown seemed grey in the depths of the fog. He turned and looked back once and saw only an empty field. Far off he thought he heard hoofbeats on the muddy ground, then all was silent.

He entered the forest, and the mist hung over him like a damp blanket, and his steps were directed, as they had been in the dream. The trees loomed over him, and vanished in the darkness above.

Then suddenly, as had been foretold, he met a stranger. One shadow detached itself from the rest and became a tall, thin man of fierce, weatherworn features, dressed in a cape the color of the fog, and a tall peaked hat. His sudden motion startled the King.

"Who are you?" Again his voice echoed, but this time he did not wake.

The other did not answer, but stood again motionless, as if he were some strange and twisted tree that had seemed by some sorcery of mist and night to be momentarily alive.

"I am sent to you," said the King. "It has been revealed that I should meet you here by one who sits behind a curtain in the tower few can reach."

At that the stranger seemed to recognize him, and still not speaking, he motioned for the King to follow. Deeper into the woods they went, along a winding way the other knew. The stranger's cape hid him until at times Anahai feared he was alone, and lost, only to hear once more the soft, steady footsteps receding in front of him.

After a while the ground began to slope upward and the trees thinned out a little. They came to a gorge in which grey-black clouds broiled. A dwarf with a long spear challenged them with a savage yell, but the one who was leading cast a jewel as big as a fist over the head of the little man and into the pit. There was an explosion like the wrath of an angry god, and a bridge of ancient wood appeared. They crossed, and when they set foot on the other side, the bridge vanished.

The trees got shorter and shorter, became gnarled and stunted little shrubs, then gave way to grass and moss, then to bare rock. The two climbed up precarious slopes, the fog clinging around them, as if the mountain wore it like a night-shirt. At last they came to the summit, and to a tiny hut. Inside was a bare table and two chairs. The stranger ushered the King in and motioned for him to sit.

Anahai looked around at the bareness of the dwelling.

"There is a pestilence in the land," he said doubtfully, "and I will give you anything you desire if——"

A long, flat box was placed on the table.

"Play this game with me."

Anahai nodded, and regretted he had spoken rashly. He knew to wait, to expect but not to ask, and hope that what he had requested of the God of Mysteries would be granted.

Inside the box was a notched board painted in black and white squares, and some glowing balls. With these they played a game, the King keeping his balls on the white squares and the other keeping his on the black. When those of one were surrounded by those of the other, they were taken, and when the stranger captured one he placed it in his palm, and the light of it would go out, leaving it a dull brown. But when Anahai took one it would glow all the brighter. He won some and he lost some. Over this game the man in the grey cape showed emotion, gloating as he hoarded each new acquisition, scowling each time Anahai made one brighter. For a time the King feared he would not win, and played on with the resignation of a general fighting a hopeless battle in which he cannot surrender, but then the tide turned, and the room glowed with his winnings which he piled on one side of the table. It seemed to go on forever. Sometimes he felt as if he were asleep, and the motions of his hands were being made by the hands, independent of his will, and at times his mind was very clear, and he schemed and made strategies and practised diversions.

At last dawn came. The sun began to melt through the uppermost mist, and the gloom inside the hut was somewhat lessened. For the first time Anahai saw that there was a window. Through it he could see the dull orange glow of the morning, diffused in the fog.

He felt confused, exhausted, irritated at having spent the whole night doing this meaningless thing.

"What happens now?"

The other spoke for the second time. His voice was deep and hollow, as if coming from far away, from beyond the form that stood before Anahai.

"You have won. You hold more worlds than I."

"Will you then drive the pestilence away, if this is within your power?"

"Do? It shall be done! It is done! Know! Recognize! See, as was randomly pre-ordained!"

"See what? Recognize what?" The King's bewilderment was now mixed with terror.

The other made a sweeping gesture with his arms, his cloak flapping out like wings. He went to a corner, picked up two things, threw the door of the hut open and stood silhouetted, the rising sun behind him.

He smiled. For the first time Anahai noticed he had a long white beard.

"Do you not know me?"

And there in the doorway, with his scythe in one hand, his hourglass in the other, and his satchel of Years slung over his shoulder, the young King knew him.

In the middle of a day measured variously according to various calendars, one dressed in rich but ragged garments wandered into a village. He called all the people around him, and some came, while others went on about their business, and when they would not bow before him he grew angry, saying, "I am your king! I am your king!" And he mentioned certain names, and the people laughed, and went away. He stood alone in their square until a very old woman came up to him and said she had heard those names before in tales told to her long ago, but that the place he spoke of had passed away ten times ten generations ago.

And on hearing this King Anahai began to weep, for he knew how his request had been fulfilled and who had done it, and he knew the answers to all the questions that had come into his head that morning, when he descended the mountain and found himself in a strange country. Somewhere the God of Mysteries was laughing perhaps, or perhaps not. Perhaps things could not have turned out any differently.

Time had driven the pestilence out of Rembathene.

JUNGLE EYES

His father had been screaming for some time. There were already tears on his mother's face when Peter sat down to dinner. He was eleven years old that summer, and he couldn't understand what his parents were fighting about. The rage in both of them built up as inexorably, as invisibly, as a storm in a night sky. He could only sit there helplessly, glancing from one parent to the other, trying to pretend nothing was happening.

But it had always been like this, as long as he could remember.

"Please," he said finally. "Please stop it."

"Shut up, you little shit!" his father snapped.

"**You** shut up, will you?" his mother said. "That's no way to talk in front of your son."

"I'll talk however I want," his father said, completely ignoring him now, all attention directed back to his mother. "Goddamned little shit!" He pounded the table with his fist, knocking over Peter's glass. For an endless silent instant, milk poured onto the floor.

"You bastard!" his mother screamed.

"It's my goddamned house——"

"That's about as much of you as I can take!"

"——and I'll talk any way I goddamned want."

Peter couldn't think of anything to say. He only wanted to make them stop hurting each other, but he didn't know how.

With a sigh his father fell silent and sat back in his chair, sweat glistening on his face.

"Peter, you'd better go to your room," his mother said.

He went, taking his plate with his hamburger and french fries, trying very hard not to cry in front of his parents. When he was upstairs, the door to his room closed behind him, he could still hear every word they said. Before long they were both screaming again.

He ate a few of the french fries, but he suddenly wasn't very hungry and left the hamburger on the windowsill. He stretched out on his bed, paging through an already familiar issue of **Jungle Man Comics,** his favorite. He tried to read it again, but couldn't keep his attention on it. Putting the comic aside, he turned out the light. In the darkness, his tears began to come.

And then the growl came from the window.

He looked up. A sleek, dark shape moved there. Two eyes blinked, stared. Yellow eyes with vertical slits in them.

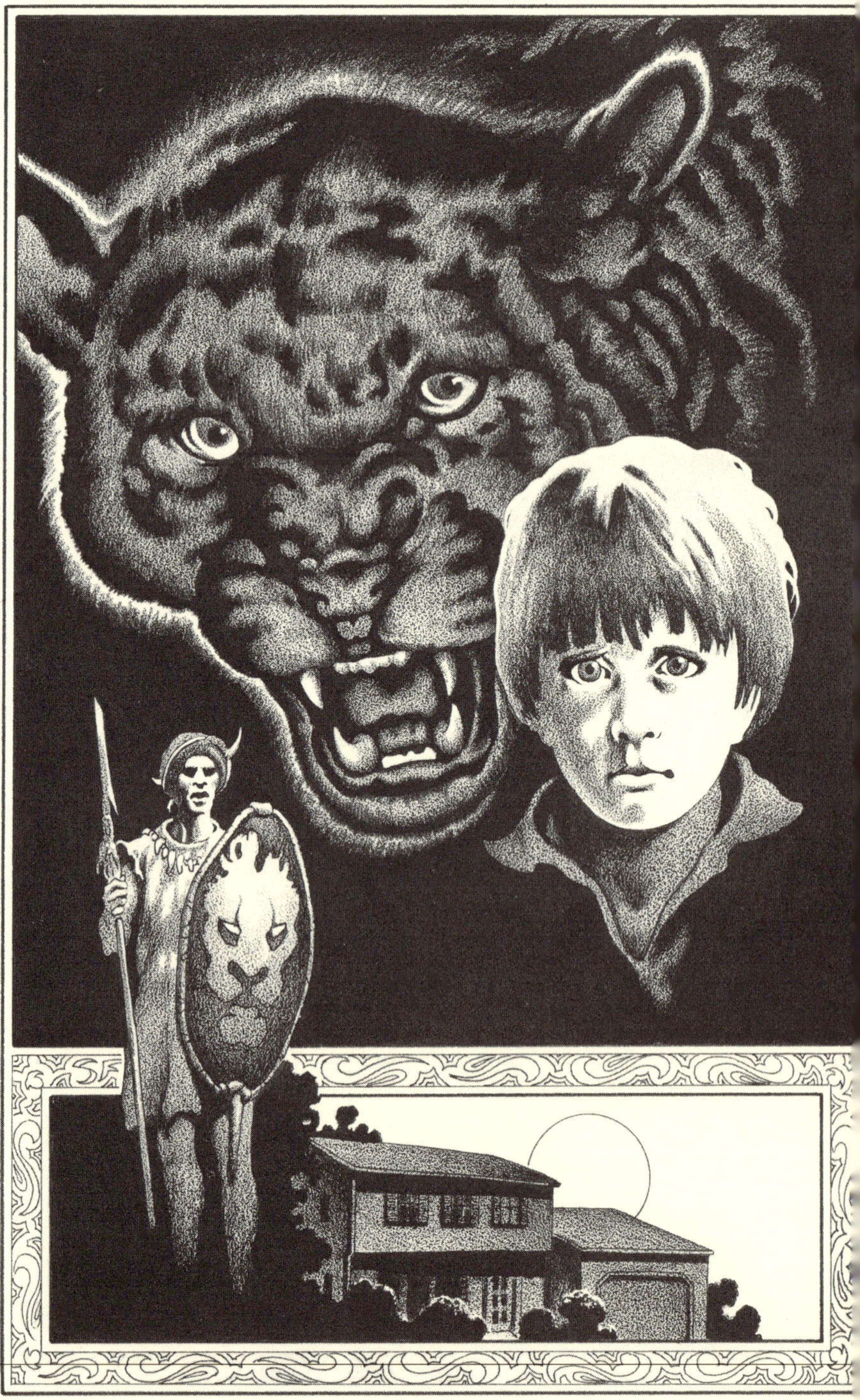

A pink mouth flashed open, exposing fangs.

It was Dkima, the Black Leopard. Peter knew him. Dkima was Jungle Man's messenger. He had come many times.

Down below, they were still screaming. Dishes crashed.

Suddenly the boy was alone in his room. The windowsill was empty. There was only the wind, ruffling the pages of the comic book.

"Wait," he whispered. "Don't go without me."

He went over to the window, raised the screen, and looked out. The night was dark and moonless, the stars clear, unwavering. The lighted windows of neighboring houses stared back at him like the eyes of jungle animals.

"Don't go."

There was a branch he could reach from the window. He leaned out, grabbed it, then swung himself free of the house. Once, in a happier time, his father had applauded his climbing and said he was part monkey.

Another dish broke. His mother was sobbing.

The tree had two trunks. He worked his way around to the farther one before climbing down, careful not to scrape branches against the side of the house.

He dropped to the ground, landing in a crouch, falling over backward. He sat there at the base of the tree, listening. The words were unintelligible now, but both voices sounded hurt, furious.

He turned and looked around him, seeing clearly now with **anoupa**, the secret jungle vision, something Jungle Man taught to all his followers. He saw the towering vine-laden trees of the tropic forest, and the eyes, the luminous eyes, all around, unblinking. Birds shrieked in the branches. Far away a lion roared.

He couldn't see Dkima, but in the jungle, in the night, nobody could. The Messenger moved swiftly, soundlessly, only his eyes visible among the many others, in the endless jungle.

Peter got up and scurried across the yard to where the bushes began, then got down on hands and knees and crawled where grown-ups could never follow, through a familiar tunnel of curving branches, along the old white fence, behind the tangled masses of raspberry and honeysuckle.

He came face to face with an owl, swaying on a thin branch. It blinked, screeched, and took off, its wings whirring, a grey blur swooping low across the lawn.

Still the voices came from the house. They were only tones now.

The eyes were all around him. The dark, hunched shapes of animals paced back and forth, stalking one another beneath the lofty trees.

Where the fence came to a corner, he had dug a hole, long ago, when he was eight. He could still crawl through, under the fence.

Beyond was a vacant lot, high with weeds, where elephants

stood asleep like black mountains, their ears gently flapping in the breeze. Grasses swayed. He moved slowly, briars catching his pants. Thistles rattled together.

When he came to his fort, the leopard was waiting, seated by the entrance, unblinking. His fort was an apple tree, bent horizontal by a storm, overgrown with vines. He had spent long hours weaving sticks and more vines into the walls of the enclosure beneath the tree.

He pulled aside the vines and crawled inside. The dirt floor was bare and dry. He could see out through the walls. He could see the stars and the thousand eyes, but no one could see in. No one could see him.

It was his favorite place. Sometimes he sat there on summer afternoons with his comic books. Sometimes he crouched around a dying campfire with his faithful band of Ugombu warriors, as they plotted the hunt of the antelopes that grazed in the grassy fields. The leopard would walk among them, growling, licking its fangs.

Now, in the darkness, he could barely see their faces, their feathered headdresses, their wide eyes. They had been waiting for him. They knew why he had come. He tried to be brave, to hold back his tears.

The wind rattled the walls of the fort.

"Have courage, Little Hunter," one of them said softly.

"I will."

He spat in the dirt and began to trace signs with his finger. The Ugombus watched, fascinated. They knew that he alone shared the deepest secrets of Jungle Man —— and that he would only resort to them when he needed one thing more than anything else in the world.

When the magic figure was complete, he spat again, giving it life. He spoke the magic words. The warriors covered their ears and averted their eyes. Then all of them waited, listening to the wind, which sometimes, even yet, brought the shrill, garbled sounds of voices raised in anger.

Then there was a tall man crouching in front of him, stooped beneath the low ceiling of vines.

The boy gazed intently at the newcomer, at the wide red eyes set in a long, dark face. The man wore a bone in his hair, a necklace of teeth over his rawhide cloak, an ivory pin in one nostril. He carried a long, broad-headed spear, holding it just below the head. The shaft stuck out through the vines. On his shield was painted the skull of a lion.

Even Jungle Man called on this one only in times of greatest danger.

"Young Hunter," the man said, in a deep, soft voice, whispering like the wind, "I am he who walks in the great forest by night. Even the lion is silent at my passing. The bravest warriors tremble when I am near. The spirit of **Umjala**, the jungle itself, is within my heart. It is swifter than the cheetah, mightier than the elephant, more cunning than the snake. I know why you have summoned me. Shall I do what I alone can do? Shall I bring silence to the place of discord?"

"Yes," the boy said. "Help me."

The other was gone. Peter broke into a sweat, filled with anticipation, with joy and terror.

He looked out through the vines, and a minute later saw the lights of the house going out, not one by one as if someone were flicking switches, but slowly and all at once, as if a huge cloak were being draped over everything. Then the helpless, hopeless dread came back. He started to cry.

"**No**!" he shouted. "I didn't understand! I——"

He looked around for his Ugombu warriors. The fort was empty. Only the black leopard sat in the doorway, yawning, its teeth gleaming. He crawled past it, scrambling through the bushes. He ran onto the lawn.

"No! Wait! I was only trying to help! Please... don't hurt them...."

The owl hooted from a bush at the other end of the yard, then stopped. There was only silence, and the boy stood shivering in the night that was suddenly cold; and the house was completely dark; and the eyes, the jungle eyes, and the hunched, swift shapes were all around him.

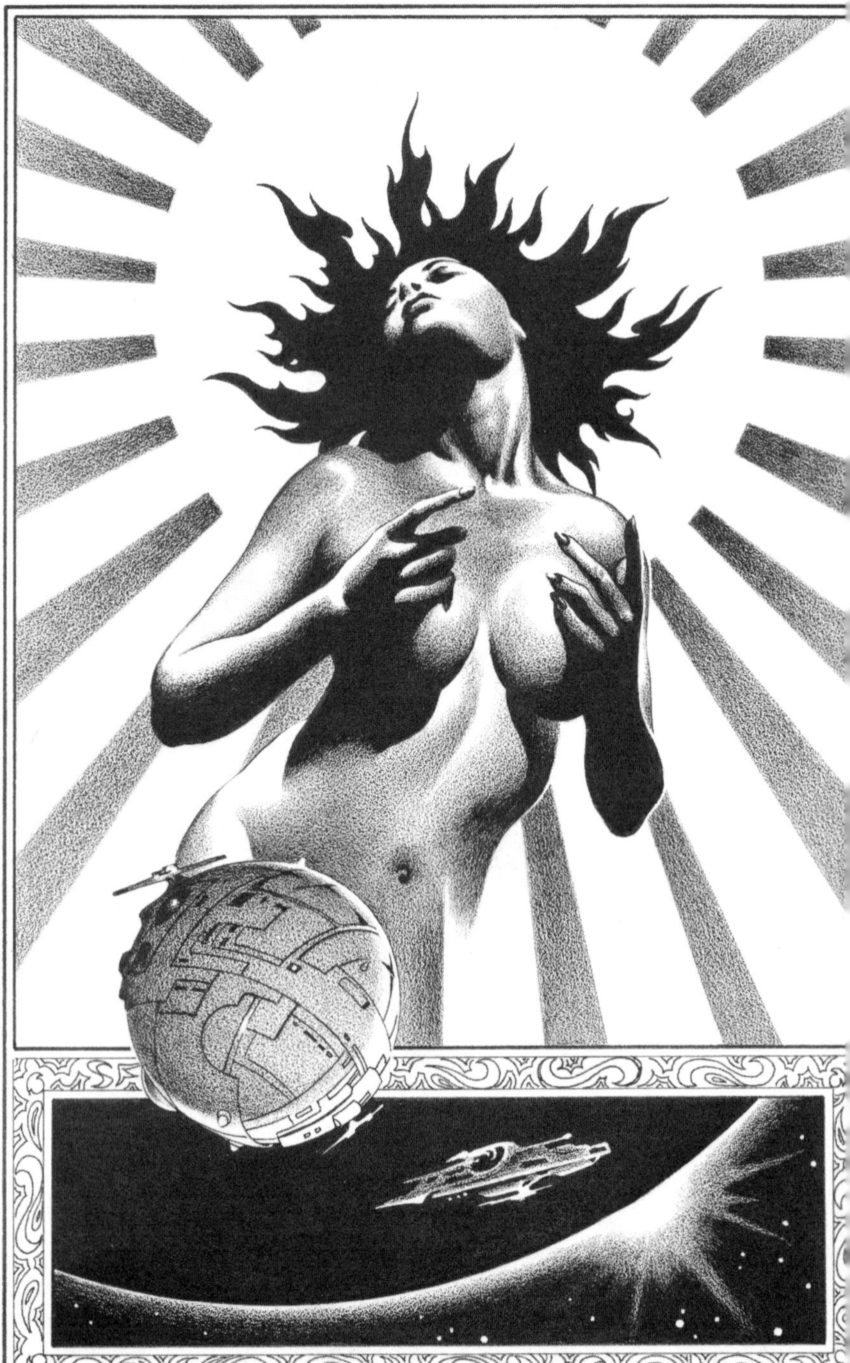

SUNRISE

In the last days, the star watcher dwelt in a tumbling metal sphere somewhere beyond the orbit of Mars, walking to and fro and up and down in it, around and around the circular corridors of his little world, gazing out ports, looking at viewscreens, jotting down readings from instruments, and even, absurd as it might have been, transmitting his findings back to Earth, even though no one would ever receive them.

Sometimes he dreamed. Once his fancy told him that the Lagoon Nebula was really a lagoon, and he a dark fish swimming in the deep, rich sea of space, splashing a froth of stars.

Another time he dreamed that he was lying on his back in the middle of a grassy plain, and that he had always been there and always would remain, the grass growing in and out of him as if he were some inscrutable mound raised by a forgotten builder. Out of his mouth, a red flower bloomed.

But all of that was impossible, since all life had been burned away from the Earth in the last days, when the sun, like mad and greedy Kronos, began to devour its children.

The star watcher's radio hummed like a swarm of bees in the springtime.

And he walked his curving corridors, performing his routines, dreaming his dreams, because like the sun, and like Kronos when he devoured the gods, the star watcher was mad. When the human race was dead, when it was obvious that he would not live much longer, his inner mind decreed the madness, banishing the news, barricading him against terror and despair.

He no longer had a name.

And there was no time. He would not acknowledge time. He was suspended between the instants. Perhaps the last days were not days at all, but hours, or even minutes.

* * *

Once, walking to and fro in his little world and up and down in it, he came to the central chamber, the innermost sphere within the sphere. There was no gravity there. He floated.

Before him, standing in the middle of the air, was one like a man, or perhaps a boy, clad in a glistening black gown, with dark, satiny wings spread wide from his shoulders. His smooth, pale face was calm.

"I know you," said the madman. "You have always been at my side. I have been expecting you. You are the Angel of Death."

"You are the last. I have come for you."

"Wait."

"You are the very last. Have I not waited long enough?"

"No. I am not ready."

There was silence in the space station, and presumably in heaven, for what might have been half an hour, had anyone been counting.

"Are you ready now?"

"No."

"Enough of this. You are the last. Come."

"Please! Wait!"

"I am not accustomed to waiting."

"What if there is someone else somewhere, someone you don't know about?"

"Then you would get a reprieve."

"Yes! That's it. There is another. Please, God, let there be another!"

The angel smiled. "What would you do with your extra time? Something worthwhile, I would hope."

"I don't... know...."

"Then I give you this charge. Learn the value of truth. Discover how you came to be what you are."

"You mean you'll——"

Even as the star watcher spoke, there came a voice through the intercom, almost lost in static, but still distinct.

"**Is anybody there? Please, come in. Do you read me? Over.**"

The angel smiled again, raised a hand, and vanished, like light being cut off when a door is closed.

* * *

The madman came to awareness floating alone in the central chamber. He was slightly less mad, peeking out of his insanity like a turtle cautiously coming out of its shell. His reason asked: Did any of this happen? The angel? The sun going nova? The voice?

He shook his head to clear it.

The voice came again. Now he could tell that the speaker was a woman, and she was frightened.

He made his way to a control console. On the curving bulkhead of the chamber there was a faint tug of gravity, enough for him to squat there. He made some adjustments, shutting out much of the static.

"Can you read me? Is anyone listening?" Now the voice had an individual quality. It was no longer the abstract archetype, Voice.

"I read you," he said into his transmitter, and the signal leapt sunward, and there was silence in heaven for another five minutes while it got where it was going, and yet another five for the reply to come back.

"Hello? Thank God someone is left!"

Ten minutes.

"Yes, there is. What can I do for you?"

"**What can you do?** You can save me. I don't want to die. Now that you're there, I don't have to."

Ten minutes.

"Yes you do," he said. "It is very essential that you do die."

Ten minutes.

"Did I read you... correctly? Are you crazy or something?"

"Madame, I fear that you are correct. I am indeed crazy. Furthermore, I have been talking with the Angel of Death. He explained the situation to me. Additionally, as the time lag between our signals would have indicated if you were thinking rationally, I am much too far away to reach you, even if I did have a shuttle craft here, which I do not."

Ten minutes later she was screaming.

Somehow the sound pushed his madness away a bit more. He could picture this strange, faceless woman, alone out there somewhere, resigned to death. Then suddenly her hope was rekindled, only to be snuffed out all the more cruelly. He wept for her. Finally he was able to speak.

"Try to be calm. Don't think about me. Perhaps if you talk about yourself, that will help."

Ten minutes.

"This is **all** crazy, so what does it matter? Gloria Bain. My name is Gloria Bain. I am——I was——a trainee. Commercial pilot. Earth-moon run. I'm in a training capsule, behind the Moon. I can't see Earth, or the sun. The moon was full to them down there. Think how bright it must have been that last night, before... I have half an orbit left. I'm still shielded by the Moon. When I come around the other side..."

Ten minutes.

"Can you land your vehicle? Perhaps a crater, or a cave——if you went underground."

"No good. It was a rendezvous and docking exercise. They were going to send someone up to meet me. But just after the launch someone was yelling over the radio that the sun had exploded, and then there was only noise. I guess it happened a lot faster than the astronomers ever thought it would. It wouldn't help if I landed anyway. My air wouldn't last. And if it did, well the Earth and Moon will be vapor before long, I imagine."

He visualized her, even more alone in her tiny silver speck against the dark face of the moon ringed with the corona of the mad sun.

"Can't you just turn around, stay behind the Moon?"

"Jesus Christ, you know better than that! Look, don't try to cheer me up with nonsense, huh? Everybody's dead except you and me. I'll die soon. You'll die a little later. That's the honest truth. I lost control back there for a while, but I can take it, so leave me alone, okay? Bug off, whoever you are."

More than ten minutes passed.

"The truth...?"

Ten minutes.

"That's right. You read me correctly. The truth."

Ten minutes. He thought of one name, then another.

"My name is Johan. Johan Faustus. You can call me John."

Another long pause.

"Very good. The way things are going, John, I almost believe you. About talking with the Angel of Death. Did you smear blood on the airlock, or just hand over your soul? Isn't something mixed up here? Look... John.... I'm sorry I yelled at you. If you're all I've got, and I'm all you've got, can't we at least be friends."

Ten minutes.

"Yes, we can be friends. Can you transmit a picture of yourself?"

Ten minutes.

"Negative. I don't have video transmission. No need for it in this bucket of bolts. I guess we'll be friends without seeing each other. Like pen pals. Let's talk."

He didn't know what to say.

"All right," she said twenty minutes later, "I'll tell you about myself. I was born in Kansas, and if you think every little girl in Kansas is named Dorothy and has a dog and gets carried off over the rainbow, you got another think coming, buster. But here I am, over the rainbow. Isn't that funny? Not quite. When I was little I wanted to be a singer, but then my father took me up in a crop dusting plane, and I knew what I wanted to do. I did. Airbreathers. Intercontinentals, but still airbreathers. I met a wonderful man. His name was John too, like you. We were married. It was hard because we both flew, and only saw each other on weekends. He flew the Earth-Moon bus, which made me feel unimportant. But he was killed in the disaster in '08. So after a while I tried to fill his shoes for him. I think I wanted to get the best of what had killed him. Now look where I am. That's all in the past, I used to tell myself, but what have we got left except the past. Hey John, you there? Over."

The madman examined his own past, and his madness left him like a cloak, dropping to the floor, but at the same time he was aware of losing it, and just now it was his most precious possession. He held on tight. More than anything else, he wanted to share it with Gloria.

"Look, I have an idea. The angel told me to find out what truth is worth, and I know. It's worth nothing. You know, I almost told you my name was Erich Weiss. Houdini. I have an escape trick up my sleeve. It's very simple. Go into your past. Deny the present. Deny everything. Lie a lot. Imagine yourself to be in some good place, with me. This is very important. If we're to die, if there is nothing beyond, what difference does it make if we face that truth or not? I think that Heaven is something our minds make up in the last second of life, and it's timeless, and we're suspended in it forever, like insects in amber. If we don't perceive something, it isn't... Consider: all those mystics couldn't be wrong. Let's go to Heaven, Gloria."

Ten minutes later, she said, "John, that's a beautiful idea. I reach the terminator in forty-five minutes. What have I got to lose? If this'll ease me through to... the other side.... It's been nice knowing you. I wish you were here."

She sounded afraid again.

* * *

Under a star-filled sky they sat, where a grove of trees opened onto a shallow pool. The full moon reflected on the unrippled surface. On the opposite shore, grass-covered ground rose to form the dark hump of a hill. Bullfrogs trilled in the darkness.

He took her hand in his.

"John," she said. "I knew it would be like this, somehow. It had to be."

"I've always liked to be out at night, looking at the stars."

"We can stay here for a while if you like and watch them go by."

Later they kissed, and made love on the soft sand at the water's edge. Her skin was white as milk in the moonlight.

"Let's swim," she said.

Naked, they waded gently into the pond. The water was very cold. It froze his shins, his knees, his thighs. They dove forward with a splash, scattering the image of the moon. With vigorous strokes he swam after her, and caught her foot just as she reached the opposite shore. Laughing, they stumbled out of the water.

She sat huddled, arms around knees.

"You know," she said. "You still haven't told me about yourself. My mother warned me about strange, silent men."

He stretched out, hands behind his head, and looked up at the sky.

"I ran away when I was twelve. Joined a circus. I really did. Then I was a soldier for a while, until I'd seen too much of that. So I wrote about it. Novels and plays. Oh, I was very very successful, but when I had reached the very pinnacle of success, climbing up the glass mountain where fortune and fame and critical acclaim are the names of the rest stops, do you know what? There wasn't anything at the top. I went everywhere and did everything, but still I was restless. I couldn't write. It was all a joke. They nominated me for a World Literature Prize, but it didn't matter. My wife left me. I hadn't been paying enough attention to her. She was a 3-V sex goddess, and that sort demands attention. So in the end I threw it all away and came to my little world on the far side of nowhere, to watch the stars."

She took him by the hand and led him up the hill. The grass was slippery beneath his bare feet. Once he stumbled, but she caught him. Her grip was strong.

"I love you, John," she said.

The stars began to fade. A line of light appeared along the top of the hill.

"Gloria... in glory."

Suddenly he paused, and he realized that he had never seen her face clearly. She had been a soft, warm shadow. Now she was a silhouette, the light at her back as she stood on the hilltop.

In a ferocious burst, the sky went blindingly white. The trees and grass withered to ash before a hot wind. The pond began to boil.

Gloria stood transfigured in the light, her hair afire.

"Wait!" he cried. "It's all lies. Everything I've told you is a lie. I have to tell the truth about myself. I wasn't a soldier. I wasn't a writer. I didn't join the circus. I didn't have a wife. Look, I lived with my mother till I was forty-two, then went into space to get away from everyone. I never had a woman because I never learned how and I was ugly and clumsy and stupid, and they frightened me, and I was the one the kids beat up on in school, and when I wanted to go to the prom they laughed and laughed and laughed. Gloria, you have to believe me."

"Isn't the sunrise beautiful?" she said.

Ash touched his face.

* * *

The radio hummed like a swarm of bees in springtime. He let go of the microphone and stood up, drifting into the center of the room. His legs were cramped.

He noticed that he was not alone.

"Isn't the sunrise beautiful?" said the Angel of Death.

THE GAME OF SAND AND FIRE

Naal han Artal is my name. I am one who wanders over the Earth, at home everywhere and nowhere, because I have come to understand the two gods. All places are the same in their sight.

Let me tell of them. Yindt-haran, He Who Caused the Oasis to be Found in the Desert, is held to be a friend of man, and all camel drivers pray to him before setting out. Yes, when I was a driver, and later, when I was master of the caravan, I prayed to him. But I did not pray to the other god. No one does. He has no name. He dwells deep in the heart of the desert. Indeed, he is the desert, the mover of dunes, and his voice is the howling of the wind in the darkness of the sandstorm. He is the enemy of all things living, and men and caravans are swallowed by him, leaving no traces behind.

Between Yindt-haran and the other, a kind of game is played, with mankind as the prize. No man may understand the rules wholly, but each must learn what is expected of him in his role. To do otherwise is to die.

Thus we have come to know the waste as an ancient enemy. We know him as a warrior knows the strength and manner of his foe, as the physician knows the symptoms of a disease. By the shape of the dune's crest, by the rippling of distant dust waves, by the sounds in the night, by the way the stars fade and the morning wind rises — by all these things we know in which direction lies the sea, and where the oasis is. By these things we can sometimes glimpse the strategems of the nameless god, and be directed by Yindt-haran. Seldom are we lost or confused, for to be lost is to be dead, and to be confused is much the same — confusion shortens the game, and it is said that even the evil one wants men to be in full command of their faculties at the height of their strength, so that his slaughter of them might prove sufficient challenge for him to enliven eternities of the game.

Yet on the day whereof I speak, I was lost, and my twelve companions were confused. The sandstorm which arose was no ordinary tempest. It blackened the sky and laughed with the voice of Chaos. It arose with the first hint of dawn and waxed wrathful into midday, and by afternoon we could proceed no further. So I gave the command, and we bade our beasts kneel, and men and camels huddled together against the wind. I could see only the vaguest outline of anything an arm's reach away from me. The camel next to me was a wavering mound. I could not make out

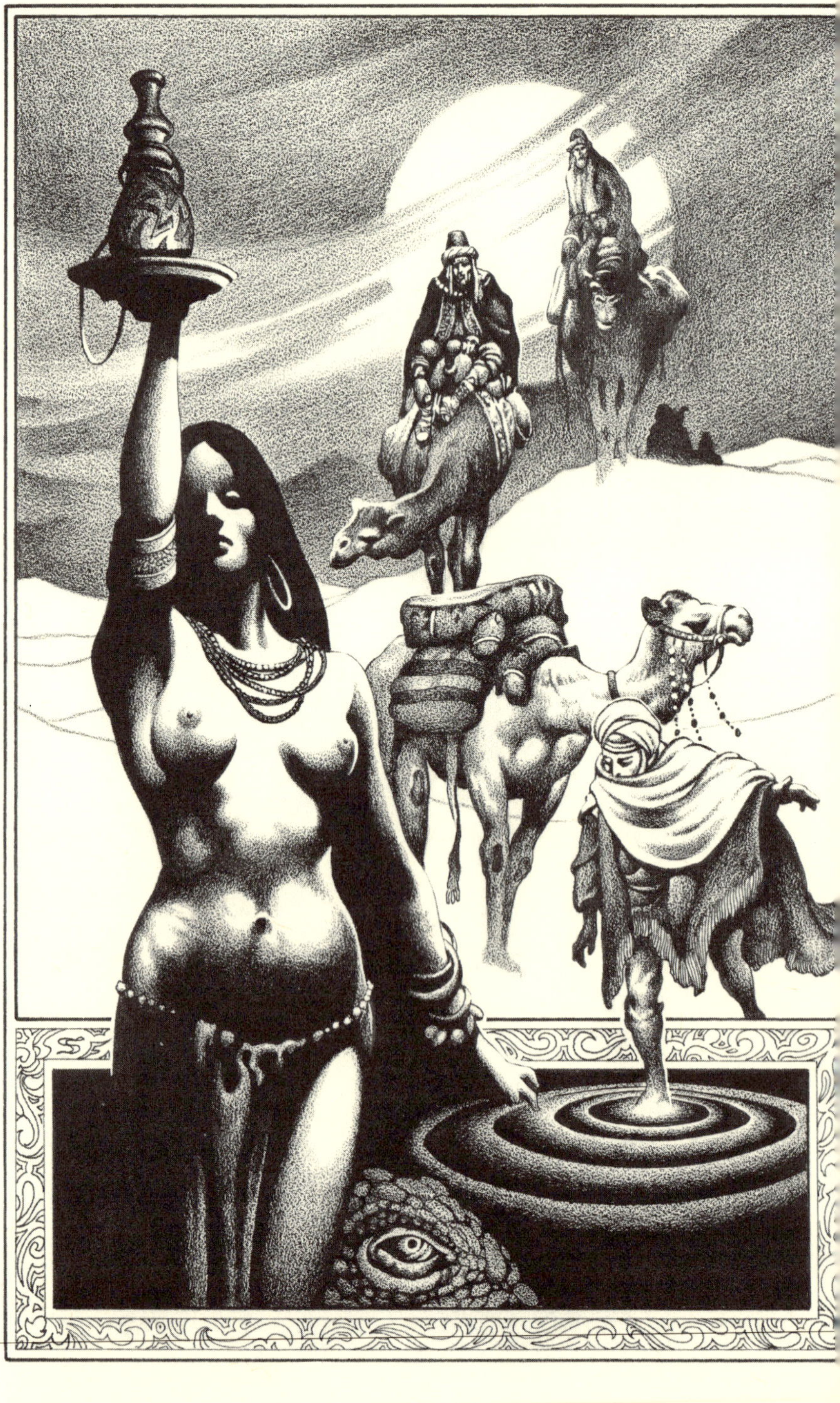

its rider, so thick was the dust in the air, though I might have taken two steps and touched him.

We saw no stars that night, and it is bad luck not to see stars, for Yindt-haran speaks to the wise through them. There was only impenetrable gloom, and sand to blast the eyes of any who peered into its depths. The gritty little grains were everywhere; one could not keep them out. We drew our cloaks over our faces, yet still there was sand in our hair, in our ears, our beards, and scratching to get under tightly closed eyelids. Sand ground between our teeth, and caked sweat-soaked bodies.

Thus the night passed and few slept, but by the approach of morning the wind began to abate. The sun rose in stillness into a clear sky.

I stood up, shook the sand off myself, and counted the crouched figures and camels. No one was missing. For this I thanked the Friendly God. We had survived the Other's move in the game, and now it was Yindt-haran's turn. I looked for good fortune.

But as I gazed about, I saw that this was not so. It was as if Yindt-haran had passed his turn. In the wake of the storm the waste had been born anew, all its features changed, all its secrets erased and rewritten. Clearly this was the work of the Adversary, and he was winning the game. We were strangers now, lost in an unfamiliar land, knowing not where the mountains stood, where the grasslands began, or how one could find those cities to which we were bound, where foreigners come in ships to buy the goods of the nomad folk.

So we wandered, for days I think, chanting litanies to Yindt-haran until our throats were too parched to emit sound. Our caravan wound like a long, dying serpent over the dunes. When the last of the water was gone, all of us became feverish. Some drank piss. I lost count of time, and know not where we travelled or what sights we saw.

When we came to the pool I was the first to see it, and I thought it a mirage. I told the others about it and they said, "The sun has touched you." And I thought, even so, for I had dreamed of nothing but water for a long time, imagining myself bathing in icy, impossible mountain streams, gorging myself from wide rivers. Thus I could well believe I had imagined the pool.

Yet when the others saw it they cried aloud with cracked voices, "What wonder is this?" and praised Yindt-haran. There was no need to turn the camels in that direction. Perhaps the beasts too, in their own way, offered thanks to the God of Necessity.

Still I feared that it was a false thing. As we drew closer, I noticed that there were no trees growing about the pool, no reeds or grasses by its banks; not even mud lay at its edge. I knew from the experience of my long years that the minds of desperate men will sometimes conjure up whatever is needed to ease their dying, eschewing all details for which they have no concern. Yet in reality there are such details. I bade my comrades beware.

They hesitated by the water's edge, and it was only when the camels began to drink in long, deep gulps that we knew it was real. Then we caused our mounts to kneel and tumbled to the ground. I was one of those whose legs were so stiff from days of riding that I had to crawl that last short distance.

It occurred to me that the water might be poisoned, and for this reason no plants grew near it, but once I had filled my mouth with a vintage finer than the cool wine of the heavenly spirits, I cared little about the danger. Far better, thought I, to die in cold, wet ecstasy than by slow degrees, with parched tongue and scorched skin, in the middle of a desert grown merciless with the knowledge that the game is won.

Yet no one went into convulsions, and it was only after all were refreshed that someone called out, and all of us gasped when we saw what had raised his outcry.

We had been too much preoccupied with drinking and washing our faces to notice the reflections on the water's surface, but when we looked again we saw ourselves, and **others** standing behind. Yet when we whirled around, there was no one. As a single body we turned back, and there again was a great marvel. In the pool, standing beyond the weary and begrimed travellers, were courtesans and kings, all in resplendent garb, surrounded by soldiers with armor and shields like those of our forefathers, who knew glory and made all nations tremble to their tread. Further, there were maidens shapely and dark beneath silken garments, and the land all of them stood on—Oh, the land!—was green and fair, with fig and fruit trees growing in great profusion, and the ground thickly covered with grass and flowers. Not a bare spot of earth was there anywhere, And in the midst of the trees there stood a wall draped with vines, beyond which one could see marble rooftops and the tips of towers. But most wondrous of all was the vast, beaten bronze gate of this city, which hung open. Ten chariots could have gone through abreast.

Once more we turned about and beheld only bare sand stretching to meet blue sky, and we turned again, and saw by the edge of the pool a thing even stranger than all that had gone before. As we watched, one of the folk therein, a lord clad in a purple gown, stepped out of the water and onto the bank, and stood among us, not as a phantasm, but a man among men. He made footprints in the sand. The wind blew his garments and beard.

"I am called Taindris," he said. "Greetings, friends."

I blinked. He remained where he was and continued.

"Brothers, weary travellers, all of us offer you greetings. We of Thalanod welcome you. Pray tell, which of you is the leader?"

"I am," I said. "I am called Naal han Artal, the caravan master. Greetings to you, friend. But one boon we seek of you. We have lost our way. Can you tell us where the city of Belhimra lies?"

"What need have you of Belhimra when there is Thalanod?

Know, all of you, that our city was built in the earliest times, in a place beyond the world, before the gods began to play idle games with men. Our land is forever green and flowing with fruit. We know nothing of sickness or pain... or even death. Strife and toil were never born among us, and it is by the will of the wisest and the most compassionate of gods, those more loving than any of the gods you know, that this gateway remains open into your world. We invite you to come and share eternal joy and peace with us. Our women are more beautiful than you can imagine and our country is filled with wonder. Come, now, out of the sun and parched land."

Then he stepped back into the water. One instant he was a man wading and the next he was a reflection on the surface, cast by nothing. The transition was too quick and too subtle for the eye to follow.

My companions looked at the pool and at one another, and then back to the pool, rejoicing and praising Yindt-haran. "Clearly the Good God has won the game," said Zad-hadoun, the eldest of my sons, even though it was that god's name which had been insulted. Recall what I said about desperate men and details.

Some of them stood in a daze, probably sure they were dead and looking on the paradise some prophets speak of. But I felt neither joyous nor dead, and I feared what I saw, thinking it either illusion or a dream. I rebuked the others, warning of treachery, and of things the mind cannot grasp. Yet they laughed and said, "Old man, you are suspicious and your thoughts are narrow. You are a fool to want to stay with the sun and the desert, with the instruments of the Other. You are a fool to want to drink only from little pools, and to strive only to move from pool to pool merely to stay alive. Remember always the joys that were offered you, and how stupidly you refused them."

Then they turned their backs on me and stepped into the water.
"Come back! I am your leader!"
"But we are not your followers."

They sank down, changing as Taindris had, in a manner beyond the seeing of the eye, and were gone, all twelve of them, my kinsmen, my friends from the earliest days of my youth. Some had lain as infants in the same tent as I, and had nursed at the same breasts, and yet they went away. Zad-hadoun was the firstborn of my children, and yet he went away.

For a while they all stood there in the pool, beckoning. Then they were surrounded by serving girls, who brought fresh and fine garments for them. For a final time they beckoned to me, but I would not join them. I feared many things: dreams, entrapments, newness. I have always been one who seeks no more than he has, to whom the desert, a camel, and a water hole at the end of a journey are the only things of importance. Even in my youth I did not dream. I imagined no ethereal kingdoms; I longed for no wonders beyond the sunset. Maidens fairer than any poet can describe I left undescribed and ignored. What need had I of these, when I had a life to live, a mortal wife to bear my children, and a tent of hides to live in?

Yet as I watched my companions pass into the pool and become phantoms, all these things I had built my life upon seemed to crumble. As the twelve and those waiting for them formed a long procession through the city gate, I felt my wisdom of leadership, my insistence on knowing no more than one needs to know — I felt my very selfhood eroding away. And as the gate shut them from my eyes and the vision faded, I was sure that I was wrong. The entrance to the new world was closed to me. The pool was just a pool again. I knelt at its edge among the kneeling camels.

I wept, and as my tears mingled with the waters before me, there happened a terrible thing, like a fantasy in a fevered dream. But it was nothing conjured out of any delirium. **In truth** the pool boiled bloody red, and when I was splattered with it I saw that the stuff was indeed blood. In truth I heard agonized screams, like cries of the damned filtering up through the ground. In truth I watched in awe and a dread superceding mortal fear as scraps of flesh and clothing floated to the surface, and I saw bobbing there a hand, like a limp, bloated spider, and on one of its fingers was a ring I recognized.

I had given that ring to my son on the day of his manhood.

I cried his name aloud, but he was beyond hearing.

I was paralyzed. Time seemed to have stopped. I don't know how long I remained there, but after a certain interval the water became clear again, and I saw, squatting in the mud at the bottom, a hunched and misshapen creature, like a toad the size of a man, its almost human face stretched hideously over its huge head, its two red eyes burning like coals in a brazier in the Hall of Pain. This thing gazed up at me and I back at it, it masterful and full of contemptuous triumph, I rapt with horrid fascination, like a desert rat charmed by the serpent about to devour it. There was no more than three feet of water between us.

The thing grinned, revealing endless rows of crooked teeth in which tatters and scraps were still stuck, and a huge throat recently distended by its meal, and from that throat and between those teeth came a deep, wordlessly malicious laugh, more subtle than the breeze that vanguards the tempest, more quiet than the trickling of dust in some ancient tomb, yet loud enough to shake my brain and fill up the entire world. Oh! How the universe reeled before it!

The camels heard even as I did, and at once they lurched to their feet and stampeded off, snorting and grunting in terror. My legs seemed fluid and invisible beneath me, and beyond any command of my conscious mind they too were moving. Thus I fled, filled with subhuman fear, far, far across the wasteland, until I was again lost, and still I ran, until all strength left me and I collapsed and slept where I lay on the sand.

I fell into dreaming. I saw all the endless centuries of pain known to mankind, and the naked, primal Earth was revealed to me, broiling beneath a red sky. Then I was swept into the depths of impossible, nighted seas, into the infinite abyss beyond the world and time, where no stars shine, where no moon ever passes, and there, in the final darkness, I saw again the face in the pool. At once the revelation, the realization, came to me that I had beheld the very visage of the Adversary, whom priests call the One Who Is Not To Be Seen. I had seen him, and I knew that from then on there would be no peace in my mind, that I would wake up screaming every time I lay down to sleep, that my pain would never end.

Even as I tell you now, I hear him whispering to me that he will be with mankind until the ending of days. Yindt-haran will never banish him. No, no, that one too craves sport, and when a man he has tried to protect dies, he mourns not, but merely acknowledges that his move has been defeated, and goes on with his gaming, wiling away eternity just like the Other. That is all. Yindt-haran loves not the men who sacrifice to him. They are but his pieces in the game.

And yet, when I awoke to see the pale light of dawn silhouetting a curving dune before me, I rose and prayed to Yindt-haran, for there is no other I know how to speak to. In time I was rewarded. A wind blew, bearing the scent of brine, and I followed it throughout the day until I came to a little town by the sea.

The game goes on. I am still part of it.

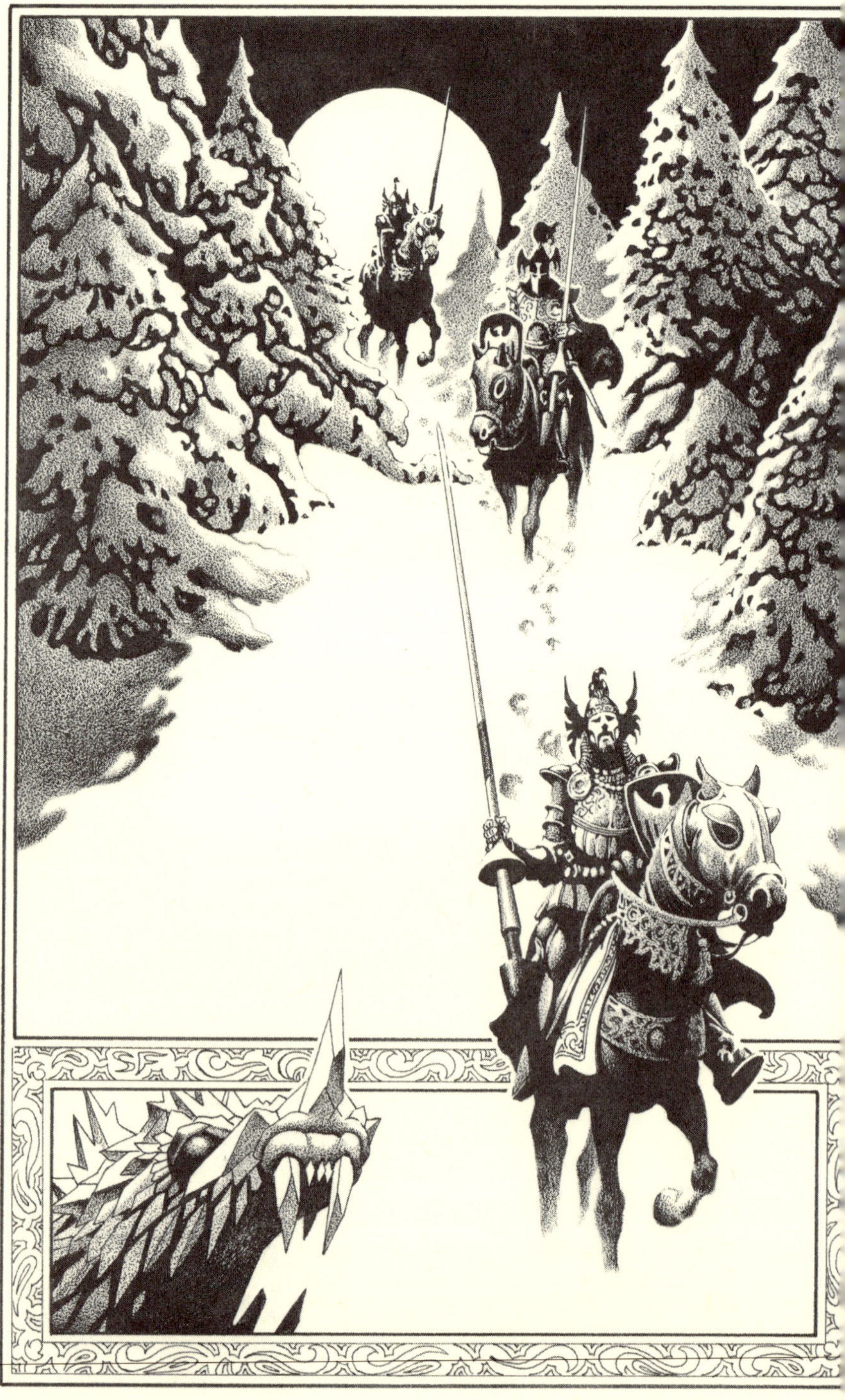

THE WINGS OF THE WHITE BIRD

In the clarity of a dream I saw them, the three knights of Mayadain, in the wintry forest beneath the moon. They rode in single file, first an old man with a snow-colored beard, then one who was younger, and a third who was truly young. Above, ice-covered branches swayed, aglow with white and silver, and the armor of the knights gleamed a cold steely-blue in the moonlight. Evening shadows drew long into night as they rode, but when the moon was high, they dismounted, and the youngest of them said, "Let us build a fire now, to drive the cold away."

The other two laughed bitterly, and ice cracked on their beards. The youngest had no beard.

"Gifallone, you are always talking in riddles," said the old knight.

"No riddle, good Lanbolir," the youngest said, his breath like a cloud of steam before his face. "We need warmth."

"This I will not deny, but what do you intend to burn? The frost itself?"

The third knight sighed, the middle one, who was younger but not young.

"I remember clearly how it was, that day long ago, when we were summoned into the high hall, where the tapestries billowed with the draught as if they were alive. I remember the darkness, how the candles guttered low. I remember the Great King sitting in his carven chair at the end of his long, empty table. I have rehearsed these things in my mind, time and time again. I can still hear him speak: 'Go, you who are my last and dearest, and bring the Bird of Summer back into my lands.' Only now do I understand the fate to which he doomed me then: standing here, freezing to death, listening to you two argue. A fitting end."

"Have you, too, ceased to believe, Jathren?" asked Lanbolir, the old knight. He shook the snow from his cloak. For a moment this seemed to occupy all his attention. Then he turned to his companion and said sharply, "Why do we still ride? Why not return to the King's hall where it is warm?"

"And admit we have failed, and bring disgrace to the Great King? No, we shall die in the snow with honor, still questing, and the King shall die a little later, when the fire in his hall burns no more. This winter is endless. The Earth is dead."

"It is not so! Nay!" protested Gifallone. "We **shall** find the Bird, and the land shall grow green again. I know this to be true, for I have seen it in the vision of a dream."

Lanbolir laughed once more, this time gently. "Then dream on, and lead on, Sir Youth, if you still find any purpose in all of this. But for tonight, we can go no farther. If we cannot build a fire, at least we can lie together among our horses, for the warmth of their bodies."

So the men and the horses huddled together in the snow against the fury of the north wind, which passed through the naked forest like a conquering army. They slept a little, and toward the morning Sir Gifallone roused them, saying, "I have dreamed another dream, and I saw the White Bird flying low over the land. The gods have revealed this to me."

"Go back to sleep," grumbled Sir Jathren.

"So it is the gods?" said Sir Lanbolir, never really awake.

The young knight slept no more. He sat up watching as clouds covered the moon. Later, he watched snow drifting almost gently down through the branches. He thought of the Bird of Summer, which he had seen clearly twice now, and also of his beloved, who had fled to the south, promising to return when the world was reborn. He smiled and softly hummed a song in his lady's honor.

With the grey dawn, the other knights roused themselves, shaking ice off their hair and beards and armor. They ate of the magic food which the Great King had given them, and stretched their stiff limbs. Then the three of them prepared to mount, but their horses would not rise. Gifallone prayed to the gods, and Lanbolir and Jathren got behind the steeds and pushed. One by one, the reluctant beasts swayed to their feet.

That day the three of them passed through a village. Nothing moved there but the wind, howling along the empty streets. Snow drifted over thresholds, and empty windows stared like dead eyes. Snow drifted in wavering curtains over the fields beyond the village. Later, the knights came to a castle guarded by a corpse frozen upright, supported by a pike. They did not pause to knock on the gate, nor did they call out to those within.

So it was in the month of July, in the year when spring and summer did not come, when the Bird of Summer flew not over the land of Mayadain. Priests begged mercy of the gods, but the gods were silent, so knights were sent to seek the White Bird. One by one they departed from the court of the Great King, until his hall was as empty as that desolate castle, and the King sat in his carven chair listening to echoes, to the footsteps of Death walking the corridors of his palace. He waited for knights who never returned, for warm days that never came. Only at the very last did he call his three dearest knights, the wisest, the hero of his greatest battle, and the most beloved. He sent them also, and they rode, and he still waited, alone.

August came, and the snows grew bold, drifting hugely upon the towns of men, snuffing them out, until all the world was white and gently sloping. The knights journeyed through all this, their horses sinking to their knees. Around them, barren treetops sticking through the snow looked like stiff grass.

The knights spoke little, but they thought of their mission,

Lanbolir never believing that the Bird could be found, Jathren ceasing to believe, and Gifallone clinging to his faith and his visions. The young knight dreamed of triumph, while the other two awaited the end and only followed him because there was nothing else to do.

And the end came to Sir Jathren in September, when his horse would move no more. The beast's legs were frozen; it could not bend at the knees. It thrashed, rolled over in the snow, and died. Jathren made his way from it, clumsy in his heavy mail, stiff with cold.

"Come now, and ride behind me on my horse," said Sir Gifallone, but before Jathren could reach him a frost dragon sensed his presence and reared up before the three, hissing pale smoke.

Gifallone and Lanbolir charged the monster as best they could, but their mounts could not gallop in the deep snow. Their lances scraped harmlessly along white scales. Then the two mounted knights threw their lances aside, drew their swords, and harried the dragon's flanks, but it bore straight down on Sir Jathren, who stood to meet it, sword and shield ready. At length the three of them did slay the great worm, but not before a long, curved tooth pierced the unmounted knight and froze his heart.

His comrades left him sitting upright in the snow, broken sword in hand, guarding the body of the dragon.

"Shall I be the next, or you?" asked the old knight.

"I beg you! Speak not of such things!" wept Sir Gifallone, the most beloved of the Great King. "You and I shall not die as brave Sir Jathren did. We shall win in the end, for this has been revealed to me in my visions."

"Beware of such visions, boy. They are masks."

"Behind them is truth," said Gifallone.

"But truth holds hidden daggers and strikes crafty blows."

"Then we shall meet it with our swords drawn and our shields uplifted. This much we must believe."

"I wish I could," said Sir Lanbolir.

* * *

October came, and deepened into November. True winter arrived in screaming triumph. Snows piled higher and higher, covering the hills, and the two knights had to dig to find bark for their horses to eat. Sometimes they ate it themselves, for the store of the magic food was very low. Once in a very great while they found a deer or a rabbit, and then had meat, although it pained them to destroy another living thing in so empty a world. They pressed on, the young knight with his dreams, the old knight with none. Hope burned like a flickering lantern in Gifallone, before the darkness of the world and of Lanbolir.

When they came to a range of mountains which stood as yet free and mighty above the enshrouded land, Gifallone asked, "What peaks are these?"

"These mark the edge of the Earth," was the answer. "We have come to the end of our quest here, for there is nowhere left to go. I see no Bird of Summer, so I think I shall lie down and sleep, and so end my life."

"Nay! Climb these hills and we shall find the Bird yet!"

"All we shall find," said the old knight slowly, "are a billion white tomorrows. This is the eastern rim of the world, where days began and the sun rose, when there really were days and you could see the sun. Then, you could peer into the abyss and see the times to come. Now, there is nothing but sameness."

"How do you know unless you have looked? I tell you we **shall** peer into the abyss, and we'll discover where the White Bird lies, and why it has not come to us. We shall see the world green again."

"Climb then," said Lanbolir, surrendering.

They climbed on horseback as far as they could, and then they dismissed their steeds, sending them back to the Great King, knowing that if the horses came home in the snow, or perished in the attempt, then nothing would matter, and all would be lost. But if they came home in springtime, the knights would not mind the walk.

They climbed, and the winds of all the world's Novembers howled in their faces, and the snow declared itself eternal in the mountain passes. Still they continued, Gifallone believing and Lanbolir trailing behind. Each night they huddled together and each morning they rose, a little stiffer, a little weaker, their armor frigid against their bodies.

The supply of the magic food was almost exhausted, and they ate sparingly, and hunger and the breath of the endless winter touched the old knight's joints until he could hardly move.

"I cannot go on," he said many times in many places, his face a pained mask of pale ice. "Leave me and continue, if you believe still. I almost believe also, because you do after all this time, but alas, I am unable to rise."

"Be patient," the young man would say, "and come with me a little ways more. It is only the winter that pains you. Winter is followed by spring. Is it not only December?"

Then they would climb some more, between peaks and over them, until they neared the highest, from whose summit they could gaze down into the starry abyss beyond the edge of the world, into the days to come. The pale sun made the sky a metallic grey, then left it black again. At last the two knights neared the top, leaning on each other's shoulders, gaunt as scarecrow stick-men, and it happened that at the very last the battle-hardened strength of the old knight, Lanbolir, held out, while Gifallone failed. The youth dropped to his knees and felt nothing when he touched the snow. His face was white and hollow, his lips blue.

"Go on without me," he said to Lanbolir. "It is not far."

"You tell **me** this now?" asked the old knight. He began to sob.

"I think you have passed your burden of faith on to me. I think I believe in the White Bird again. But now, now, you tell me——"

"I have had another dream, my friend, and I saw the Dancing Man. I knew then that my journey was at its end, for one sees him only when he has already arrived. But your limbs are sound yet, so I beg you to fare on a little ways and look over the edge. Then come back and tell me where the Bird of Summer lies. Go quickly now."

"I shall," said Lanbolir, but his words fell on frozen ears, for the young knight was already dead. He left him and walked to the top of the mountain at the edge of the world. It wasn't far. It only took him a few minutes. When he reached the summit, he paused and looked back. Far away, gliding over the snowy slopes, he saw two dark figures, neither of them leaving footprints, both as nimble as a mirage. They danced slowly, gracefully, to music the old knight could not hear. Just before they passed from view, one of them pointed up at something behind Lanbolir.

The knight turned and looked out over the abyss, and there spread before him was the future, all the days ever to be, stretched out in an endless procession. He gasped at the wonder of it, for the days were not filled with snow and ice as he had expected, but only a snow that melted with the coming of spring, with a summer to follow. He saw flowers in the fields and crops growing, birds in leafy branches deep in forests, and he saw men also, knights parading beneath bright banners, tradesmen and peasants, kings and slaves. Lovers met in walled gardens. Old men died in their beds in darkened rooms. All these things he saw, and then he looked away, back to where Gifallone lay half-buried in the drifting snow.

"This was for you to see, not I," the old knight said. But later he said, "I think I understand."

He took off his cloak and his war helm, his hauberk of mail and his iron gauntlets. His sword he drew and snapped over his knee and cast into the abyss. The pieces glittered as they fell. He stood unarmed and waiting, and he called out to the Bird of Summer.

And the Bird came to him, to accept the sacrifice he offered. It rose slowly as a cloud out of the Days That Shall Be, with its white wings spread far across the sky. It bore Sir Lanbolir up and flew high over the world. Sharp claws cut into his flesh, but he hardly felt the pain. His blood rained down upon the Earth, and wherever it fell, the snows retreated and the ground was green again. Spring came early, on the first day of the new year, and buds opened to the touch of the blood of Sir Lanbolir, and all the lands of men were redeemed. In the end, when there was no blood left, the bird dropped him into the sea, and continued on to the ultimate west, where it rested in the glow of the sunset and the dying of days, until another year arrived and it was time to venture forth again.

These things I saw in the clarity of my dream, and I know they are true. They happened long ago, in a time near to the beginning of the world.

ABOUT THE AUTHOR

Novelist, short-story writer, essayist Darrell Schweitzer is the author of two well-received fantasy novels, **We Are All Legends** and **The Shattered Goddess,** plus numerous short stories which have appeared in **Twilight Zone, Fantastic, Weirdbook, Whispers, Fantasy Book,** and other publications, including several hard-cover anthologies. He has also written **Conan the Deliverer,** which is "less a solo effort than a collaboration with the ghost of Robert E. Howard." His nonfiction includes author interviews, reviews, critical articles and books, as well as a few polemics on the current state of the fantasy field, which, he feels, has "retreated from its real potential as the most universal form of literature in favor of endless look-alike and read-alike paperback trilogies in which, to borrow Brian Aldiss' phrase, the universe is saved from utter evil by a Peter Pan figure, a girl of high birth, and a moron." To some extent, Schweitzer writes because no one else is writing the stories he would like to read.

Schweitzer was born in New Jersey in 1952. His hobbies include backyard astronomy, medieval and ancient literature and history, and book collecting. He is also an amateur cartoonist.

He has been an assistant editor of **Isaac Asimov's Science Fiction Magazine** and holds a similar position at **Amazing.**